Praise for *Mutant City*

Mutant City will be happily received by Feasey's many fans and will find an equally appreciative audience in anyone who enjoys *X-Men* and the other superhero universes
thebookbag.co.uk

I'd recommend anyone who loves a bit of sci-fi to read *Mutant City*, especially if you're a fan of *X-Men*
thebritishbooknerd.blogspot.co.uk

A really well delivered story set in a fantastically dark and futuristic world with imagination and creativity at the height of the genre. This is amazing stuff; I am really looking forward to the next instalment
Mr Ripley's Enchanted Books

Daaaaaamn this book was amazing!!! :)
George Lester, goodreads.com

Mutant City is the only mutant book that I can say I and X-Men would approve of
Kirsty-Marie Jones, goodreads.com

What a brilliant book!
Kulsuma, goodreads.com

I really cannot recommend it enough. There's only really one thing left to ask you: whose side are you on? Are you Pure or are you Mutant?
Leah, goodreads.com

If you are looking for a cracking action-packed story and some wonderful characters then you don't need to look any further

Paul, goodreads.com

MUTANT RISING

MUTANT RISING

STEVE FEASEY

BLOOMSBURY
LONDON OXFORD NEW YORK NEW DELHI SYDNEY

Bloomsbury Publishing, London, Oxford, New York, New Delhi and Sydney

First publish… Great … Bloomsbury Publishing Plc
50 Bedford Square, …

www.bloomsbury.com

BLOOMSBURY is a registered trademark of Bloomsbury Publishing Plc

A CIP catalogue record for this book is available from the British Library

ISBN 978 1 4088 5572 0

Typeset by RefineCatch Limited, Bungay, Suffolk
Printed and bound in Great Britain by CPI Group (UK) Ltd, Croydon CR0 4YY

1 3 5 7 9 10 8 6 4 2

This book is dedicated to my daughter, Hope.

Keep your chin up, kiddo.

Prologue

Rush stood perfectly still, eyes narrowed as he squinted out on to the shadowy landscape. The measly light from a crescent moon did little to illuminate the murk, but without it Rush would not have spotted the glint – a brief flicker – in the distance a few moments ago.

Since that time he hadn't moved. Like a statue he stood atop the elevated platform that must have once been used to hoist straw or some other feed up into the roof space of the dilapidated barn at his back, and he focused all his attention on the area out there where he thought the glint had come from. A cold wind blew in from his right, tousling his long hair and whipping it across his face.

Maybe it had *been a trick of the light?* There had been no repetition; the night was as dark and ordinary as it had been before. *If not a trick of the light, maybe the moonlight glinting off an animal's eye*. Could something like that be spotted this far away? He doubted it. No, the reflection seemed to come from something not of the natural world: a shiny surface, something man-made, possibly metal.

Behind him, through the rotting timber walls of the abandoned outhouse that had been left to decay like the rest of the farm, he could hear the sleepers. One particular noise, a deep bass rumble, much louder than the sound of the other sleepers, could only be Brick, the mutant man-child they had managed to rescue from City Four. The incursion, however, had made Rush and his mutant friends public enemy number one. It had also had the effect of uniting City Four's Pure inhabitants behind President Melk, who was only too eager to order that Rush's small band of mutant teens should be hunted like animals by the Agency for the Regulation of Mutants. Because even in the mutant world outside the Pure cities, Rush and his friends were different. Their gifts made them powerful – and dangerous.

There was a moan from inside the barn, followed by mumbled gibberish that presumably made sense to whoever was experiencing the dream or nightmare. Rush's own dreams had been vivid and unnerving of late, no doubt thanks to the continual state of stress he found himself in. That and the hunger.

He continued to stare out into the darkness.

Rush wanted to wake his friends – just in case there *was* anything out there – but he knew how tired they all were. They'd been out hunting most of the day, although they had little to show for it. After cooking and eating whatever they'd managed to catch, the group had gone to bed with their bellies far from full.

The old telescope was on the deck at his feet. He opened his hand, and the device sprang up from the wooden floor and slapped into his palm, as if pulled there by some invisible string. He lifted it to his eye and scanned the shadows again. Nothing. Not even a hint of movement. He sighed. Phantoms in the darkness.

Relaxing a little, he lowered the spyglass and slowly sank back down into his seated position on the floor. Retrieving the blanket that had dropped to the wooden deck, he pulled it around his shoulders, suddenly all too aware of the cold now the adrenalin charge he'd experienced was dissipating. He considered everything he'd been through since that fateful night when the ARM had turned up at his own farm all those months ago – the things he'd experienced and the things he'd discovered. Rush had always thought he was just another grubby mutant. But in fact he was the result of a secret scientific experiment to create mutant hybrids with extraordinary powers, and there were others like him. Eventually they found each other: Rush, Anya, Brick, Flea and Jax. Like a strange, broken family, they'd fought a battle and survived – hiding from the ARM, learning to use their powers, waiting for the moment when they could fight back. How could all that have happened in the space of a few months? It hardly seemed possible. One minute he was living on a remote homestead in the middle of nowhere with his guardian, the next he was a member of a renegade band being pursued across the lands of Scorched Earth – rebels with large bounties on their heads. Dammit, if all that wasn't enough to make you think you were seeing things in the dark, he didn't know what was.

He settled back against the cold timber wall, the coarse material of the blanket making his neck itch a little. Taking in the stars on the far horizon, he allowed himself to wonder how long it was until dawn and gradually felt himself relax a little.

Then he saw it again.

This time there was no doubt in his mind. Out there in the dark, something was moving around, and it was moving slowly, as if it was aware he'd almost spotted it. Whatever it was, it was man-made. *It's a gun*, he thought. He didn't know why he knew that, but he did.

He wanted to jump to his feet and shout out to wake his friends. His heart was thumping wildly again, but he forced himself to move calmly, convinced that whatever was out there was watching him every bit as closely as he'd been looking out for it. He rose, made a big show of stretching and yawning and went inside.

Although long abandoned, the place still had a faint whiff of animals and straw. On the floor, curled up in blankets, were the vague, indistinct shapes of his slumbering friends, and he hurried over to the closest of these amorphous mounds. Dropping to his knees, he shook the thing awake.

'What is it?' Jax was instantly on the alert. Despite the dark, he could clearly make out the worried look on the younger Mute's face. The albino, fully clothed beneath his blankets – all in black as always – threw the covers to one side and got to his feet. He was much taller than Rush, and in the darkness of the barn his ghostly white flesh seemed even starker than usual.

'Something's outside.' Even as Rush said it he began to feel the return of the same doubts he'd nursed while on lookout. What had he really seen, after all? 'It might be nothing – just a vehicle passing by on a routine patrol somewhere way off in the distance – but I'm pretty sure there's something moving about out there.'

'When did you first see it?'

'A few minutes ago. I thought I might have imagined it, but I've just seen it again, and it's definitely not a trick of the light.' He paused, then nodded, mainly to himself. 'Somebody is out there.'

'Show me,' Jax said.

'Shall we wake the others?' Rush hissed.

Jax took a moment to look about him. 'Not yet.'

Captain Rourke held the night-vis set up to his eyes, zooming in to fill the display with the green-and-black image of the two Mutes on the wooden platform.

It still wasn't completely clear to him if his squad's presence had been discovered, but he didn't like the way the younger one had gone inside and then come back out with this other, taller freak.

Rourke's squad had been tipped off as to the whereabouts of the mutant terrorists thanks to a random spotting from a surveillance drone that had flown off course and ended up lost somewhere over this wilderness. The drone's operator had, for some reason known only to himself, decided to check the footage stored on the device, and he'd seen the images of the Mutes at the derelict farmhouse. Knowing there was an order that any sightings of small groups of Mutes should be reported, he'd taken his findings to his commander and, after reviewing the footage, the powers-that-be proclaimed that this was almost certainly the group responsible for the bombings in

City Four. After that it was simply a matter of identifying which ARM unit was nearest and deploying them at top speed. Rourke's squad *was* that unit, and the captain was delighted to be the one tasked with meting out some ARM justice to these terrorist scumbags. It had been a tough journey. Even with their all-terrain vehicles, they had had to travel all day and night to get across the broken lands known simply as the Shattered Zone.

Now here they were. Although exhausted and sore from being bounced around in the back of a troop carrier for all that time, he could sense the excitement and anticipation in his men. Under cover of darkness they'd started to move into position, everything going well until something spooked the kid sitting watch up there on the platform. Now there were two Mutes up there on the high ledge, scanning the landscape for whatever it was that had caught the boy's attention. The captain zoomed in closer, frowning. Actually only the shorter one was looking out; the tall white freak at his side was standing perfectly still, his eyes closed as if he was meditating or something.

Rourke felt a strange sensation inside his head, a moment of slight vertigo that made the world around him shift and his stomach roll uncomfortably. He had the weirdest feeling – as if somebody was looking out through his eyes. It passed as quickly as it had started, and he shook his head, wondering if it was his body telling him to take on board some food or fluids. Reaching for the water canteen at his hip, he became aware of movement beside him as somebody skilfully belly-crawled through the brush, followed by the familiar voice of his second-in-command, a promising young soldier called Henderson.

'What's happening, sir?'

'Not quite sure. The kid went inside and came out with this other freak. They've been standing like that for a while now.'

'Our options?'

Rourke had been weighing these up for the last few minutes. For his liking, he and his men were still a little too far away from the ruined old farmhouse to go for an all-out assault. With no way of knowing what means of transportation the Mutes might or might not have, he ran the risk of losing all of them if he went down that route. Even so, he knew the longer they were forced to hide here in the dirt, the brighter it would soon get, and the advantage of a night attack would be lost to him.

'Where are Sax and Franco?'

Rourke had ordered the two men to break away from the rest of them and head off to the left, instructing them to use some low hills on that side as cover and make their way round towards the back of the outhouse. If he'd had them in place, he could have launched his attack and relied on the pair to trap any escaping Mutes. But the two men, like the rest of them, had been forced to take what meagre cover they could find when the young lookout got twitchy.

'Dammit, we might just have to go in. Take the fight to the Mutes and hope we can engage with them before they have a chance to get away. Go and tell the men to –'

Something flew overhead. It was only a whisper of a sound, but it was picked up by the highly trained military man nonetheless. Rourke craned his head around just in time to catch a glimpse of a large dark shape against the night sky. This was followed by the sound of leathery wings flapping once, as if whatever it was had suddenly braked against the air and come to a halt up there.

'Sir?'

There was a dull *thump* to the rear of his squad, that to Rourke's mind could only be something hitting the ground. Twisting around again and lifting the night-vis back into position, he trained the device back on the platform. The two Mutes were gone.

'Quick, Henderson! Get on the comms and tell everyone we're under attack!'

The actual 'fight', if it could be described as such, was thankfully short. Anya had morphed into a hideous-looking winged serpent, coiling her lower half around Brick and Rush, ignoring the latter's complaints that she was crushing him, and carrying them both out of the back of the barn and into the night. At the same time, Flea had set off in the direction of the two men who were working their way up the flanks. Despite her being the smallest of the group, nobody thought for a second Flea would be in any sort of danger from the two soldiers – it's hard to fight with someone who moves so quickly you can't even see them. Jax stayed behind and monitored the others' movements.

The *thump* the captain had heard was the sound of Brick as the giant mutant hit the ground. Anya was a little more careful with Rush, but not much; she swooped in lower, dropping him close to Rourke and using her terrific momentum to slam, head first, into the ARM officer. Issuing a weird ululating cry, she shot back into the air.

Only a short while after the encounter had started, the ARM squad surrendered and had their weapons, comms devices, uniforms and other paraphernalia taken from them.

'What are we going to do with them?' Rush asked, looking across at the men, who were now all restrained using their own cuffs.

'Kill them,' Anya shot back, staring defiantly at each of the others in turn. She still had a feral look in her eye, despite being back in human form now. 'What? They have guns and knives and heaven knows what else. They were on the point of attacking us in our sleep. You think any of us would have been alive when the sun came up if they'd got to us first?' The anger was clear to hear in her voice, but there was something else: fear.

'That's enough, Anya,' Silas said, pulling up on the harg-drawn wagon. The man who'd saved the mutant children way back when they were babes in arms quickly scanned the scene, giving each of his young wards a nod of approval. Jax and Tia climbed down from the back of the vehicle. 'We'll have no more talk of that sort, thank you.'

'You're kidding me, right?'

'No, I am not kidding you. We will not be stooping to the levels of our enemies, and that's final.'

Anya looked on the verge of answering him back, but held her tongue. Instead she turned her back on them all, shrugging off Jax's attempt to console her, and walked off into the shadows, muttering under her breath.

Silas approached Rourke and his men. 'I have little doubt that my young friend's assertion of our survival chances had you not been discovered is correct. But we will not respond in the way she suggests. We will, however, be requisitioning your vehicles. You'll be left out here to make your own way back as best you can.'

'But we're miles from civilisation,' Rourke complained. The captain had a harrowed look about him and was finding it difficult to look his own men in the eye. How could he have allowed himself to be caught out like that? And how the hell was he going to explain all this to his superiors?

'Civilisation? Is that what you call it? What kind of civilised race sends armed men out to hunt down and kill children?' said Jax, standing beside his guardian. 'I'm sure you'll be picked up by your own people soon enough. They sent you here to find us, so they have a pretty good idea of where you are.' He paused, narrowing his eyes at the captain. 'After all, they know where the surveillance drone was when it fortunately spotted us.'

Jax was right. The next day Rourke and his team found themselves on a transporter heading back to the nearest city. When they arrived at the ARM headquarters, they described how they hadn't stood a chance, how there were dozens of Mutes out there, and not just the five they'd been told to expect – although all of the men agreed during the journey back how it was strange these 'others' had disappeared as soon as they'd surrendered, and how none of them had managed to hit any of them with their weapons, the rounds appearing to simply pass straight through them as if they were ghosts. One man told how he'd thrown a grenade at a teenager, staring in disbelief as the boy raised his hand and the thing had hung in the air halfway between the soldier and its intended target. The kid's hand had shot up, and at that the grenade had flown straight up into the night sky too, only to detonate harmlessly somewhere high overhead. The youngster had turned his attention back to the man, and the next thing the soldier knew, he was flying backwards through the air, the entire front of his body feeling as if it had been hit with a giant hammer. That wasn't all. The men reported dark, hideous flying creatures that morphed into other even more terrible beasts when they landed, striking terror into them; some told how their night-vision equipment had been ripped from their faces by a girl that seemed to appear and disappear again before they had a chance to react. Strange visions had been implanted in their heads – things that weren't there but for all the world had appeared to be. Perhaps the strangest tale had come from the one ARM agent who'd been seriously injured during the skirmish – the man's leg badly broken when, on the run, his foot had gone into an animal's burrow all the way up to the ankle, snapping the bone like a toothpick. He'd lain there wailing in pain, unable to free his injured leg from the hole. Then, when the contact between the two groups was over, a colossal Mute had approached the man, the giant holding out his hands in a placating gesture as he slowly came towards him saying the word 'Brick' over and over. Quaking with fear, the soldier flinched as the hulking figure went down on his hands and knees next to him, fully expecting the brute to deliver the final killing blow. Instead, the Mute reached out and gently placed one of his shovel-like hands on the man's head. That was the last thing the man remembered before blacking out. When he opened his eyes a few seconds later, and removed his leg from the burrow, he was astonished to find it was healed, completely pain-free. He rotated his foot, blinking in disbelief. As he did so, he caught sight of the huge mutant walking off. He was limping badly.

The accounts of Rourke and his men were supposed to be classified, the captain and his squad ordered not to repeat what they'd reported. But even in an organisation as regimented as the ARM, these things have a way of getting out, and word quickly spread that the mutant children out there in the Wastes had strange powers – superpowers.

And as these rumours grew, the enthusiasm of individual members of the ARM to be assigned the role of catching these Mutes shrank.

Melk

From the darkened penthouse complex at the very top of the Bio-Gen tower, President Melk looked out over the metropolis that was City Four. Above, corpulent clouds, their fringes gilded with silver light, drifted lazily in front of the moon. The floor-to-ceiling wall of glass before him provided a stunning unbroken vista, and he had none of the apprehensions or feelings of vertigo he knew many felt when they stood this close to the transparent barrier. If he felt anything, it was the desire to lean forward, to reach out towards the city he and his ancestors had built and sweep it up into his arms.

Lights shone from the windows of most of the huge tower blocks again now – lights that, along with the heating, had been extinguished thanks to the terrorist attack the city had suffered. To make matters worse, the winter had been a harsh one for C4's citizens. Reinstating these crucial services had been beset with delays, but he was pleased power had now been restored to well over seventy per cent of the city, with assurances that the rest would follow in the next few weeks. Of course this wasn't good enough for his critics, who had the nerve to suggest he'd been dragging his heels over some of the work. There was truth in the accusation, but still . . .

He glanced down at a small table by his side, on top of which lay the report he'd been reading. His secret project. It was a work of such Machiavellian genius that even he'd baulked at putting it into action at first, but needs must when the devil drives. And the devil was driving Melk, driving him on to find a solution to the ultimate problem faced by his people.

A sigh escaped him, and he reached for the glass of water on the table.

There was still much to do to repair the damage done – not just to the infrastructure, but to the minds of its citizens – seven months ago by the mutant terrorist group. A group of five mutants with freakish powers, led by Melk's own brother, Silas, who it turned out wasn't quite as dead as the president had believed him to be. Melk had been forced to call on the aid of the other cities, and his handling of the rebuild and its progress were being closely monitored by both his political opponents and those who had re-elected him. There was, however, one guarantee he'd made to the citizens of the Six Cities that he'd not been able to honour. Despite his best efforts, he had still not managed to recapture the renegades responsible for the carnage wrought on C4. And that bothered him like nothing else.

He'd come close on a couple of occasions – sightings of the Mutes, particularly in the slums on the outshirts of the other cities – had almost led to their arrest by members of his elite Agency for the Regulation of Mutants. But each and every time, the ARM had been thwarted and the rebels had escaped. Recently, however, these 'sightings' had almost ceased. After that debacle in the Shattered Zone a few weeks ago, his hybrids – he still thought of them as 'his' – had disappeared. They were out there, making occasional forays to ambush transportation vehicles for food and other supplies, but the rats had gone deep underground.

He watched as a surveillance drone descended from the skies to investigate something. The skies were out of bounds to citizens and mutants alike. Only unmanned drones were allowed access to the heavens, a law that still rankled with him. He wondered what the device was investigating; it was probably just some Pure kids up to no good on the streets.

In the slums beyond the City, the mutant problem was growing. Rallies demanding mutant rights, equality, access to the privileges of the Pure. He had his rabble-rousing brother to thank for that too! Something needed to be done. And now Melk was ready to put in place the means by which to do it.

Melk swore to himself that when he *did* finally capture Silas and his band of freaks he would bestow upon him the most heinous punishments imaginable.

Below, a brightly lit advertisement for a soft drink of some kind momentarily caught his attention. *Be Happy!* the vivid neon hoarding suggested, but Melk found it difficult to comply. Despite all the good reports he'd received from his officials about life in the city returning to normal; despite Melk silencing the critics of his unprecedented fourth-term return to office; despite his latest, most secret project about to come to fruition, he was not happy.

Things, strange things, had started to occur. Things that, as a man of science, Melk should have been able to laugh away as ridiculous. Things like the shadowy figure that had appeared by his bedside the other evening. A figure that for all the world looked like –

Stop it!

He took another sip of his drink and forced himself to

think of other things, like the most recent satisfaction polls that had come in this morning.

He swirled the glass in his hand, the ice cubes chinking softly against the sides. Glancing down, he caught sight of citizens moving along a clear-roofed walkway far below – filing along obediently in countercurrent streams. Like ants. And just like ants, the attack on their colony had changed them. Before the bombings, the mutants beyond the wall surrounding City Four had been viewed as little more than a pest by the city dwellers: an out-of-sight, out-of-mind nuisance not taken too seriously. Despite his own efforts to warn people, they'd refused to listen. His citizens had become soft. Spoiled and overindulged, they'd dismissed his protestations about 'the enemy at the gate' as rhetoric. Well, they were listening now. He had to hand it to his brother – Silas had managed to accomplish something he'd almost failed to. And all it had taken was a few strategically placed bombs. Melk smiled to himself. If he'd known that was all that was required, he might even have planted the damned explosives himself!

There was fear now. The good, Pure citizens of City Four were frightened of the mutants surrounding their safe, privileged world. It was time to act. Never one to look a gift horse in the mouth, Melk was determined to use the new state of affairs to his advantage and –

Father . . .

Melk whirled around, the cold drink splashing up out of the glass and on to his hand.

'Wh-who's there?' he said.

His eyes went to the spot where his son, Zander, had been standing when he was killed on the night of the attacks. There had been blood on the carpet then, a black pool that slowly spread outwards from beneath the prostrate body. He shook his head. The carpet had been replaced, but a part of Melk fancied he could still see that inky stain.

He swallowed, the noise sounding unnaturally loud in the silent room.

'Hello?' He didn't like the tremor in his own voice. It sounded . . . weak.

It must have been somebody outside his office. Some member of his staff who had decided to work late, that's all. His aide! Of course, that's whom he'd heard. He'd asked the man to stay behind a little later this evening. It had been nothing more than that.

It didn't sound like someone outside the office though, did it? And what about the other night, when you woke up?

Shut up.

It was the look on Zander's face that he couldn't get out of his mind. There was none of the slack emptiness the dead were supposed to exhibit once the 'essence' housed in their body had departed. Instead, in death, his son's expression had been one of outrage and surprise.

Telling himself to stop being irrational, Melk absently wiped the spilt liquid against his trouser leg. Without knowing he was doing it, his gaze returned to the carpet and the ugly blackish stain that wasn't really there.

Except it is there, Father. I will always be there.

This wasn't the first time he'd heard the boy's voice. Walking to a meeting the other day – in broad daylight – he could have sworn he heard Zander shout out to him. Then, like now, when he turned around to look, there was nobody.

Pull yourself together, he told himself. *It's the stress you're under, that's all.* The pressure on a man in his situation was enough to make anyone a little jittery. *There's nothing there.*

The carpet hadn't been the only thing he'd had torn up. The entire room had been refurbished – everything thrown out and replaced – with the exception of the battered metal plaque on the wall, the one with the number four. It was a relic, a historical artefact from ARK #4 – the vast underground facility that had sheltered his ancestors when humanity had tried to wipe itself out. Melk found it strangely comforting somehow to know it was all still down there, buried beneath the earth. They all were. Each of the Six Cities had been built atop the subterranean Arks when their creators had emerged from beneath the ground like new life rising from dormant seeds.

That had been a new beginning. Now he was on the verge of another.

He took a deep breath, forcing himself to close his eyes and be calm. He was acting irrationally. This nonsense was beneath someone like him. He was, when you stripped away his political achievements, a scientist, and there was no place in science for ghosts or phantom voices from the grave. Claptrap like that was the stuff of the weak-willed or the Mutes outside the walls.

When he opened his eyes again, the carpet was one uniform shade.

You see? Stress, nothing else. A small sound – not quite a laugh – escaped him.

On unsteady legs, Melk walked over to the desk from which he would deliver his ultimatum in two days, skirting the place where Zander had fallen. The speech would be broadcast not just inside the walls but outside too – on a huge vis-display that was being lowered into place at this very moment. It was a speech that would leave those on both sides of the divide in no doubt that their neighbourly relations were about to change forever.

Placing the drink down on the plaziglass surface, he pressed the fleshy part of his palm beneath the thumb, activating the comms unit implanted just beneath the skin. He lifted the hand, forefinger resting against his ear, a purplish light illuminating the side of his face. His assistant, who worked in an office next to Melk's suite, answered immediately.

'Bring me another drink,' Melk said, noting the slight catch in his voice.

'Is . . . is everything all right, Mr President?'

'Of course. Why wouldn't it be?'

'It's just that I thought I heard you speaking to somebody.'

Had he been talking out loud? He wasn't aware he'd done so.

'No, er, that was just me going through my speech. You know, getting the juices going.'

'Of course. I'll bring you that drink straight away, sir.'

Tia

Tia was being jostled to within an inch of her life in the back of Tink's wagon, the rigours of the long journey creating a host of aches and pains in her young body. A heavy tarpaulin stretched across a metal frame created a half-tunnel of canvas over the rear of the wagon that hid her and the mutant trader's merchandise from anyone who might take an interest in the vehicle. The only other passenger, Silas, was somehow managing to sleep.

She pulled the canvas back to get some air. Despite repeated warnings from Tink, Tia couldn't help but occasionally pop her head out the front to take in the stark and often inhospitable landscapes they'd crossed over the last few days. The world outside the cities, where until recently she'd spent her entire life, was so very different she might as well be on another planet. There was a wildness to it she loved; the people, the flora and fauna, the land itself, everything felt more . . . alive.

Looking out on a windswept tundra, she found herself thinking about the group she had thrown her lot in with now. They owed their continued existence to her slumbering travel companion, Silas, who'd rescued them from his brother when most of them were little more than babes in arms. Like the terrain she was travelling through, they were wild in a way she found exciting. They had to be: despite the incredible powers they'd been created with – each of them cooked up in a top-secret laboratory by the evil Melk – their lives had been harsh and unforgiving, and just about as different from her own childhood as could be imagined. She'd been sheltered from the *real* world. Even as a journalist and daughter of a rebel, she'd been kidding herself when she told people she understood what it was like to live outside the protection of the city walls. Well, she wasn't kidding herself now, was she? Out here, away from her own people, the plight of the mutants was much worse than even she'd imagined.

It was cold now. The sun had begun to dip towards the horizon, taking with it what little warmth it had contributed to the day. Tink, wrapped from head to toe in unidentifiable animal furs so only his face was exposed to the elements, stared ahead stoically. In his mouth, jutting out beneath his bushy white moustache, was his pipe. The thing had long since gone out, but he kept it clamped between his teeth, as if the fiery embers that had no doubt warmed him for a while were still burning.

'You should come inside,' Silas said to her. She hadn't registered his waking.

Tia turned to look at him before nodding and withdrawing back under the canvas.

The trio's trip had served two purposes. First, they'd been to City One, the southernmost of the Six Cities, to listen to a mutant rally Silas had helped to arrange. He'd spent years campaigning for Mute rights, and even though he now had every ARM agent on Scorched Earth looking for him, he still insisted on attending many of these events. She admired him for that. He reminded her of her own father, a man whose determination and pig-headedness had undoubtedly rubbed off on her. Like Silas, Tia had quit the safety of City Four to be with the group of young rebels, documenting the events leading up to, and those that followed, the discovery of the mutant children with special powers. It was work she believed to be important – a documentary that would ultimately expose President Melk and his Principia as liars and hypocrites – even if there was a good chance it would never be seen by anyone inside the Wall. Because she doubted she'd ever get inside any of the cities again. Tia had had her CivisChip – a device all Pures had embedded in their thigh bone at birth – removed. In doing so, she'd also ended her ability to get past the formidable security in place at each and every entry point to each and every city, as well as most of the buildings inside them.

After the rally – a subdued affair thanks to the heavy ARM presence – the three set off on what was the more important leg of their journey and continued south, heading in the direction of a region so devastated in the Last War that it had been forsaken by almost everyone on Scorched Earth. Tink had convinced them that there was somewhere close to the Blacklands that might provide Silas and his group of extraordinary mutants with a place they could make their own, where they might remain safely hidden from their pursuers – for a while at least.

Despite being lost in her thoughts, Tia noted the shift in the rhythm of the monotonous noise of the harg's hard hoofs hitting the ground as it pulled the wagon along. Tink's voice, expressing urgency without betraying any fear, called back to them.

'Er, you two might want to get inside that secret cubby-hole like we practised,' he said. 'And quickly. We've got company coming up the road behind us.'

Ignoring Silas's hissed warnings, Tia peeked through a

gap to get a glimpse at whatever it was Tink was talking about. Her heart sank when she saw an ARM troop carrier speeding up the road in their direction. Sliding away a number of boxes to reveal a hatch in the floor of the truck bed, she watched as Silas prised his fingers into the gap and swung the flap up, allowing access to the concealed hold beneath. It was a terribly tight squeeze, but Silas and Tia *could* both get in there. And as long as the ARM didn't look too hard, they could stay hidden until any search was over.

Holding the hinged section up, Silas let Tia in first, and was about to follow her when Tink gave a little laugh. 'Well, what d'ya know. Silas, Tia, you can forget crawling into that tiny little box. Looks like our Agency for the Regulation of Mutants has itself been deregulated a little.'

The pair looked quizzically at each other before getting up and pushing back the canvas to see what he was talking about. There, climbing out of the troop carrier and waving their hands at them, were Rush, Jax, Flea, Anya and Brick. Bringing up the rear, snuffling and *hurghing* with indignation at having been cooped up, was the rogwan, Dotty.

They pulled the vehicles well off the main road, into a hollow that would provide them shelter from the wind as well as any prying eyes that happened along the route.

Around a large fire they discussed everything that had happened during the twelve days they'd been apart.

'So did you find it?' Rush said, addressing Silas and Tia. It must have been a trick of the light, but Tia fancied he looked more mature than when she'd set off. His jaw seemed squarer, his shoulders a little broader.

'It wasn't quite where Tink thought it was, but, yes, we found it,' the older man responded.

'And it's really uninhabited? An entire city?'

Tia answered this time. There was something about the way she pulled the blanket tight around her shoulders as she remembered where she'd just returned from that left Rush feeling slightly uneasy. 'Well, I think you'd be hard pressed to call it a city, once you've seen it.'

'Still . . . it's hard to imagine a place like that remaining abandoned for so long.'

'I guess the only good thing about planning on living with the dead is that nobody else wants to.'

'It is a lot further south than Tink remembered,' Silas continued. 'It's on the edge of the Blacklands. "Remote" doesn't even begin to describe it. That could work for, but also against, us. It'll be hard to find food there that won't make us all sick or even kill us, and I'm not sure how we'd go about supplying ourselves for the winter.' Silas had been opposed to finding a base somewhere so remote, stating that it would take him away from his mutants' rights work and the rallies he was still so keen to keep going. However, he'd insisted they put it to the vote, and when he'd been outnumbered he'd grudgingly accepted the majority decision.

Rush looked over at the armoured troop carrier, a sly grin slowly forming on his face.

'The cities have no trouble supplying each other.'

'What are you talking about?'

'If Melk wants to label us as guerrillas, I say that's how we start acting. We'll steal everything we need. They ferry supplies between the Cities in those large transporters. How difficult could it be to liberate some of that stuff?'

'That could be dangerous.'

The youngster gave the older man a bemused look. 'Haven't you worked it out yet, Silas? Everything we do is dangerous now.'

Dead City

Tia crested the hill and pressed her foot on the brake to bring the troop carrier to a halt. Although she had seen the place already, the shock of what lay before her was no less than it had been that first time. Silas, sitting in the passenger seat by her side, seemed to be having the same thoughts. She glanced in the wing mirror at the transporter behind them, waiting for it to catch up. When the two vehicles were side by side, everybody got out and stood on the ridge staring down on the vast, open mausoleum.

'Behold. Man's inhumanity to man,' Silas said in a low voice.

'Wow,' Rush said, knowing the exclamation sounded lame and inadequate as soon as it had left his lips. He glanced over at Brick, who had made a low groaning noise at about the same time.

A bridge, or a flyover of some kind, had once linked the place down there with the hill where they stood. That, like everything else associated with this place – the tower blocks, the shops, the houses and whatever else had once stood down there – was long gone. The fact that the scene greeting their eyes had once been a city, a city teeming with people, a city perhaps not unlike the six that the Pure inhabited on this rebooted version of Earth, was not obvious at first glance. Now it looked as if an enraged god had smitten the place, transforming everything into broken stone, corroded metal and ash – a cracked and broken place. Burnt-out shells (Rush guessed they must once have been vehicles of some kind) were everywhere, thousands of them, not an inch of space between them; most of them were covered in the same debris and rubble as everything else.

Grey.

The place hadn't always been so; once it must have been a multitude of colours and lights, but not any longer. Now everything was grey and lifeless.

Tink had not accompanied them. He'd told them that he had 'business to attend to' way off to the south and would go there on his own, refusing both their pleas for him to stay and their offers to go with him. Rush had noticed the odd look in the older man's eyes when he'd told them of his plans the evening before his departure, and a little later, when they were alone, he'd asked his friend if the business had anything to do with one of Tink's 'visions'. 'Maybe,' was the foreseer's enigmatic response. 'But I hope to hell I'm wrong on this one.'

Rush had been sad to see Tink leave, but knew it was the older man's way. Whatever it was he was up to, he hoped he was safe.

'There's a path of sorts over there,' Tia said, gesturing to their right. 'It's the only way down from here.'

'I'll fly,' Anya said. There was none of the spiky attitude she'd exhibited so much recently. Instead she, like the rest of them, seemed aghast at the scene before them.

'Brick stay here,' the big guy said.

'You can't,' Rush said, putting a reassuring hand on the hulk's ham-like forearm. 'This is going to be our new home.'

'No,' Brick said, shaking his head. 'Dead things down there.'

'Well, yes, I guess there are. But they can't hurt you if they're dead, can they?'

'Dead things and the dark. Brick get frightened.'

'Not this again!' Anya blurted out. 'Have a look at yourself, Brick. Just for one second. Look at the size of you! Afraid of the dark? Don't be such a dummy.'

'Don't call him that,' Rush responded angrily. 'He's not a dummy. He's –'

'Ridiculous!'

'What is your problem, Anya?' Rush took a step towards her, suddenly angry on his friend's behalf. 'For weeks now you've been a pain in everyone's arse. Sulking all the time. Snapping at the least thing anyone says. OK, so Brick doesn't like the dark. So what? You've no right to call him names, so don't.'

'Or what?' She showed no sign of backing down. 'What are you going to do, hmm?'

Silas stepped between them, holding his arms out to separate them as best as he could. 'I hardly think this is helping. Squabbling and fighting among ourselves. What is that going to achieve?' He turned to Brick. 'There are lights where we're going, I promise you that. Besides, you have your torch, don't you?' The older man looked over at Rush and gestured in Brick's direction. 'He'll need your help.'

Rush watched as the huge man-child fished inside his pocket for the dynamo-powered device he'd given to him all that time ago when they'd first met. It made him smile to watch the big man's shovel hands, topped with the fattest fingers imaginable, deftly spin the tiny handle on the side of the thing, whirling it around with perfect dexterity before flicking the switch at the side. Brick hated to be without the thing, and Rush guessed it was a security blanket of sorts. Something the big guy relied upon whenever the night demons that haunted him threatened.

'We'll just go and see what it's like, eh?' Rush gave Brick a nudge with his shoulder. 'If you don't like it, you and I can sleep in the transporter tonight, and we'll work something out tomorrow.'

Brick seemed to relax a little. 'Rush shouldn't shout at Anya.'

'Well, Anya shouldn't be so mean to people. What do you say? Will you give it a go?'

'Down there?' Brick still looked miserable at the prospect.

'Everything'll be fine.'

'Rush promise?'

'I promise.'

Rush was filled with a strange feeling of dread as they made their way through the devastation that they were proposing to make their home. Brick was right; there were dead things – more than any of them could count. Corpses stared out at them from everywhere. Some of those trapped within the cars were surprisingly well preserved, as he found out when he wiped a thick crud of grey ash from a windscreen and looked inside. Sunken-eyed, with mummified lips drawn back over ghastly toothy grins, they stared back out at him. Others were little more than skeletons, but these too seemed to track the group's progress through the derelict streets, as if to ask who the newcomers were and what right they had in coming here. He hated it here, but he put on a brave face for Brick, who walked along with his head down, humming tunelessly in a voice that threatened to crack at any moment.

Nobody spoke. That it had been rush hour when the attack occurred was obvious from the sheer number of bones and skulls littered on the ground. Either that, or everyone in this place had come out on to the streets to die together.

'This is it,' Silas said, coming to a halt before what appeared to be a large rectangular opening in the ground. From the look of the earth around it, he, Tink and Tia had already cleared a large amount of the rubble and wreckage to open it up properly.

'Down there?' Jax said, looking dubiously down the steps that led under the cracked and broken concrete of the streets. Although he didn't know it, the albino was standing on what had once been the pavement of the busiest junction in this former city. At that time – before humankind had unleashed the ultimate storm of death – great glass and concrete structures had loomed over this spot on all sides: a giant commercial Mecca that drew consumers from all over the world.

'There's almost as much of the city below the ground as there is above it,' Silas told them. 'Down there are miles of tunnels that interconnect and criss-cross everything you see up here. There were underground trains, powered by electricity, to transport vast numbers of people around the city. The main benefits are that we'll be out of sight and sheltered from the weather. The temperature down there is fairly constant all year round. Don't get me wrong, I'm not saying it's warm, but it is better than being exposed to the elements.'

'Brick'll freak out.' Rush said. They'd left the big guy a little way back, and the younger mutant glanced across to make sure his friend wouldn't overhear him.

'No, he won't.' Silas gave him a strange look. 'Tia and I didn't just clear this entrance. Like I said, we were busy. Just keep him occupied up here for a few moments, and I'll go down and make it possible for him to join us.'

Once they'd powered them up, the fumes from the generators filled the place with an acrid stench, but the lights rigged up to them cast their harsh illumination across the vast open space at the bottom of the steps. It was only once this was done that Rush and Brick were summoned. They stared around in wonder.

It must once have been a ticketing hall, no doubt for the trains: windows with counters were set into the walls, alongside the rusted remains of machines whose purpose was no longer clear. Bisecting the vast space were a series of barriers arranged side by side with little gates between them, some of which were open. Beyond these, on the far side of the space, where the shadows deepened, there appeared to be stairs that led down into a much greater darkness.

'This is where we're going to live?' Anya asked, not even attempting to hide her distaste.

'For now,' Silas said. 'We agreed we need a base, and this is the safest place we could find. Of course, if you think you can do better you're welcome to try.' He raised an eyebrow at her, only continuing when she declined to answer. 'We're going to need more supplies. We need fuel for the generators, bedding, warm clothing. The food we have will only last a month or so at best, but this is a good place for us. We can make this into something. There are plenty of raw materials we can use, and it's a lot safer than constantly moving from place to place out there.'

'I think I preferred it when we were being hunted by the ARM,' Anya said, unable to resist sniping again.

'If you think that's stopped, you're kidding yourself.' Silas turned to the others, choosing to ignore her. 'Now, let's at least attempt to make this place a little more comfortable, shall we?'

'What's it called?' Tia said, speaking for the first time. 'The city, I mean. If we're going to make it a base, we should give it a name.'

'How about Deadville?' suggested Anya, still sulking.

'What about Brickville?' Rush suggested, giving the big guy a playful punch on the arm, the suggestion greeted by the big man shouting out his name at the top of his voice before treating each of them to a wide, toothy grin.

'I think that's an excellent name,' Silas said, nodding his approval. He hooked a hand into the crook of the big man's elbow and gently led him away, suggesting ways they could make Brickville a good place for them all to stay.

Ambush

Stubbs, the driver of the escort vehicle, saw the massive boulder tumbling down the hillside before him in plenty of time to stop. It cartwheeled end over end, making harsh cracking sounds as it splintered and broke up into smaller rocks which in turn smashed through the scrubby undergrowth, kicking up a vast dust cloud as they went. As large as the rocks were, Stubbs knew they posed no real threat to either his vehicle or the larger transporter behind it. Even if they'd been hit full on, both transporter and escort were built to withstand almost anything this harsh landscape could throw at them. Besides, the rockfall wasn't even that close – the stones and rubble spewed out over the road surface about fifty metres or so in front of him and finally came to a halt.

Stubbs sighed. In the same way he cleared snow in the

winter months – when this area was so deep in the white stuff that a person could sink in it up to his waist – he'd now have to lower the large metal plough over the front of his vehicle to create a path for the transporter to pass through.

He waved a hand over the comms unit on top of his dashboard, a holo-image from the interior of the cab behind him instantly appearing.

'Did you see that?' he said to the transporter driver, a surly woman named Horst.

'I'm not blind,' she sighed. 'Why the hell did they insist on us taking this route? This gorge is a nightmare.'

'I'm with you on that one. I'll have to use the scoop to get all of that crap out of the way. Bear with me.' Stubbs pushed down a lever and there was a loud whining noise as the hydraulic arms on either side of the cab slowly lowered the formidable-looking shovel into place.

'How long do you think it'll take?' Horst asked.

'Not so long. Sit tight.'

'Well, get a move on. I'm in a hurry.'

Stubbs flicked a hand out and turned the comms device off before swearing out loud, declaring *exactly* what he thought of the sour-faced bitch in the other vehicle. Who the hell was she to speak to him like that? His usual partner on this run had fallen sick, so Horst, whom nobody in the depot appeared to have heard of, had been assigned to the transporter vehicle. Now, instead of having his buddy to talk to, he had this harpy.

'Get a move on,' he said, mimicking her under his breath. He hadn't even wanted to take this job from his own city, C3, to the capital – not when there wasn't even the prospect of a good time to be had at their destination. C4 used to be a fine place to overnight, but since the terrorist attacks a few months back, all passes to visit Muteville had ceased.

There was a loud *clunk!* and Stubbs's cab rocked a little as the scoop came to a halt, just off the ground. He peered out through the windscreen. It was still a little hazy out there, so he waited a few moments for the dust from the rockslide to clear. When it did, the figure of a solitary boy was revealed on the hill ahead of him. The sun was at the youngster's back so he was a perfect silhouette – his long hair blowing wildly in the wind as he swung the long rope sling round his head.

'What the hell . . . ?' Stubbs hit the button to activate the robotic cannon on top of his vehicle, reaching up with his other hand and pulling the goggles sitting on top of his head down over his eyes, his hands shaking as he fumbled for the button to turn them on. He was supposed to keep the eyewear on at all times; the gun was synced with them and would lock on to targets via the visual feed.

He peered up in time to see the stone as it left the sling and raced through the air like a tracer bullet. Stubbs flinched as it hit the windscreen with a *crack!*, transforming the toughened glass instantly into a shattered mosaic which was impossible to see through. At the same time something dark, flying very low to the ground, flashed past his passenger-side window. Although it was gone before he could get a proper look at it, it was clear that the boy on top of the hill was not alone.

What was going on?

The loud *bang* on top of his cab made him jump in alarm – something had landed on the roof. Looking up, he heard the servo-engines that powered the turret gun swinging the weapon up in the same direction. There were three loud *thunk!* sounds above his head and the noise of the servo-motors cut out. This time, when he swung back around to face the shattered windscreen, the guns did not respond.

'We're being ambushed!' Stubbs shouted into the comms unit, at the same time hitting another button that would override the automatic targeting and cause the guns to fire anyway, hoping it would be enough to scare away whoever was out there. He waited for the low *flump-flump* sound of pulsed-energy rounds, but nothing happened. 'Get the hell out of here, Horst!'

'I can't!'

'What? Why?'

'Take a look!'

Stubbs could hear the strident whine of the other vehicle's engine. He stared in the large side mirror at the vehicle behind him, his mouth falling open at what he saw. The biggest guy he'd ever laid eyes on – a huge colossus of a man – had taken a grip of the front of the haulage vehicle, just below the grille, and was lifting it up off the ground, the tyres on either side spinning furiously in the air as Horst tried in vain to get away. If he hadn't seen it with his own eyes, Stubbs would not have believed it possible to lift the thing; the engine alone must weigh at least –

All thoughts of Horst and the colossal mutant were banished from his mind when the *thing* suddenly appeared at the window on his side, hanging upside down only inches away. Face to face with the stuff of nightmares, Stubbs screamed and threw himself back from the glass on to the passenger's side, his feet scrabbling on the seat he'd just vacated as he sought to get as far away as possible. The creature staring in at him was a vile monster. Multiple eyes, like big black berries, blinked in unison. The mouth – filled with long, dagger-like teeth – seemed to be grinning at him. Gibbering incoherently, Stubbs tried to retreat further, but his head and shoulders were already jammed up against the door on the passenger's side. As quickly as it had appeared, the monstrous thing was gone, and he thought he could hear its clawed feet scrabbling about on the roof again.

He'd forgotten to lock the doors!

As if his thoughts had been read, the driver's-side door flew open, letting in cold air and dust in equal measure. Stubbs thought he saw something – not the dark monster, but a glimpse of a small girl with long red hair; the vision gone almost as soon as it had formed. There was the unmistakable rattle of keys, and the engine died.

Something had taken his keys. Something that was there one second, gone the next. The door remained open, and he wanted nothing more than to slide back over there and lock it shut, but his body wouldn't respond and he remained where he was, frozen with fear. He thought he might be in danger of having a coronary if his heart continued to hammer away inside his chest as it was now. *What was happening!?* Until today he would have scoffed at the suggestion ghosts or monsters might exist, but what he'd seen in the last few moments . . . Well he'd –

'Hello.'

Stubbs jolted as if struck by an electrical current. Standing outside, looking in at him, was a tall black-robed figure with the whitest skin and the bluest eyes Stubbs had ever seen. Due to the height of the escort vehicle, only the albino's upper half was visible, but that was more than enough for the driver, who found he couldn't even speak.

Anya landed on the ground beside Flea, morphing back into her human shape as soon as her feet touched the ground. She was wary of staying in any other form for too long – she'd become 'trapped' on occasions in the past, and although Jax was trying to help her find ways to overcome this she was still nervous. As always, she felt the physical toll of reinhabiting her body: a dull ache that permeated deep into her bones. Ignoring it as best she could, she turned her attention to the driver, who was gawping out of his cab at the white-skinned figure before him.

'My name is Jax,' the albino said with a slight nod of his head. 'My friends and I are hijacking you. Would you be so kind as to step outside?'

'Hijacking?'

'I believe that's the correct term. We're rather new to all this.'

Stubbs – that was the name embroidered on to the pocket of his shirt – shifted his eyes from the albino to the area immediately around the door, as if he was expecting something to suddenly appear again. Jax nodded sympathetically. 'If you're worried about the hideous creature that appeared at your window? You don't need to – she's gone now. She wouldn't have hurt you anyway; she was merely a distraction.'

The description stung Anya. *A distraction? Hah! She'd terrified the guy. He'd been fit to pee his pants when she'd looked in the window at him. And now Jax was belittling her contribution – yet again – by describing her as a 'distraction'!*

'Come down,' the boy – Jax – said. 'I promise you you're quite safe as long as you do as we say.'

Reluctantly, not sure what else he *could* do, Stubbs slowly climbed across the seats and got down out of his vehicle. He glanced across at Anya, his eyes flitting from her to Flea – who jangled his keys at him – and back again. The man clearly had no idea it had been her up there on top of his vehicle. She morphed, only for a second, back into the multi-eyed creature and gave him a wave, almost laughing out loud when, for the second time that day, she saw the colour drain out of his face. She liked the feeling of power it gave her.

'Anya. Enough.' Jax shook his head at her.

'Who are you people?' Stubbs asked. 'What's g–'

The sound of someone calling out, as if to a pet, made him spin to see the figure of a mutant boy hurrying down the rutted, uneven road towards them. Anya followed the man's gaze and tried hard not to blush when Rush gave her a nod. Instead she returned the gesture, trying to look as nonchalant as possible. Her heart beat a little faster.

Not for the first time, she asked herself why he had this effect on her and why she had feelings for him. Especially when it was obvious he didn't feel the same way about her.

He was tall for his age. Tall and handsome. Kicking a stone out of his way, he did that thing with his head, a little flick that sent his long locks out of his face, and called again for the beast accompanying him to catch up.

Anya forced herself to look at the driver again. The man's attention was fully on Rush's pet now. The weird mutated chimera – part dog, part lizard and part something completely unidentifiable – huffed and *hurghed* as it padded along on short legs to catch up with the fifteen-year-old boy who was coiling a leather sling about his hand.

Noting the man's growing unease, she stepped forward. 'It's a rogwan,' she said.

'What?'

'The creature. It's a rogwan.'

'Does it bite?'

Jax smiled at the driver. 'She, like the rest of us, doesn't want to hurt you in any way.'

'So what *do* you want?'

'First we need you to talk to your friend,' the albino said, nodding in the direction of the other vehicle. In his panicked state, it was clear Stubbs had almost completely forgotten about Horst. 'Tell her to cut her engine, please. Our friend Brick must be getting a little tired of holding that thing up like that.'

The wheels of the transporter were still rotating wildly in the air. The giant Mute, however, hardly appeared to be struggling under the immense weight. On unsteady legs, Stubbs walked over so Horst could see him clearly through the windscreen. He waved his arms about to get her attention and gave her a nod, swiping the air in a signal for her to stop.

When the wheels came to a halt, the big guy in front of the vehicle slowly lowered it to the ground, glancing momentarily at the bloody gouges on the palms of his hands where the transporter undercarriage had cut through the flesh. His friends knew the wounds would already be starting to heal, and that pretty soon they'd be gone altogether.

'Are you OK?' Rush called across to the man-mountain.

'Brick!' the big guy answered in a loud voice. He gave the others a broad grin and a thumbs-up before strolling over to the edge of the road, where he sat cross-legged and started to pet the rogwan.

'Signal for your friend to come out, please,' Rush said to Stubbs.

It took a few moments, but eventually the female driver left her vehicle and joined them.

'What's in the back of the transporter?' Rush asked her.

'Supplies,' Stubbs answered, when the woman refused to speak. Anya noted the bemused look on the driver's face as he tried to work out why the younger Mute had taken over the questioning, and why the albino, now standing silent by his side, had his eyes closed.

'What type of supplies?'

'Foodstuffs and clothing for the ARM.'

'Why does food and clothing need an armed escort vehicle to accompany it? That never normally happens.' It was a question the mutant children had pondered when they'd seen the vehicles coming.

Stubbs couldn't hide the sarcasm from his voice. 'Well, apparently there have been cases of Mutes ambushing vehicles bound between the cities lately. Maybe that could be it, eh?'

Anya stepped forward. Both she and Rush stared at the albino, Jax. 'Well?' she said.

'He's telling the truth,' Jax said. 'At least, he's telling us what *he* knows.' His eyes were still shut. 'The woman, however, is an ARM operative, and she knows a whole lot more. For instance, she knows there's a hidden section in the transporter . . .' He paused, his white eyebrows beetling together for a moment. 'She doesn't know what's in it, only that it's extremely important to President Melk. It's destined for . . . the Bio-Gen labs at City Four.'

'How the hell did you . . . ?' Stubbs looked from the Mutes to his colleague. 'Is it true?' He took her silence for an admission. 'An ARM operative? Just what is going on here, Horst?' Then, to the mutant children: 'I don't know this woman. I've never worked with her before. She was assigned to me.'

'Tell us about that hidden compartment,' Rush said to Horst.

Instead of answering, the woman made a grab for a gun concealed in the waistband of her trousers. Anya morphed, but she knew she would never get there in time. She didn't need to. Rush, raising his hand, flicked his fingers to the right and the gun flew out of her grasp. His other hand, palm out, shot forward and Horst flew back off her feet, landing in an unconscious heap a short distance away. The gun, turning end over end, never got a chance to hit the ground. It seemed to disappear in mid-air, and although none of them saw the little redhead move, she reappeared in front of Stubbs, gun in hand, the barrel pointing straight at his chest.

'Whoa!' he said, arms raised. 'Don't shoot! I had no idea she was carrying a gun. Hell, like I told you, I had no idea she was with the Agency.'

'Rush? Anya?' Jax said, gesturing for them to join him before addressing Stubbs. 'We're going to take a look inside that transporter. If you move, little Flea here will shoot you, won't you, Flea?'

The freckle-faced kid nodded, the gun held unwaveringly out before her.

'I ain't moving,' the support driver responded, his eyes glued to the weapon as the other three strode across to the back of the transporter and opened it up.

Ignoring the large metal cages crammed with supplies on either side, Anya and Rush followed Jax up the central aisle towards the wall at the back of the hold area. A perfectly smooth, brushed metal surface greeted them. Jax rapped at it with his knuckles.

'No obvious way to open it,' Anya said, examining the wall and the area all surrounding it.

'The other guy, Stubbs, genuinely had no idea about this?' Rush asked.

'Not a clue. When I dipped into his mind, he was as surprised as we were to find out Horst was an agent.'

'So what do we do now?'

'We take this thing, find a way to open it up and discover

what's behind here. If it's important enough to have a secret agent transporting it, maybe it'll be useful to us.'

'OK,' the Mute called Rush said, smiling at Stubbs, who was standing in the exact same spot they'd left him. 'Here's what's going to happen. *We* will be taking *this* vehicle.' He indicated the transporter. '*You* are free to leave in the other one. We've already disabled the robot gun turret of your escort vehicle, so don't bother trying to open fire on us as we drive off.'

Stubbs frowned as if expecting the boy to say something else. 'That's it? I'm free to go?'

'Uh-huh.'

'Just like that?'

'What did you think? That we'd stake you out on the dust and leave you for the scavengers? That we'd kill you?' The boy gave a sad shake of his head. 'Despite what your leaders tell you, the mutant people are not your enemies, Stubbs. And we are not like your trigger-happy ARM friend over there.'

'She's not my friend,' Stubbs said, looking across at Horst as she let out a little groan, slowly regaining consciousness. 'What about her?'

'That's up to you. You want her, take her. If you don't, leave her behind. Whatever you decide, you wait here for an hour, then you go to wherever you want to go, as long as it's not in the same direction we're heading.'

'The windscreen on that escort is broken.'

'Improvise. I'm sure you'll manage somehow. Oh, and you've still got some rocks to clear out of your way.' He nodded at the little redhead, the one called Flea. She threw the keys back at Stubbs, who caught them despite the tremors in his hands.

Without another word, the Mutes jumped into the other vehicle, some in the cab, the others in the back, and drove off, leaving the two drivers behind.

Stubbs watched them go before wandering over to help Horst sit up. She was bleeding a little from a small cut at the back of her head, but she didn't seem too bad. When she asked him where the transporter was, she followed the line of his finger, squinting into the distance as the thing slowly disappeared.

'This is not good,' she said, her voice more than a little shaky.

'You should have told me you were an agent. You endangered my life, dammit!'

'Stop your whining and help me up.'

'Do you think they're the Mutes who attacked C4 and killed the president's son?' he asked once she was able to stand on her own two feet again.

'If they're not, there are two groups of mutants with special powers wandering around out here on Scorched Earth.' She moved her head from side to side, testing her neck for any pain. 'Come on, let's get the hell out of here. I need to make a report to my commanders.'

Melk

The screen that had been positioned in front of the south-facing section of the Wall – lowered into place by two huge cranes from inside City Four – was vast. Despite its size, the vis-display was dwarfed by the colossal metal-and-concrete curved bulwark reaching up into the air behind it. The landscape immediately in front of this section of the Wall, beyond a heavily fortified and guarded no-man's-land, was dominated by the sprawling slums of Muteville. The live presidential address that was shortly to appear on the screen was directed at the inhabitants of that place, but it would be watched by everyone on either side of the Wall. Giant white numbers were ticking slowly downwards on the vis-display: a countdown that had been going on since the thing had been put in place.

As the numbers switched to indicate three minutes

remaining, a klaxon sounded, the harsh, jarring noise pumped from the speakers mounted on the sentry points all around the no-man's-land. Like the countdown, the klaxon had accompanied the arrival of the screen. It would be followed by the announcement – the announcement that by now everyone in Muteville could probably recite word for word. At first the klaxon had sounded every hour on the hour, the noise penetrating deep into the inner wards of Muteville and waking everybody in the thin-walled hovels and shacks that made up the vast majority of the dwellings there. Every hour. When one mutant unfortunate enough to live close to the fences had tried to disable a speaker by throwing rocks at it, he'd been shot, his body left close to the razor-wire-topped barrier as a warning.

When an hour remained, the intervals between the braying alarm and its accompanying message had started to be repeated every ten minutes. When only fifteen minutes were left, it was every five. Now it was every sixty seconds.

The deafening noise of the klaxon – specifically designed by scientists to jar and set teeth on edge – stopped, and was replaced by a flat and emotionless female voice:

'Inhabitants of Muteville, your attention. The leader of the Principia, President Melk, will address you from this screen at

the end of this countdown. It is in the interest of every mutant to hear what the President of the Six Cities has to say. Ensure your fellow mutants are aware of this. That is all.'

There was a brief squeal of feedback, and the announcement stopped.

The countdown and proclamation had had the desired effect. Most of Muteville appeared to be gathered before the razor-wire fences now that the countdown was almost at an end, anger and fear in equal measure on their faces as they stared up at the screen, wondering what this was all about. Some held young children, but others, wary of the armed guards in the sentry towers and their habit of opening fire on any mutant getting too close to the fences, had opted to leave their offspring at home.

Most of the Mutes weren't obviously deformed or disfigured. Minor abnormalities abounded: an extra finger or toe; asymmetrical facial features; lumps or growths under the flesh. But the more obvious defects – those that were far more common in those unfortunates born topside immediately after the Last War – weren't so prevalent now. Regardless of this, most of those inside the walls viewed their neighbours with disdain and revulsion.

Sixty seconds turned into thirty, into ten, five . . .

The screen blinked, the harsh white numerals replaced by the stern face of perhaps the most famous man on

Scorched Earth. Up on that enormous screen he seemed to loom over his audience, as if at any moment he might reach out and swat them away or squash them. Although only his head and shoulders filled the picture, it was clear he was sitting in an office of some kind. In the background, hanging on the wall, was a huge metal plaque; scratched and battered, a large number four could clearly be made out on its surface.

The man looked straight into the camera, the intensity of his stare making some people in the crowd shift nervously.

'You know who I am. If you didn't before, I guess our little countdown message must have put you straight, but I'll introduce myself anyway. We are, after all, neighbours.' He drew this last word out. 'My name is Melk, and I am the president of the Six Cities – cities that were built by the Children of the Arks – the door to one of which is hanging on the wall behind me.' His eyes shifted for a moment, as if somebody behind the camera had said something to him, before he continued. 'This, however, is not a history lesson. Far from it. Scorched Earth needs to look forward, not back.' He paused, staring straight into the lens again as if to emphasise this point. A small child, picking up on the tension in the crowd, began to cry, but otherwise there was silence. 'Ghettos similar to the one you are watching this broadcast from exist close to each of the Six Cities. Yours, however, like the metropolis whose shadow you inhabit, is the largest. Despite the huge wall that separates us, the growth of your . . . community has not gone unnoticed. You Mutes seem to crave our company.' The corners of his mouth twitched, but whether it was a smile or a grimace was impossible to tell. 'We, on the other hand, do not crave yours.'

The picture on the screen crackled with static for a moment, but quickly returned. If Melk was aware of this, he didn't show it.

'It is common knowledge that City Four, the place I'm talking to you from, was recently attacked. Mutant terrorists found a way inside our walls – something I swore would never happen – and bombed us. My own son was killed as a result of this attack.' Another pause as he let this sink in. 'Now, some of you out there might be feeling good about that. Some of you may think we had it coming. That we *deserved* it. The more intelligent among you will understand that an act like this could easily be seen as a declaration of war, giving *us* the right to punish *you* in the most extreme ways imaginable.'

A nervous babble swept through the crowd, many eyes turned instinctively towards the armed men in the towers as the President's voice boomed on.

'But what would that prove, hmm? That we're superior to you? We already know that.' His brow furrowed. 'So I have thought long and hard about how to respond to this attack. And today I am going to share my conclusions with you.

'As you are no doubt aware, I'm a man known for his hard-line policies. Indeed, the *old* me would almost certainly have reacted in the way I've just described: by lashing out at the entire mutant community in retribution for what a few of your members have done. But then it occurred to me that there might be another way.' He paused for a moment before continuing.

'My late son, Zander, believed a possible solution for the mutants of Scorched Earth might be to give you your own space in which to live – settlements designated as mutant land. He'd looked into this in some detail and had started to set up reservations for Mutes to inhabit. Places where you could build houses, where you could grow crops and raise livestock. Where you could begin again, out of the shadows of the cities. I'm ashamed to say I poured scorn on these ideas.'

A map appeared on the screen. On it the positions of the Six Cities were marked, but also, well away from them, were six new separate areas. One by one these flashed up, accompanied by visuals of rivers and fields. An image of a tall multi-storey building was shown, a family of four standing before it, smiling at the camera.

'It was an olive branch my son wished to extend to the mutant people. And even though, as a father, I am hurting from his loss, I know how important it was to him. He felt it was the right thing to do. It should be him, not me, addressing you now. With that in mind, I intend to follow through with the plans he set in motion. I may not like them, but I'm willing to be proved wrong.'

The map was replaced by Melk's face again.

'Once completed, each of the six reservations you've just seen will have enough housing for thousands of mutants. To date, the only one finished is the reservation designated to house *you*, the Mutes of the slums outside City Four. You have been chosen as the pioneers for this project. You will be the first to be resettled. My offer is simple: take up these places. See this for what it is – a chance to start again, a chance to get out of the slums, out from the shadows of a city that does not want you.' A pause. 'Following this broadcast, a registration bureau will be set up near the fences on the western side of City Four. You can enrol yourselves and your families there. Rules for registration will follow this announcement. You have five days in which to register, and another two days to gather your things together. We have arranged comfortable transport to your new lands.' He narrowed his eyes, his look cold and stony. 'Those Mutes who refuse to register will be declaring their allegiance with the terrorists and will be arrested. A week after the deadline for registration, Muteville will be burned to the ground.' He paused, letting this last bombshell truly sink in. 'You have been warned.'

The screen went blank.

'Cut!' the director responsible for the live address shouted.

Melk leaned back in his chair, steepling his hands before him and resting his chin on the tips of his fingers to accept the congratulations and plaudits of the broadcasting team. Feeling pleased with himself, he watched them for a few moments as they busied themselves around his office space, dismantling equipment and coiling wires. The lights were still on, their harsh beams directed straight into his face, so the space behind them appeared to be in deeper shadow than it really was. One of the crew came over and began to unclip the microphone from the lapel of his jacket. She was young and, like almost everyone in C4, ridiculously good-looking.

'Great speech, Mr President. I'm ashamed to admit it, but I haven't always agreed with your views. I realise that was foolish of me. I'm right behind you now.'

The lights were making him sweat a little. He was about

to ask that they be turned off when his attention was caught by a figure hanging back in the shadows beyond their glare. Unlike the rest of the crew, who were busy packing up their stuff, this person stood unmoving. Melk narrowed his eyes against the harsh light, trying to get a better view. *The way the shadowy figure stood, its arms folded in front of it, head set at that angle . . .* The president's pulse quickened. The intense heat thrown out from the bulbs suddenly seemed to increase to an almost unbearable level.

'Zander?' Melk whispered.

'I'm sorry?' the young woman said, but the politician swatted her away and rose to his feet. The shadowy figure tracked his movement.

'Is this some kind of joke?' the president said in a loud voice, turning to look at the members of the film crew, all of whom had stopped what they were doing and were staring back at him. 'Do you think this is funny? Hmm?'

The director eventually broke the silence.

'Mr President? I'm sorry, sir. What . . . what seems to be the problem?'

Melk glanced at the man before hurrying around the desk, pushing people out of the way until he was beyond the lit area. He stopped. There was nobody there. 'Where did he go?'

'Sir?'

'He was here. He was . . .'

'Who was there?'

Melk looked at the coat stand bearing one of the crew's jackets and a peaked cap.

'Get out,' Melk said, his voice quiet at first. 'Are you deaf? I said get out. All of you. Now!'

Leaving their equipment behind, the film crew hastily scrambled out of the room.

Melk balled his hands into tight fists and closed his eyes. For the second time in as many days, he'd felt his grip on reality loosen. He would not, could not, let that happen. The people relied on him, just as they'd always relied on the Melks.

He was about to change Scorched Earth forever. This broadcast was just the start, the opening move in his quest to provide a solution to one of their longest-standing and most difficult problems. He would not buckle under the strain!

Hands still a little shaky, he took a small yellow pill from a dispenser in his inside jacket pocket and swallowed it.

Get a grip on yourself! You are a leader!

And a leader did not allow shadow phantoms or disembodied voices to distract them from what was needed. Especially now, when he was on the verge of leading the people of the Six Cities into an all-new era. There was no place for weakness, not now. And when the true nature of his mutant relocation was revealed, all of Scorched Earth would see his strength and resolve.

Silas

Snow had started to fall in Brickville. A few small flakes drifted lazily out of the sky, dancing on the wind. Silas looked up at the heavy grey clouds and sighed. He doubted this would turn out to be a full-blown storm, but it would surely be followed by increasingly unpleasant weather.

From his position at the top of the wreckage that might have once been an office complex or maybe a shop of some kind, he could see out towards the route the teens would use for their return, if they hadn't done something reckless and got themselves captured or killed. He reprimanded himself for having these thoughts. He was being foolish; they were more than capable of looking after themselves – they'd proved that from their last two successful raids, not to mention their heroic rescue of Brick from City Four. He couldn't help but smile at the memory of that day when their audacious plan had come together so that they not only liberated their friend, but also sent a message to Melk and the people of the Six Cities: that the mutants were no longer going to sit back and put up with the mistreatment they'd endured for so long. His smile broadened further as he was reminded of the look on his brother's face when he'd realised that Silas had not been bluffing, and the explosions, carefully placed to cause the maximum damage without costing a single life, had begun.

A noise made him look up again, but it was nothing but a large ugly bird taking to the skies from one of the ruins. *Where were they?* He glanced off into the distance again, willing his young charges to come into view.

'No sign of them yet?' Tia called up to him. She was working at a small makeshift table she'd set up not far from the underground entrance, trying to get some of her damaged equipment to work.

'Not yet,' he replied, and she turned back to her task.

He had come to admire the Cowper girl immensely. At first he'd wondered why she'd stayed with the group. She was a Pure, and although she'd illegally removed her CivisChip – the device that allowed citizens to be recognised as such and granted them access inside the Walls – he thought there must be some way she could have used her father's power and influence to get back inside. Instead she'd remained with the mutant company, claiming her work documenting the group's struggle was nowhere near finished. It was only when Silas began to notice how she looked over at Rush at night as they sat round the fire to eat that he began to think there was more to her staying put. Of course, somebody else in the group had also spotted these stolen glances, and from the way Anya had been treating Tia recently, there was little doubt in his mind that she was none too happy about it.

Just what we need, Silas thought. A*n already volatile shape-shifting teenager with bad feelings towards a telekinetic's potential girlfriend. What could possibly go wrong there?* The only good thing to say about the situation was that Rush appeared to be oblivious to it all. Since their big argument on the evening they'd all arrived here, Rush and Anya had hardly spoken a civil word to each other. That was good in some ways, but bad in others, and he knew he'd have to try to do something to resolve the situation. The longer it went on, the more resentment would grow between the two, and the more likely something other than just a shouting match would occur.

Movement at the edge of his vision made him turn his head again.

'What the . . . ?' He stared in disbelief as an enormous

vehicle hurtled across the rubble-strewn landscape towards him.

'Now, I know what you're thinking,' Rush said, before Silas had a chance to speak. The young mutant had climbed down out of the cab almost before the transporter unit, driven by Jax, had come to a halt, and now he stood in front of his guardian, hands out before him in a placating gesture. 'Give us a chance to explain.'

'What is this?' Silas said, barely able to control his anger. 'Maybe you could bring a whole fleet of stolen vehicles here next time, eh? Closely followed by every ARM agent on the face of Scorched Earth! How the hell are we supposed to hide this thing?'

'I know we agreed no more vehicles, but we wouldn't have brought it back here unless it was important.'

Jax had joined him and nodded in agreement. 'It's true, Silas,' he said.

Rush knew Jax's opinion carried more weight with the older man. It was understandable; while the other mutant infants had been hidden in the far corners of Scorched Earth following their rescue from the secret facility where they'd been created, the older albino boy had stayed with his liberator, growing up in the shadows of City Four's walls. Jax was almost like a son to Silas. 'We would have taken what we wanted and let this thing go. But the vehicle's driver was no ordinary delivery woman. I took a peek inside her head and discovered she was an undercover ARM operative.'

'Why would an ARM agent be driving a supply vehicle?' Tia asked, coming up to join the others.

'That's what we wondered,' the albino continued. 'At the same time I discovered that she was not who *she* seemed, I also discovered that this vehicle isn't all *it* seems either.'

Brick opened up the large doors at the back and they all walked round to look inside.

'Look how far back all this stuff goes,' Rush said, pointing to the cargo stacked on either side. 'Now go back outside and see how long the hold really is.'

When Silas and Tia came back, puzzled looks on their faces, they climbed inside and approached the far end of the hold. The others joined them.

'This wall is a dummy,' Silas said, nodding at the metal barrier. Copying what Jax had done when he first came across the barrier, he rapped his knuckles against it, noting how solid the sound was. 'The question is, how do we get it open?'

'Did the woman have one of these on her?' Tia asked, removing her omnipad from her pocket and showing them. The thing had stopped working a few weeks back because of a problem with its internal power supply. Despite this, the teenager still carried it around with her at all times.

Rush grinned at her. He knew how much she missed using the device, and how cut off she felt without it. He dug into his pocket and fished out the one he'd taken from the ARM agent before sending her away. 'I figured you'd want this. I thought you maybe could use the power supply to get your own working.'

Tia turned the thing on and waved her hand over the pad, quickly scanning the display for unusual applications. One caught her eye, and when she opened it a holo-keypad appeared in the air. She let out a frustrated sigh. 'Security protected. You have to enter a four-digit code to gain access, and that could take me forever to –'

'Try 7648,' Jax said, shrugging as the others turned to look at him. 'It was a number the ARM agent was trying very hard *not* to think about once she realised I could read her thoughts. I had no idea what it might mean – until now.'

Tia entered the code and was immediately rewarded by the sharp noise of automated locks being withdrawn on the other side of the transporter's false wall. A staccato series of harsh *clicks* followed and then, with a noise like a sigh, the entire wall slid up and back over their heads.

A weird yellowish-green light spilled out of the revealed space, painting the onlookers' faces in the same ghastly hue. The illumination came from the glass-fronted cabinets that lined the walls, each of them filled with what appeared to be hundreds, if not thousands, of syringes, hanging point down. Each hypodermic appeared to contain the same light blue liquid.

'Medicines?' Silas said, stepping forward and depressing a small button at the side of one of the cabinets so the front slid back with a *hiss*. He reached in and picked up one of the hypodermics, tapping the vial and peering at it as if this inspection might reveal the nature of the liquid. Removing the rubber bung covering the needle tip, he applied gentle pressure on the plunger, squirting a small jet of the contents into the air. He sniffed, it was odourless.

'Why all the cloak-and-dagger stuff if this is just any regular medicine?' Anya asked. 'The convoy we hit last week had medical supplies on board, and they weren't hidden away like this.'

'Maybe something in here will tell us,' Tia answered, holding up a heavy-looking metal case she'd found beside one of the cabinets. This too had a small keypad on the top. Trying her luck, she entered the same four-digit code Jax had previously revealed to them. Once again they were rewarded, this time with the satisfying *clunk!* of locks disengaging. Inside the case, nestled down among protective foam, was a holo-image player. Placing the device on a shelf, she activated it, stepping back so the others could get a view of the image that immediately appeared in the air above it. The figure of man in his fifties looked back at them.

'President Melk, felicitations from City Two. As promised, here is the second batch of the N22 DNA marker. I must say, I rather like your name for it: Crimson Tears – very good, Mr President. There are twelve hundred syringes pre-loaded with product, and we are manufacturing more as quickly as we are able, as per your instructions. In line with your suggestions, we have made some changes to the transportation solution, and I think you'll be happy with the results. Following this holo-mail is a short film demonstrating our most recent tests. I'm sure you'll agree it is quite impressive. Just speak the words "Play N22 research file number forty-six", followed by your security code, and it will begin. I trust you'll find it most enlightening. I hope to see you the next time I'm in City Four. Until then.' The man disappeared.

'Where was this shipment bound?'

'C4.'

Silas looked about him. 'So unless we know my brother's

security code, we have no way of knowing what these syringes are for? Great.'

'Not necessarily,' Tia said. 'I know a man in Muteville who might be able to tell us.' She looked at the case. 'He might also be able to get us access to that research file.'

'Who is this man?'

'His name is Juneau. He's a scientist. Quite brilliant, but he's chosen to set himself up as a backstreet surgeon, carrying out all manner of dubious work for money.'

'Can we trust him?'

'No.' She shook her head. 'But he's about the best chance we have of discovering why all this is so important to Melk.'

'Then I think we need to make a visit to the C4 slums.'

'Great,' Anya said. 'I'm sick to death of this place.' She grimaced, realising what she'd said.

'No,' Silas said firmly. 'We will not all be going. For this, I think we should keep the numbers to a minimum. I suggest Jax, Rush and Tia.'

'What?'

'Think about it. It makes sense. While Tia goes to find Juneau, Jax can go on a fact-finding mission in other parts of the slums. He knows them better than the rest of you. After all, he grew up there. Tia is the only one who knows this Juneau character, so she has to go –'

'Why does *he* have to go?' she said, pointing at Rush, and doing nothing to disguise the contempt in her voice.

'Because if anything untoward happens, Rush will prove useful.'

'*Useful.* So what am I to infer from that? That you consider the rest of us to be use*less*?'

'Now I didn't say that. In fact –'

'To hell with you, Silas! To hell with all of you! This is just so typical of what has been going on here recently. *She* –' Anya thrust an angry finger in Tia's direction – 'has been manipulating you ever since she wheedled her way into this group. Don't you see what she's doing? She doesn't care a damn about any of you; she's only interested in us as a narrative for her precious documentary! A freak story that will make her famous!'

'That might just be the most stupid thing I've ever heard!' Rush said.

It was clearly the wrong thing to say. The look on Anya's face went from indignation to outright fury. She transformed. One second an angry teenager was there, the next a huge winged monster with a broad serpent head and an ape-like body loomed over the group, its jaws wide open to display row upon row of black curved teeth. It hissed, turning this way and that to direct the angry sound at everybody present. Unfurling the leathery wings, it bent at the knee and leaped into the air, the wings filling the air with a loud whooshing as they beat faster and faster, lifting the creature up into the air.

'Anya, wait!' Silas said, ignoring the dust kicked up from the earth. But it was too late. The creature took off into the air, flying away without so much as a backwards look.

Melk

'I said I was not to be disturbed! Come back when –'

'Sir?'

Melk recognised the voice. He turned in his chair to take in the face of his most trusted aide, General Razko. Well built and still an imposing figure, despite his years, it was clear from the military man's expression that whatever news he bore was not good.

'What is it, General?'

'We have a problem.'

'Well . . . ?'

'There's been another ambush on a transporter.'

'The mutant children? Another food shipment?'

'Yes to the first, not quite to the second.' He hesitated. 'They hit the vehicle we were expecting from C2. The one carrying the latest batch of injections.'

Melk sat unmoving, his eyes fixed on the general's.

'Unlike the other raids, they didn't just unload the stuff they wanted. They took the transporter too.'

'DAMMIT!' Melk roared, getting to his feet and smashing his fist down into the electronic equipment mounted into his desktop, shattering the screen. 'How did they know?'

'It's not at all clear that they did. At least not at first. We think it started as another opportunist hit like the previous two. But the albino . . . he read our agent's mind.'

'Jax.' Melk's lip curled and he shook his head. 'How much did *she* know?'

'Very little. She knew the shipment was covert, but not the nature of it.'

Melk, deep in thought, rubbed at his chin, oblivious to the cut on his hand and the tiny droplets of blood oozing from it. When he spoke again, it was mostly to himself. 'Even if they manage to find out what was hidden in there, it'll mean nothing to them. This is just a . . . blip.'

'There's something else,' the general said.

'What?'

'The laboratory's findings? The videos and data you requested? They were supposed to be sent on a separate vehicle. It appears somebody got lazy and stored an omnipad with the information along with the shipment.

The files have an extremely high level of security, as does the device itself. We should be safe.' Razko looked over at his boss, his eyes drawn to a bulging vein that had appeared across the top of the man's head. 'I do have a piece of good news.'

'Oh?'

'Agent Horst managed to activate a small tracking device inside the transporter before it was taken. We'll know where the vehicle is very shortly.'

'Why not now?'

'We're having a few technical problems with our equipment.' He put his hands up. 'Nothing we can't fix,' he quickly added.

'I want whoever is responsible for allowing that data to be transported along with the other cargo found. You are personally to see to it that they're punished. I also want the transporter located within the next thirty minutes. Is that clear?'

'Might I make a suggestion, sir? I think this is the perfect time for us to deploy our other recent project.'

Melk frowned, trying to figure out what the military man was alluding to.

'Not the cyborg?'

'Yes, sir.'

'He's not ready. The scientists are still worried about

various systems. They want to rework the haptic feedback on his legs, and –'

'With all due respect, Mr President, the scientists *always* want more time. I'd have thought that you, as a man of science yourself, would appreciate this. They'll never be satisfied with the 'borg until it is, in their eyes at least, perfect. I've looked into this myself, and in my opinion it's as ready as it's ever going to be. I also believe it's our best chance to capture these young mutant rebels. Every time we send an ARM team after them, they manage to get away. Maybe a lone hunter would stand a better chance of trapping this prey.'

'I'm not comfortable with that, not on the first mission at least.'

'Then maybe a small hand-picked support team?'

Melk thought for a moment, an ugly smile slowly forming on his lips. 'I'd want to see the 'borg before we let it loose.

'Of course. When would you like to do that?'

'Now seems like as good a time as ever, don't you think?'

Registration

Principal Physician Groll glanced up as the woman, her partner and their twin teenage children emerged from the doorway of the treatment room to his left.

How long had he been here, in this place? And how much longer did he have until he was relieved?

He and his staff were all cooped up in the hastily erected structure set up to register the Mutes prior to their relocation, and he hated it. It was about as far from his sterile, high-tech laboratories back in the Bio-Gen building inside the City walls as could be imagined. It was the smell: even the harsh surgical disinfectant he'd insisted the place be cleaned out with couldn't dissipate the terrible reek of these mutants. And here he was, the senior health advisor on the Principia, forced to deal with the unwashed masses. The Mute family were almost at the exit now, the twins – it was strange how many of them were born to Mutes – rubbing at the top of their arms near the shoulder and grimacing a little. The father said something, no doubt asking if they were all right, and the pair nodded. All four made their way through the exit.

From the device on his desk, a message from the operatives in the other room flashed up before him, confirming that all of the preceding family members had been injected without any problems. If he'd seen that same screen text once this morning, he must have seen it a hundred times. The message, like this entire process, was grating on his nerves. 'Monotonous' didn't even begin to describe it. The Mutes in the line outside were ushered in, each family group clutching their papers as they looked nervously about them. He checked their names, asked them some questions about their medical history, confirmed they had their travel dockets and then pointed them in the direction of the treatment room for their 'vaccination'. And it was this last act that was bothering him more and more as the day went on.

Put it out of your mind, he told himself, giving the nearest guard a nod so the man could bark out an instruction for the next in line to approach the desk. Groll had given up on doing this himself after about an hour; his throat was already sore from all the talking he'd done this morning, and he guessed it might still be at least an hour before he was due a break. While he was still inputting the details of the last entry, Groll became aware the Mutes were already standing before his desk.

'Excuse me?' a woman said.

'Wait,' he replied, without looking up.

Eventually he raised his head and took her in.

Standing before him was a mother and her two children. One, a male infant, was balanced on the woman's hip, the thumb of his grimy left hand jammed into his mouth. The drool on his lips and chin, coupled with the rosy colour of his cheeks, suggested to Groll that the child might be teething. He guessed that the other child must be a little girl, but couldn't be sure as she was hidden behind the folds of her mother's skirt, a wild spray of long curly hair into which a number of coloured ribbons had been interwoven all that was visible to the scientist. Using a system of shorthand he himself had devised, he entered this information into the device before him. He estimated the woman must be in her mid-twenties, and was surprised to discover how attractive she was – for a Mute. She was petite with elfin features, and her skin was the colour of sand, but her eyes were truly startling: the irises a deep purple hue with a fine ring of green just around the pupils. He was about to speak, when the little one – she was indeed a girl – appeared from behind her mother, leaning out to the side and staring at Groll warily as if she thought he might leap out at her at any moment. And it was the sight of the young girl that took Groll aback, causing his breath to catch in his throat. The resemblance was uncanny. In fact, apart from the hair and the child's inheritance of that fantastic eye colouration, this little mutant urchin could almost have been his own beloved Megren fifteen years ago! The realisation brought with it painful memories, memories that he could not allow himself, not here, not now.

He cleared his throat and glanced at his screen, trying to pull himself together.

'Family name?' he said, when he'd recovered enough to start the interview.

'Feld.'

'How many of you will be travelling to the reservation?'

'Just the three of us.'

'No partner? No Mr Feld?'

'No. My partner disappeared last year. The ARM claimed they apprehended him in the act of selling black-market goods.' She said this with no small amount of venom, looking at the armed guard standing behind Groll as if he might have been one of the men responsible for her man's vanishing. 'They took him away from his family and we haven't seen him since.'

Groll glanced at the little girl again. She was of an age that, should she indeed make it to adulthood, she'd have no memory of what her father might have looked like. More unbidden memories flooded in. He remembered how his Megren would sit on his lap and ask endless questions about the world. Every answer he gave was followed by yet another 'Why?' until he would give up and, laughing, resort to the only response left to a parent of a precocious child: 'Because it *is*, that's *why*.' He missed her so very badly. His life had never been the same since she'd been taken from him.

'Have any of you had any contact with another mutant with a communicable disease in the last three years?'

'Er, yes, I guess. I mean, out here in the slums people are sick all the time.'

'Quite.'

It was the question to which there was no right or wrong answer; say yes and you went through to the treatment room; say no and you went through to the treatment room. He glanced at the small girl again. As he entered the data, he noted how his usually precise notations were riddled with errors.

'Is there something wrong?' the mother asked.

'What?'

'It's just you keep looking over at my daughter.'

'No. Nothing wrong. She . . . er, she just reminds me of somebody.'

'Oh?'

'Yes. Somebody who was very dear to me.' He cleared his throat. 'My daughter actually. She was . . . she was killed in an accident.'

'I'm sorry to hear that.'

For some reason, her sympathy irked him. What right did this raggedy Mute have to feel pity for him? A Pure. A man at the top of his chosen field.

Get on with your job, Groll, he told himself, and was about to proceed with the registration when the little girl stepped forward and placed a small item on the edge of his desk. Made of twisted wire, with a glass bead for a head, the thing was fashioned to look like a tiny person standing on wire legs, its arms sticking straight out at its sides. With delicate little fingers, she nudged it towards him before disappearing behind her mother's skirt again. He heard her whisper something from her hiding place, but her voice – little more than a whisper – made it difficult for him to catch what she said. He thought it might have been, 'For the sad man.'

Groll stared at the thing on the desk surface and made

his mind up. Letting out an exasperated sigh, he flashed a sad smile at the mother. 'I'm afraid your request for registration is denied, Mutant Feld. You and your family must leave.'

'What?' She stared at him incredulously. 'D-do you have any idea how long my children and I have queued up outside to get in here? There must be a thousand people in that line out there and some, like me, have slept out overnight so we wouldn't lose our place. And now, just like that, you tell me that my request is denied!'

Groll met her angry look with what he thought was his most icy stare. 'Your partner, the male Mutant Feld, is missing, presumed under arrest. Families were told to report with all immediate members present. You are clearly missing one important member. Therefore your request is denied.'

'And how am I to report with my children's father if I have no idea where he is?' Her voice was much louder now, and had a desperate quality to it. She looked back at the next group of people standing behind the rope barrier before rounding on him again. 'This is ridiculous.'

'If you don't leave of your own free will, I'll have the officer here escort you away. I'm sure both of us would rather spare your children that.'

'This was a chance to give my children a new start. You're denying them that chance.'

Groll tapped something into the screen and waited while the plexiprint below his desk finished. He removed the small transparent sheet and handed it to the woman. 'Take that to the ARM. It's a request for them to let you know the whereabouts of your partner. Once you have the information, come back here and reregister.'

'But –'

'Next!' Groll shouted, wincing at the rawness in his throat.

After a moment or two of standing there glaring at him, the woman and her children finally made their way out.

Her exit prompted the guard behind Groll to step forward, the man leaning down to talk to the clinician. 'Excuse me, sir, but I couldn't help but overhear what you told that woman. We've already accepted a large number of Mutes that didn't have all family members present. Shall I go and retrieve them so you might –'

'When I want your input, soldier, I'll ask for it. Until then, I'd appreciate it if you kept your mouth shut. In fact, I'd like you to swap duties with the other guard over there at the barrier. Perhaps he knows how to keep his nose out of matters that do not concern him.'

The soldier made a disgruntled noise, but proceeded to do as he was told, striding off to relieve the other man. As he walked away, Groll reached out and picked up the little handmade toy the mutant child had left behind. He turned the thing over in his hand, allowed himself a small smile, then carefully placed the item inside his jacket pocket.

A fresh group of Mutes presented themselves in front of his desk.

Tears of anger and frustration fell down the Feld woman's face as she exited the registration building, pulling her little girl along. She wanted nothing more than to storm back inside and give that pompous buffoon a piece of her mind. She would have too, if the place wasn't jammed with armed guards.

She looked down at the plexiprint in her hand. Coming to a halt, she studied it more carefully, not quite able to understand what she was reading:

Do not try to reregister your children on this scheme. Instead, leave the slums and stay away from C4.

For the sake of your daughter, please heed this advice.

* * *

Jax arrived at a hill overlooking the western side of the vast slums outside City Four. His chosen vantage point afforded him the chance to observe what was going on below without drawing attention to himself. The only thing he wished was that there was some damned shade where he could take refuge. Jax disliked being out in direct sunlight; the intensity of the light hurt his eyes, and if his skin was exposed for even a short time, it would burn and be painful for days. Clothed in his usual black garb, he pulled his hood down over his head to cover his face as much as possible. It provided some relief, but he still squinted as he cast his eyes over the vast sprawl hovels laid out chaotically below him. At first glance the place appeared to have no organisation at all – dilapidated shacks seemed to be piled up almost on top of one another with little apparent thought to access or personal space – but in reality Muteville had a complex system of living, involving distinct wards that jealously guarded their limited space and resources.

Tia and Rush were somewhere on the other side of the slums, trying to get a meeting with the backstreet bio-engineer the girl had first met when she was still a citizen. Something told Jax it was important they find out what the substance in those syringes was. Melk was planning something sinister, he was sure of it. What he couldn't work out was if the scene directly below him – a huge queue of people waiting patiently to be called into a large marquee-like building – had anything to do with the president's plans.

'What are you up to, Melk?' he muttered to himself. He'd toyed with the idea of simply joining the line, but the sheer number of soldiers and security guards down there made that unsafe. Even with his ability to 'cloak' himself from view by altering other people's visual feedback – a power that meant he could appear as an old beggar woman or a street urchin to somebody who was looking directly at him – he would struggle to avoid being noticed by that many eyes, especially as Melk's spies would be on high alert. No, it would be better to go down into the slums and quiz somebody there as to what was going on.

Jax had only ventured a small way into the shanty town when it became clear from the minds of those around him that the residents were preparing to pack up and leave following some kind of edict from President Melk. There was almost too much excitement and nervousness, and he found it difficult to filter out a coherent signal from the myriad of people hurrying to and fro among the maze of alleyways linking the various wards and enclaves. Halting at a particularly busy junction, he watched as families packed what meagre possessions they owned on to make-shift carts set up outside their ramshackle homes. Barrows and trolleys were piled high with stuff, the precarious towers secured with old ropes or cord. Here and there, families were bickering about what was and was not essential; others were fighting about whether they should be going at all.

He approached an elderly woman standing outside her hovel next to a ridiculously overloaded sled contraption. He was only a few strides away from her when, quick as a flash, she swung a weapon up and shouted at him to back off. Jax took one look at the makeshift thing – a pole with long, rusty nails hammered through one end – and decided he was already plenty close enough.

He raised his hands. 'I'm not looking for any trouble, and I have no intention of trying to rob you, if that's what you think.' It was. She'd already had to deal with one youth who had tried to go off with her stuff when she'd popped inside her shack for a few moments, and he could tell by reading her mind that she was deeply suspicious of him.

The woman had no teeth, but she puckered her lips in his direction and drew her grey eyebrows together. 'That so? Then what *do* you want?'

'I was just wondering what was going on here. Why are so many people packing up their stuff?'

'You kidding me?'

'No, ma'am.'

'You weren't at the announcement?'

'The announcement?'

'That president.' She spat into the hard-packed dirt beside her. 'Melk. Up there on the giant screen.'

The albino gave her a shrug. 'I've just arrived here. Been out of the slums for a few days.'

She narrowed her eyes at him. 'Well, you picked a helluva time to return, youngster! Muteville is being relocated. Everyone's gotta put their names down to be settled in these new reservations. There's a place set up on the west side to register everyone. I went in yesterday with my people.'

'So that's what it is?' He nodded his head as if this confirmed something. 'I just came from over there. Lots of ARM on display.'

'It's crazy, isn't it?'

'What did this registration involve?'

'Not much. Got asked a load of stupid questions about this, that and the other. Then they stuck us all with a needle and sent us on our way with a little card which is supposed to be our ticket to the Promised Land.'

Jax tried to keep his voice level. 'They gave you an injection?'

'Yep. Something about trying to minimise the risk of disease prior to us being resettled. If you refuse to have the jab, they don't let you put your name down.'

'This injection – can you remember what colour the stuff was?'

The old woman gave him a searching look. 'Blue. Why?'

'No reason.' He paused for a moment, considering what her information might mean. 'When does all this happen? And why is everyone so keen to be shipped out like this? Surely there are some who want to stay?'

'There are three more days left to register, and two more after that to have all your stuff packed and be ready to go. Anybody left after that will be viewed as an enemy of the Six Cities: a terrorist. So if I were you, I'd get myself in that queue, because there isn't going to be a Muteville soon.'

'What?'

'Melk and his thugs are going to have it destroyed after they've moved everyone out.' She sniffed and looked around her. 'It's funny, but I've always said the best thing that could happen to this place was for it to be razed to the ground, but now it looks as if that's actually going to happen, I'm not so sure.'

'Those all your possessions?' he asked, giving a nod at the tower of what appeared to be junk behind her.

That suspicious expression quickly returned, as did her fear. She raised the club again.

He sighed. 'Like I said, I'm not here to rob you. Honest.' He pushed a thought designed to assuage her fears in her direction. It seemed to work, and he saw her relax a little.

'Each family is only allowed to take what it can carry or load up on to one cart. According to the man who registered us, the housing at these reservations is much better than anything here, so there's no need to take our old place down and load it up.' The thought of this seemed to upset her, tears welling up in her rheumy eyes. 'My children and grandchildren were born in this place, and now we've got to go to some place we don't even know.' She sniffed and visibly pulled herself together. She was typical Muteville stock: tough and resilient, and Jax couldn't help but admire the old bird. '"A new start" – that's what my son says it is. A new beginning for us all.'

'I hope so. Thanks for talking to me.' He gave her a nod and wandered away, thinking through everything he'd heard. One thing was certain: Rush and Tia had better find out what those syringes contained, and quickly.

Juneau

The ‘surgery’ was off a dingy, rubbish-strewn alley in one of the less inviting areas of Muteville. Rush, Tia and Dotty on either side of him, approached the passageway from one end, but they’d taken no more than a few strides between the buildings that made up the lane when a group of men and women emerged from the shadows. Rush didn’t like their body language as they moved in front of the trio, blocking their way. The rogwan, sensing her teenage owner’s apprehension, responded by *hurghing* loudly, pulling back blackened lips to reveal rows of vicious-looking teeth.

That a girl, Rush thought, enjoying the look on the men and women’s faces at the sight of the rogwan.

‘All right, Dotty,’ he said, patting her on the head without taking his eyes off their would-be accosters.

One mutant, a tall woman with high cheekbones and

hair so black it seemed to suck in the light, was clearly in charge. Stepping in front of the others and approaching the youngsters, she pulled aside one side of the long leather coat she wore to reveal a large knife hanging from a scabbard at her waist. 'Your little freak pet there isn't the only one with "teeth". Best you turn around – I think you must have taken a wrong turn somewhere.'

Rush stood his ground. He felt a familiar sensation inside him, a swirling coalescence or power that he knew he could tap into almost instantly if the group chose to follow up their words with actions.

'How can you know we've taken a wrong turn when you have no idea where we're going?' he replied. He was about to say something else when Tia halted him with a touch at his wrist with her fingers.

'We don't want any trouble, remember?' she said to him under her breath, before fixing her most winning smile and addressing the tall woman. 'We're here to see Juneau.'

'He expecting you, Pure?' The woman eyed the younger female slowly, her expression suggesting that she wasn't particularly impressed with what she saw.

'No.'

'Then I suggest you turn your pretty little rear around and go back the way you came. Juneau don't see anybody without an appointment.'

'Maybe you'd give him a message for me? I think you'll find he'll waive his "no appointment" rule if you tell him that Tia Cowper wants to talk to him about her CivisChip.'

The woman gave her a cold stare, but didn't move a muscle. When it became clear neither of them was going to back down, Rush stepped forward. 'It's important. We wouldn't be here otherwise.'

That stony look was turned on him. 'You look like a Pure. Like a City dweller. You're not though, are you? She is, but *you* are one of us. A pretty one, but one of us just the same.' She reached out a hand, touching his face and gently dragging one of her long nails across his cheek. When Dotty *hurghed* threateningly at her, the left side of her mouth twitched a little. 'I like your beast,' she said without taking her eyes off the boy.

'She's a rogwan. When she's upset she's every bit as terrifying as she looks. I think the two of you probably have a lot in common.' He was pleased when her mouth twitched again, this time a little higher, in response to this. 'It's important that we speak to Juneau.'

The woman thought for a moment, then seemed to make up her mind up. 'Grub!' she called out, and a man who'd been hanging back unseen at the rear of the group shuffled forward. Deformed and misshapen, the man craned his head up so she could whisper something into his ear. Then he limped off, surprisingly quickly, in the direction of a building set halfway along the passageway.

A moment or so later, he appeared in the alleyway again and gave a nod.

'Well, what do you know?' the woman said, addressing Rush as if the girl was not there. 'It seems as if Juneau's got a slot available for you after all, honey lips. That thing – the rogwan? – can't go in though. She'll have to stay out here with me.'

Rush narrowed his eyes at her. Food was always scarce in the slums, and anything on legs could be considered fair game to hungry eyes.

'If you hurt her in any way, I'll hurt you. Is that understood?'

'Why would I hurt her?' the woman responded. 'Like you said, she and I are quite alike.' Her face softened a fraction. 'She'll be safe here.'

The building was much larger than it first appeared, and although, on the outside at least, it was as dilapidated as everything else around it, the room immediately inside the entrance was relatively clean and tidy – a waiting area of some kind. Furniture that had probably been rescued from one of the city's dumps lined the walls, the chairs facing a small table with leaflets and other reading matter on it.

The room hardly registered with Rush though; his attention was fully on the bizarre-looking individual waiting for them in the centre of the space.

Thin to the point that his face had the look of a skull, the backstreet bioengineer, Juneau, stared back at the pair, his expression conveying both amusement and ire. His unkempt hair stuck out in all directions as if he might have just woken up, and he was in need of a shave. Judging from the smears and spatters on it, he'd not bothered to change his green surgical shirt following his last procedure. But none of this was what made Rush stare so openly at him; his astonishment was due to the extra pair of arms that emerged from the man's back – two strangely long limbs, ending in hands with spindly, delicate-looking fingers which were clasped together at his waist, as if some unseen person was hugging him from behind.

'Do you like 'em?' he asked the staring boy. 'In my line of work, two pairs of hands are definitely better than one, and it saves on having to employ a theatre nurse. I designed and grew them myself, then had them surgically grafted in place. Neat, huh?'

'Er, yeah, I guess.'

'Now let me see if I remember this correctly,' he said, a broad grin revealing a mouth full of perfectly white teeth that looked at odds with his otherwise shabby appearance.

'Young Ms Cowper, right?' He pointed with one of those long digits on his 'extra' arms.

'Juneau.' Tia nodded back at him.

The man lowered his arms again and looked at Rush.

'And who's the rather startled-looking young man with you?'

'This is my friend Rush.'

'Rush,' the bioengineer said with a nod, as if he was logging the information. 'Well, now we've got the pleasantries out of the way, perhaps you'd like to explain just what the hell you are doing here.' The smile still adorned his mouth, but there was no humour in his eyes any longer. 'The work I did for you –'

'Work for which you were paid an extortionate fee.'

'That's completely beside the point.' He sniffed. 'The procedure I performed on you involves certain dangers for the person carrying it out, should their work be discovered. As the punishment is *death*, and the person in question is *me*, you'll understand why I'd rather *not* have former clients calling in at my place of work! I thought I made that very clear to you, Miss Cowper.'

'You did. And I'm sorry to have turned up like this. I wouldn't have come if I thought there was anybody else with half the brain power and intellect you possess, Juneau.' She swung the backpack off her shoulder and undid the zip. 'We need you to look at something. Something that has been made by Melk. Something I think your unique abilities and knowledge can help us with.' She pulled a syringe from the bag and held it out to him.

If he was flattered in any way, he didn't show it. Instead he peered at the item in her hands.

'What is it?'

'We don't know. But we think it's dangerous and we'd like to know if there's a way it can be rendered harmless.'

'Why?'

'Why what?'

'Why do you think it's dangerous if you don't know what it is?'

'Melk and his people went to great lengths to hide it.'

Juneau sniffed. 'What's in it for me? Handling stuff that's been taken from the Cities is a serious crime.'

'Another one?' Rush said, but quickly shut up again when Tia shot him an angry look.

'We'll owe you a favour.'

'I can't eat favours.'

'Juneau, please. This is important.'

The scientist paused, but it was clear his curiosity was piqued. Without saying another word, he leaned forward, reached out with one of those long arms and took the vial from her. Crossing the room, he pressed a button on a small device hanging around his neck. Perfectly disguised to look like the rest of the wall around it, a door slid away to reveal a laboratory on the other side. Juneau walked through, leaving Tia and Rush looking at each other, not sure what to do next.

'Are you coming, or are you staying out there all day?' the scientist called out to them. As the pair followed him inside, the door slid shut behind them.

Juneau was already seated at an impressive-looking piece of equipment that was almost as tall as the room was high. Staring at the device, Rush took in the bewildering array of buttons and numerical keypads, unable to guess what on earth any of them did. Juneau, taking the syringe, put a tiny droplet on to a glass slide which he placed into a small square opening in the front of the device. With a flip of a switch, the slide disappeared into the guts of the machine, accompanied by a sharp *hiss* and a series of staccato *taps*. The scientist peered through two eyepieces set in front of him. 'OK, let's see what we've got here,' he mumbled to himself. The extra pair of arms reached up and began to press a series of buttons on a panel overhead, without the apparent need for Juneau to look up.

'Wow,' the scientist said.

'What is it?' Tia asked, crossing the room towards him.

'I mean, seriously. Wow.'

'Juneau . . .'

At the press of another button, an image appeared on a screen beside the equipment, a duplicate of what the scientist was looking at.

At first glance they looked like a weird jellyfish of some kind, although it became immediately apparent that the things were man-made and had nothing to do with the natural world. The microscopic medusas had an ugly look about them. The body was egg-shaped with a flared 'skirt' around the bottom. Emerging from beneath this were a series of tentacles that were almost twice as long as the body. Some of the tentacles had what appeared to be hooks at the end of them, others what could only be described as blades and drills. Suspended in solution, they were inert and unmoving, as if in some kind of stasis and awaiting reanimation.

'Impressive, eh?' Juneau said, swivelling round on his chair to look at them for the first time since entering the lab.

'What are they?' Rush asked, unable to take his eyes off the screen.

'That, my young friend, is a miracle of engineering. It's a nanobot of some kind.'

'A whatbot?'

'A nanobot. Each one of those things is about six microns in size.' He paused when he noticed their baffled expressions. 'About the size of a red blood cell?' He shook his head in dismay. 'Imagine a perfect little robot so small it's invisible to the eye. Brilliant. And like blood cells,' he continued, 'you can get an awful lot of them in the tiniest drop.' He thumbed a small toggle switch and the image slowly began to zoom out. The three machines in the tiny area they were looking at became ten, a hundred, a thousand, tens of thousands, and then a haze of indistinguishable specks in a sea of blue. It was clear the number of the things was colossal, and the image was still zooming out. 'There are hundreds of millions of red cells in single drop of blood. I have no way of knowing for sure, but I'm guessing there's a similar number of these nanobots on that slide. They appear to be utterly inert at the moment.'

He lowered his head to the viewing apparatus again, and when he spoke it was more to himself than to his visitors.

'Fascinating. Way more advanced than anything I've seen before. You've got to hand it to the Pure scientists, they really are quite innovative. The big question is, what are these things doing in your syringe, and what's their ultimate purpose? If I were a betting man, which I am, I'd say cellular nanosurgery of some kind.'

'This might give us the answer,' Tia said, removing the holo-image player she'd taken from the case. 'There's a file on it that shows what these things are for. The trouble is, it's encrypted. It needs Melk's very own passcode.'

'It's a private message to the president?'

'Yes.'

'Then it's not just the password you need; it's Melk's voice too. For about a year now, the government has been using an advanced form of speech cryptology as an additional cipher.' Despite this revelation, Juneau held out a hand, gesturing for Tia to pass the equipment over to him. 'Shouldn't be too hard to get access.'

'But I thought you just said –'

'You want to see what's on that file or not?'

'How are you going to break the code?' Rush asked. If he was honest, he was far from sure they could trust this crazy individual. There was something about the man that just wasn't . . . right.

'Kid, I work with the greatest encryption known to man – DNA code. Compared to that, I tend to regard most other ciphers as relatively easy to crack. Having said that, something like this might take a little time to figure out.'

'How much time?'

'A day or so.' He paused, removing the slide from the machine and placing it carefully on the side. 'But I haven't said I'll do it yet.'

'What do you mean?'

The Mute scientist sighed and settled back in his chair,

crossing both pairs of arms over his chest as he regarded the two teenagers. 'What's in it for me?'

Tia met his stare with her own stony look. 'Ten thousand credits?'

Rush gaped at her. In total contrast, Juneau didn't even blink at the figure.

'Do you have it?' the bioengineer asked.

'My father does.'

Juneau narrowed his eyes at her as if he was gauging if she was joking. Rush couldn't read the strange expression on his face. 'You don't know, do you?'

'Know what?'

'Dammit! I'm sorry, kid.'

'Know what?'

'Your father? Melk had him arrested last month.'

Tia stared at the four-armed man for a moment as she took this news in. 'W-what was the charge?'

'Treason.'

'What?!'

'Melk's had him declared an enemy of the state, and has accused him of being in cahoots with the terrorists who bombed C4.'

'That's absurd! Melk can't do that. The people of the Six Cities won't stand for it!'

'Things have changed while you've been outside the

Wall, kid. Even those citizens who might once have been sympathetic to the Mutes have hardened towards their neighbours.' He gestured to himself. 'Your father must have sensed this. He broadcast a feature in which he suggested those inside the walls deserved what they'd got, that the explosions were the fault of Melk's ongoing inhumane treatment of the mutant underclass. Some of the things in the piece appear to have angered a whole bunch of people. And you know Melk: never one to let an opportunity slide, especially if that opportunity gives him a chance to silence one of his biggest critics.' The bioengineer gave her a sad smile. 'The trial is in a couple of weeks.'

Tia stood perfectly still for a few moments as she took this in. It was clear the revelation had rocked her to the core.

It was Rush who finally broke the silence by coming up with a possible solution. It was simplicity itself, but as soon as the words were out of his mouth, Tia grabbed him as if he was a life preserver thrown out to a drowning woman.

'Your film,' he said.

'What?'

'The documentary you made of everything that happened in the build-up to the bombings. That's the proof your father needs to expose Melk as the monster he is. You've got a Get Out Of Jail Free card, Tia. You just have to find a way to play it.'

She turned to Juneau. 'You know how rich my father is, right?'

'Sure.'

'I'll triple my original offer. Thirty thousand credits, if you can get me back into the City.'

'I just told you, your dad's –'

'You get me in, I'll get him freed. Then the money's yours, Juneau.'

'Us,' Rush said. 'Get us in. I'm going with her.'

'Rush, you can't. You –'

'I look like a Pure. Dammit, I almost am one! Wasn't I created from an embryo taken from the City Four stock?'

'What's all this about? Who is this kid?' Juneau asked.

Ignoring him, Rush continued. 'Get me some citizen clothes, and I'll pass for one of them every bit as easily as you.' It was true. As far as looks went, Rush could easily have been born inside the Wall. His expression told her there was no talking him out of his decision, and he watched as her resolve crumbled. She nodded before turning back to Juneau.

'So how about it? Do we have a deal?'

'Twenty-four hours. That's all I can give you. And it'll be fifty thousand credits. I don't quite know what you two kids are up to, or what this film you have contains, but if I'm going to risk my neck re-chipping the two of you for what sounds like a crazy scheme, I need it to be worth my while.' He paused as if expecting them to protest.

'Why the time limit?' Tia asked.

'The CivisChips I'll be embedding in your thigh bones? They have that time constraint.'

'Why?'

'They're from dead people.' He held up all four hands when Tia started to protest. 'It's the only way! And don't ask me how I come by them, because you don't want to know. All you need to know is that when a citizen dies it takes the authorities roughly two days to deactivate the CivisChip. If it's removed quickly enough from the corpse, it can be reused during that period. However, it usually takes about a day for me to get my hands on them, so the best I can offer you is about twenty-four hours. Take it or leave it.'

'You've done this before?' Rush asked. He tried not to show it, but he was more than a little freaked out by the prospect of having a dead person's private microchip installed into his skeleton.

'Plenty of times,' Juneau said with a wink. 'How do you think I got all this scientific equipment? Mutant Santa Claus?'

Steeleye

The mutant known as Steeleye Mange sat on the edge of the metal examination table, looking towards the doorway. Superimposed over the image of the steel door transmitted to his brain via his human visual apparatus was a constant stream of data from the heads-up display installed in his right eye socket. The visual data, like the feedback from his other bionic augmentations, had become so much a part of him he hardly noticed it any longer. It was like background noise, filtered out most of the time until it was needed. When he *did* tune into it, the range and depth of information available to him was astonishing.

Having scanned the areas beyond the entrance – his ability to use microwave to do this, like so many of his other abilities, no longer filled him with wonder – he knew that Melk, Razko and Dr Svenson were out there, and the presence of the last person in this trio was enough to put him on edge. Like a dog who's been kicked and beaten by an unkind owner, the mere thought of the female doctor sent a shiver of fear running through him. *Svenson*. Of the three doctors responsible for his 'rehabilitation' over the last five months, she was the worst. Tall and beautiful, with dark, curly hair and model's cheekbones, she looked – like so many of her fellow citizens – a picture of perfection. On the outside at least. However, as the surgeon of the team, she had shown herself to be a brutal sadist. It wasn't enough that Svenson had initially been responsible for chopping him up and putting him back together again: minus both his old legs, his left arm and half his face and head. She'd then gone on to perform her very own special brand of Frankenstein surgery on him at every opportunity. 'Mech and tech upgrades,' she called them. To her, he was nothing but a plaything. Like a child with a toy doll she could pull apart and put back together in new and wonderful ways. So each time the manufacturers came up with a better, newer bionic augmentation, she didn't hesitate to put him back under the knife. Steeleye had no say in these matters. At first he'd protested, raging against those sent to fetch him. But they would 'shut him down' and drug him, and when he woke up in a world of pain and discomfort he knew that she'd tinkered with her plaything again. Svenson was always there at his side when he came round. She would loom over him, her face expressionless as she fired questions at him, recording his responses on her omnipad. Then later they'd take him down to a testing area, where they'd put him through his paces.

She'd be the first. Steeleye had promised himself that. If – no, *when* – he could get his hands on his three white-coated torturers, Svenson would be the first to go. He'd show her what his robotic arm could *really* do by ripping her pretty head clean off her shoulders. He might use the offending article to beat the other two to death. A warning flashed across his HUD, the information accompanied by a high-pitched noise. He looked down. Oblivious of doing so, he'd curled his titanium-and-steel left hand around the edge of the thick slab of metal that was the examination counter, and now it was a ruined and twisted mess. The warning was to let him know the bionic hand was approaching the peak pressure it was able to exert; any more and he was in danger of damaging it, and if he did *that*, Svenson would have another excuse to chop him up with her scalpel and her cutting saw.

He stood, eyeing the walls of the place, frustrated in the knowledge that they stood little chance of holding him if he really made a concerted effort to escape. A few kicks and blows and he could smash his way out of this room.

He knew because he'd tried. The problem wasn't the walls or the doors of the rooms he was confined to – it was the safety mechanisms Svenson and her colleagues had installed inside him so they could 'shut him down' – either through a spoken command or via one of their fancy gadgets – at any point. Not just that, but the shutdown was automatically activated whenever he was in an area he was not supposed to be in, and that meant just about everywhere in this place. He was a prisoner. A very expensive one, but a prisoner nonetheless.

He turned as the door opened and the three walked in, the examination table separating him from them.

'Ah, Commander Mange!' Melk greeted him as if they were long-lost buddies. The old man stood, his head tilted a little to one side as he took in the cyborg. 'You look . . . formidable.' It was true. The former mutant mobster had been an imposing figure to start with – at nearly two metres tall, with long hair plaited halfway down his back, one eye socket filled with a ball bearing and every inch of his skin covered in tattoos, he'd always had the ability to strike fear into the hearts of his erstwhile enemies. Now, with more than fifty per cent of him machine, ugly hydraulic pipes exiting flesh and entering metal, riveted sections where flesh met steel, he was a thing straight from the pages of a horror story.

Steeleye gave Melk a stony look. 'And you look like the liar I've come to know you are,' he said.

'Now don't be like that, Commander.'

There it was again, that title. Commander? Commander of what? And the way the loathsome politician said it with no sign of humour on his face made Mange want to crush him. Steeleye gauged the distance between the two of them, calculating whether he could get his hands on the president before Svenson managed to shut his systems down. He decided to bide his time.

'Five months. That's how long I've been kept here. That was not our agreement, Melk. You said you'd let me have my revenge, not lock me up here to be the ongoing experiment of this psychopath.' He pointed at the surgeon, but his eye never left Melk.

If Svenson was at all bothered by being referred to in this way, she didn't show it. She didn't even look up in his direction, just stared down at the device in her hands as if he didn't exist. Maybe he'd tear her arms off first. Then her legs. Then –

'It's taken longer than we all anticipated, I'll grant you that. But the good doctor here tells me that you are now fully operational and glitch-free.'

'Actually,' the white-coated surgeon said, finally lifting her head, 'I said that there were –' She stopped almost as quickly as she'd begun when Melk lifted a hand and shot her a withering look.

'I thought we'd agreed you wouldn't speak, Doctor,' the politician said, turning his smile back on the Mute. 'Now, remind me again, Commander, what it is you want so badly.'

'Besides my real arm and legs back?'

The politician remained silent.

'I want out of here.'

'Why?'

'You know why.'

'Indulge me.'

'I want revenge. I want to know that the operations, hard reboots, software upgrades, equipment checks I've had to suffer at the hands of that . . . woman over there have been worth it. I want –' now he'd started speaking he found it hard to stop; the bitterness and rage that had been building up inside him could be heard in every word – 'you to give me the chance to take care of those kids once and for all.'

'Hmm.' Melk nodded. 'You must accept my apologies for the delay, Mange, but it was unavoidable. I've had the not inconsequential task of rebuilding my city.' Melk paused, weighing up his words. 'As a politician, I have to prioritise, and I can't let my desires get in the way of my duties. The Six Cities come first. They always have and they always will.' *Well, equal first with my other secret project,* Melk thought to himself. 'I wouldn't expect you, coming from the gutters of Muteville, to understand that, but it's true.' He paused and glanced around the room. 'Not only that, but I was led to believe you were not fully functional, that there were difficulties with your systems and that the doctors –'

The words stuck in Melk's throat as Steeleye lunged forward and smashed his arm through the top of the examination table. The limb passed through the metal slab as if it wasn't there. It continued downwards, crashing through the heavy struts and hydraulic lifting mechanism beneath until the entire thing caved in beneath the force of the blow.

Svenson looked as if she was about to jab something on her omnipad, but she was halted again by a shake of the president's head.

There was a whine of servo-motors and Steeleye jumped, coming down with all his considerable weight on the ruined counter, the remnants of which collapsed beneath him. Raising one leg, then the other, the mutant cyborg stomped at the metal, crushing it into the floor until it was almost unrecognisable. There was a moment of silence while the 'borg glared back at the two men from the ruined mess. 'Does *that* look as if I'm not fully functional, Mr President?'

If Melk was intimidated in any way, he didn't show it. Instead that smile slid into place again.

'I'm glad to see you still have that anger in you, albeit a little . . . misdirected. I'm not your enemy. Neither is General Razko, or Dr Svenson. *We* are not responsible for you ending up here in this place. No, it was those children – the ones with the strange abilities, the ones who in trying to kill you injured you so badly that you'd be dead had we *not* intervened – *they* are the ones to blame for everything that's happened to you, and it would pay for you to always keep that in mind.' The smile fell away and the politician stared unflinchingly at the huge half-man, half-machine before him. 'You are about to get your wish. In a moment we are all going to leave this place. You won't be returning. I'm going to set you loose on this world with the mission of finding and destroying the very people you have to thank for being the way you are. Your wait is over, Commander Mange. It's time to see what you can do.'

The eight ARM agents stared at the mutant cyborg who'd just been introduced to them as their new commander. Then they looked at each other to see if this might be some kind of joke. It wasn't.

Steeleye scanned the faces before him to try to figure out who was going to give him the most trouble. He didn't think he had too much to worry about. Despite their uniforms, they were just soft city dwellers. That was how he thought of them and their kind, because when you stripped away all their fancy high-tech gadgets and weaponry, they couldn't hold a candle to most of the Mutes. Hell, his kind had survived the apocalypse *topside*, not hiding away for generations in underground Arks, sucking in each other's recycled farts while the world above boiled and burned. Their hard-earned survival had made the mutants of Scorched Earth tough, and Steeleye reckoned he was the toughest of the whole damn lot. He cleared his throat and addressed the seven men and one woman who'd been assigned to him.

'All right, listen up. Now I know you Pures might find it difficult to accept me as your leader, but believe me when I say that I want *you* along on this assignment every bit as much as you want *me*. That is to say, not at all. I would prefer to work alone, but I've been told I have to drag your sorry arses along with me on this mission.' They were in a briefing room inside a wing of the ARM headquarters. Steeleye had been told to address the squad from the raised platform, and each step he took as he paced back and forth made the structure shake, the heavy, thumping footfalls providing a percussive accompaniment to his speech. 'So let's start this thing off as we mean to go along, lay out some ground rules. You are to stay out of my way as much as possible. The people we are going up against are extremely dangerous, and I do not want you screwing this mission up. My previous experience as part of an ARM unit did not go well. In fact, the reason I look the way I do now is because of the blundering ineptitude of that unit. So let's be clear: if I need you, I'll call on you. Otherwise, you stay back and let me get on with what I'm supposed to do.'

One of the agents barked a harsh laugh.

'Something funny?' Steeleye asked, rounding on the man; he eyed the insignia on the officer's uniform. 'Captain?'

'Well, yes, Commander,' he drew this last word out, leaving everyone in the room in no doubt as to what he thought of their cyborg guest. 'Since you ask, this whole thing strikes me as funny. Because you have got to be joking if you think I'm taking orders from a freak Mute like you!'

A number of the other men began to grumble their agreement.

'Is that so?'

'You bet your metal arse that's so.'

There was a high-pitched whirring sound, as a device on Steeleye's shoulder swung round to point at the ARM agent. Without any warning, the small pulsed-energy gun fired, knocking the man backwards out of his seat and to the floor, where he lay perfectly still.

For a moment there was silence, and then the room exploded in uproar as the agents nearest the captain jumped to their feet and gathered round the prostrate figure. One man reached forward and checked for a pulse, he turned and stared at Steeleye. 'He's alive, but only just,' he said.

'Yeah?' The 'borg gave a small theatrical sigh, tapped the energy weapon reproachfully and shook his head. 'You know, I only had this thing fitted yesterday, and I'm having a bit of trouble getting used to the settings. Must have dialled it almost to max there by mistake. My bad.'

'He needs medical attention.'

Another theatrical sigh. 'You –' Steeleye addressed one of the men – 'take him to the infirmary. Tell them he was shot for disobeying orders. And tell them that there is no rush to get him patched up; he's off the team.'

Mange turned to face the rest of the room's occupants, his face, the human side of it at least, changed from one of feigned regret to menace. In a voice that left nobody in any doubt that he was indeed in charge, he ordered the remaining six agents to return to their seats. 'Now, where were we? Oh, your erstwhile captain's unwillingness to take orders. Does anybody else have the same problem?' Except for the sound of a few shuffling feet, there was silence in the room. 'Good. Who's the lieutenant here?'

He grinned at the man who reluctantly put his arm up. 'Congratulations. You've just been promoted. What's your name?'

'Blake.'

'Well, *Captain* Blake, have this squad ready to leave in an hour. We're heading out towards the wastelands between here and City Three. There's a dangerous group of young Mutes that we have to find and eradicate. You will all travel in one of your fancy armoured troop carriers that is being equipped as we speak. Any questions?'

Blake put his hand up. 'How will you be travelling . . . Commander?'

'I'll be on foot. Try to keep up.'

The men looked at each other again.

'We'll meet at the vehicle depot in one hour. Dismissed.'

The sun was beginning to set on Scorched Earth as the ARM unit approached the edge of the Wastes, three hours after setting out from C4. The seven agents were travelling in an armoured troop carrier. Outside, running at about two-thirds of his top speed, Steeleye was enjoying his newfound freedom. His bionic enhancements worked even better than he'd imagined, and he grudgingly had to admit that Svenson had indeed done great job. He was still going to kill her at the first opportunity he got, but at least she'd die knowing she'd been at the top of her game. Running on an electronic treadmill inside an air-conditioned laboratory hadn't prepared him for the sheer exhilaration he now felt. Off to his left, he was aware of the vehicle, but he paid it no attention. He was enjoying himself. Out here, despite the cold harsh wind, he felt alive in a way he hadn't for months. The wind in his face made his human eye water and he blinked the tears away as he raced across the ground, his hair streaming out behind him like a tail.

Onboard systems scanned the landscape ahead, giving him constant feedback about the topography, superimposing the visual image with contour lines and highlighting potential dangers. Steeleye largely ignored the data. When he came to a group of pre-Last War relics – gnarled concrete and rusted metal – jutting out of the earth in front of him, he simply amped up his speed and jumped them. The highest of them was easily twice his height, but he knew from the data in his HUD that he could clear it. It was only as he was on his way down that he realised he might have overdone it. This was his first attempt at such a manoeuvre, and he'd misjudged the leap a little. Feeling himself tipping forward as he began to descend, Steeleye let out a shout, a wild mixture of anxiety and exhilaration. One foot crashed into the ground, and his leg, despite its tremendous strength, buckled under the impact. As the earth rushed up to meet him, there was no fear in the mutant; the computers had already made the necessary calculations about how best to deal with the situation, and Mange simply dipped his left shoulder, the metal arm sweeping down in front of him as if he was taking a high-speed bow. The forward roll he performed was perfect, and he was back on his feet and moving again almost without breaking stride.

The newly promoted Captain Blake looked out of the small viewing port on his side of the troop carrier, staring in amazement at the running figure of the mutant cyborg. The 'borg's legs were almost a blur as he gobbled up the landscape in front of him. Blake couldn't help but wonder what had got into the heads of the Principia by putting this . . . thing in charge of him and his unit. What he did know was that the cyborg didn't care a jot for those in his command. The feeling was entirely mutual. At the first chance, Captain Blake would rid himself of the Mute, take revenge for what the freak had done to his predecessor and get this ARM unit back under the control of Pures.

Despite his hatred of the 'borg, he had to admit the thing was remarkable. He watched as it jumped over some ruins, quickly bringing the vis-gogs he held up to his eyes as he saw the Mute wasn't going to make the landing. He smiled. Maybe he wouldn't have to worry about his new commander after all because he was about to crash head first into the ground and –

When the 'borg rolled up out of the impact and carried on running, Blake could hardly believe his eyes. He zoomed into Steeleye's face, expecting to see that smug look wiped off. He frowned, lowering the device. The cyborg was laughing like a maniac.

Rush and Tia

'Try not to walk so funny,' Tia said under her breath as the pair approached the entry gate.

'I *am*,' Rush muttered. 'But for some reason, having my leg cut open and a microchip inserted into my thighbone has affected my usual ability to swagger fearlessly up to an entry point manned by half a dozen armed guards!'

'Shhh,' she hissed. 'Unless you've forgotten, we are trying not to draw attention to ourselves.'

'Seriously? In this stupid get-up? How could I *not* draw attention to myself?' He gestured at the yellow-and-black jumpsuit he was wearing, the only item of citizen clothing Juneau had been able to find in the teenager's size. 'I look *and* feel ridiculous.'

'Oh, please stop moaning. It's all the rage.' She paused, before adding, 'At least, it was last year.'

'You know what I think? This is the very outfit that the corpse was dressed in when they brought it in for Juneau to dissect? It makes sense – the guy must have died of embarrassment.'

'Here we go,' Tia said, her demeanour and bearing changing as they walked the last few metres separating them from the guards. To Rush, she seemed to grow in height in those last few strides, and if her leg was hurting her as much as his own was, she no longer showed it. He did his best to do likewise, but he found it hard not to be intimidated by the surroundings as he took one last look up at the Wall, the vast and forbidding barrier that separated the two surviving societies of the Last War. From down here, at its base, it looked even more intimidating. The entrance he and Tia were to walk through was about three metres long – the thickness of the wall here – and set into it at exactly halfway was a black metal frame, like a doorway with no door. Instead, a series of flashing red lights and figures shone out at various points across its surface.

'Step through the detector,' the man nearest the structure said. Although his voice sounded bored, his eyes never left the pair as they approached. Neither did the PEG weapon he held.

As Tia, closely followed by Rush, walked through, another guard, this one on the other side of the device, looked down at a screen. Tia had already told Rush that if they were going to be shot, this was when it would happen. Right now he kind of wished she'd kept that little nugget of information to herself. The teenage mutant's heart was hammering away inside him, and he wondered if the tremors were visible through the thin, slightly shiny material of the jumpsuit. The guard behind the screen waved them over. When the man eventually looked up from the monitor, the expression on his face did nothing to assuage Rush's fear.

'Adams and Stark?'

'Yes,' Tia said.

The guard peered at Rush, eyebrows beetling as he did so. Juneau had managed to reprogram certain aspects of the CivisChip data, like the image of the civilian's face that popped up when the chip was scanned, as it was happening now, but some things were not possible to alter. 'It says here that Citizen Adams is twenty-four years of age.' He left the statement hanging, as if there was no need to add anything further.

Tia was ready for this. 'My friend's father – he works at VieTech.' This much she knew to be true from the information Juneau had managed to acquire from the Civis-Chips. 'They're working closely with Bio-Gen at the moment to produce what they're calling the "Dorian Gray" gene, and lucky old Citizen Adams here is one of the first to try it. It's supposed to considerably reverse the ageing process.' Rush noticed the way Tia was talking to the guard. Ditzy and excited, she sounded younger and less sophisticated than she usually did. 'Isn't it great what the scientists can do? I wish my dad worked in one of the big labs. Adams here gets to try out all the latest stuff. I had the rate at which my hair grows changed last year so I could get it *really* long, you know? I wanted it for my prom.'

'Dorian Gray gene? Never heard of it.'

'Apparently it's a reference to some ancient text.' She waved her hand in the air as if batting the sentence away. 'I don't pretend to understand what it means, but from your reaction, I think the treatment must be working!' She leaned in closer to the man. 'My mother is already signed up for it. She's an early adopter of most of VieTech's stuff. She's worried she's looking her age.'

The guard looked over at Rush again, his expression still sceptical.

Rush joined in the conversation. 'It's got some weird side effects though,' he said, ignoring Tia as she snapped her head around to stare at him, her eyes wide. He was supposed to keep quiet throughout their entry in case he said something that would mark him out as a non-citizen. 'I'm prone to vomiting. A lot. It's like . . . projectile. Dad says it's real important I don't get sick on anyone else. Something to do with the sneckocites and the way they . . . ungh!' He grabbed his stomach and groaned. 'Oh no. I think I'm gonna chuck again!' He puffed his cheeks out and clamped his hand over his mouth, looking urgently from the guard to Tia and back again.

His elaborate pantomime seemed to do the job. The guard, ignoring whatever data was still being displayed on his screen, hastily declared their CivisIDs were valid and waved them through.

'Sneckocites?' Tia said to him under her breath once they'd passed the last armed sentry.

'It was the first thing to come into my head,' he said with a grin. 'Sounded good though, huh?'

'Don't keep doing that,' Tia said. They were well clear of the entry point now, having emerged from the tunnel into a glass chamber where they were 'decontaminated' by various mists that were sprayed from all sides. Rush could still smell the stuff on his clothes and skin. It had a nasty, medicinal whiff to it.

'Doing what?' Rush said.

'Gawping at everything as if it's the first time you've seen it.'

'Er, it *is* the first time I've seen it.'

'No, it's not. Because you are Citizen Adams, remember? At least, you are for the next twenty-odd hours we have inside the Wall. Adams grew up with all this stuff, so stop acting like you've just arrived here from outer space.' She grasped his arm and pulled him out of the way of an unmanned road sweeper that he was about to step in front of, mumbling under her breath something about a 'country mouse' as she did so, although he instantly forgot about it when she nudged him on to a moving walkway, almost knocking him off balance in the process.

There was a sound, a deep sonorous gong. Rush looked up and saw a gigantic video-advertising panel dominating one side of a skyscraper not too far from where they stood. Moments earlier the thing had been clear, the windows behind it visible, but now it was filled with an image of an extraordinarily beautiful ebony-skinned woman who was staring out, a hint of a smile creasing her lips and eyes.

'*Bio-Gen,*' the woman said in a voice like silk. '*We make you the people you were meant to be.*' The voice was accompanied by the image of a baby lying on a white blanket. This in turn was replaced by a series of images that faded, one into the next, of more beautiful people, until eventually these were replaced by the company's logo.

'Everything looks so new. It's all so . . . clean.'

'On the outside maybe,' Tia responded, pulling him

across the road and on to another travelator. 'But scratch the surface, and the Six Cities are as grubby as anything you find outside their walls. And believe me, this one, C4, is about as filth-ridden as they come.' She paused, giving him a brief smile. 'Look, I'll show you some of the sights if we get a chance, but right now I need you to look as if all this –' she fluttered her fingers, taking in the looming towers and their vast illuminated hoardings – 'is something you've seen a million times.'

'I'll do my best. So what's the plan?' He forced himself not to look at the woman with silver-and-purple hair coming towards them.

'I need to hook up with my father's friend Eleanor. If anyone can help me to help him, she can. Here,' she said, taking him by the hand and stepping off at a gap in the side of the walkway.

'Where is this?' Rush asked.

'This is Downtown. A5.'

'Downtown?'

'One of the poorest areas,' she said, looking about her until she spotted a glass-walled booth not far from where they stood. On a sign above the booth was a white letter *i* in a blue circle.

'Wait here,' she said, moving towards the cubicle. 'I just need to check something out.'

Rush stared about him. There were none of the looming glass and steel towers that he had seen on their way here, but compared to the terrible poverty and squalor of Muteville, 'Downtown' looked positively opulent. Clearly those inside the walls had too much wealth if a place like this could be considered 'poor', and this realisation made him angrier than he'd been since first entering the city. The citizens of C4 labelled this place as poor, while turning a blind eye to the terrible conditions endured by their mutant neighbours. *What kind of world was this?* He looked over at Tia in the booth, remembering what she'd said about scratching the surface of the cities to find out what they were really like, and realised that you didn't even need to do that. All you had to do was recognise the chasm that existed between the two societies to know that this was an ugly place run by even uglier people.

A nearby shout made him turn around. Approaching a gap between two buildings, Rush peered down the alley to see what the cause of the commotion was. What he saw was a group of young boys and girls surrounding another, smaller child. The older group was teasing this individual, taunting him with a toy they'd clearly taken from him. One, the ringleader, kept holding the toy out, only to snatch it back when the target of their fun reached for it. Each time this happened, the other members of the group laughed and jeered until the bigger boy, finally bored with his game, threw the toy up in the air so it landed on a ledge far above their heads. The anger that had boiled up inside Rush moments earlier resurfaced as he watched the small boy start to cry. There was no hope of the youngster retrieving his property. Slapping the tall boy on the back, the bullies made their way up the alleyway in Rush's direction.

'That wasn't nice,' he said to the tall boy as he passed.

'What did you say?'

'I said that wasn't very nice.'

'What the hell has it got to do with you, hmm?' The boy squared up to Rush. They were about the same age and height, but the bully was bulkier. He'd clearly never had to worry about where his next meal might come from.

'Nothing.'

'That's what I thought,' the bully said with a sneer. He turned and began to walk away.

Nobody could work out how it happened, but as the bully approached the moving walkway it appeared as if one of the paving slabs lifted a little, catching his foot and sending him off balance, at the same time as a nearby refuse bin tipped over on to its side and fell into his path. There was a crash and the boy flew over the thing. The split lip and grazed forehead he suffered could have been much worse if he hadn't got his hands out of his pockets in time. As it was – his friends laughing raucously at his extraordinary tumble – it seemed the damage to his pride was the worst of his injuries.

Rush turned his back on them and peered down the alley. The small boy, having given up on retrieving his toy from the ledge, was trudging away from it in the opposite direction.

'Hey, kid!' Rush shouted. The youngster turned fearfully, frowning back at the stranger who was pointing at the ground and asking if he'd 'dropped something'.

Rush's smile matched the boy's as the youngster hurried back to retrieve his toy, hugging it to him before scampering away.

'What are you grinning at?' Tia asked. She glanced up the now deserted alleyway, then round at a group of youths who were busy picking one of their members up off the pavement.

'Nothing. Did you find what we need?'

She led him to a shop called Cybergonk, the sign over the door looking decidedly amateurish: spray paint on two crudely joined panels, five metres in length. Walking in, Rush had to force himself not to stare again. The interior was poorly lit, but this didn't seem to bother the dozen or so people inside. Neither did the entry of two new visitors, who barely drew a glance from most of the clientele, engrossed as they were on the high-tech machines in front of them. The devices seemed to be displaying an impossibly fast series of holo-images, text and symbols; these appeared and disappeared in the air before the users in what seemed a blur. The users, however, sat engrossed in this tumult of visual data.

'What are they doing?' Rush asked.

'Gonking. You take a mind-altering drug that makes the brain believe time is being slowed down. The holo-images and data are transmitted at eight or nine times the usual speed, but to the gonker it seems perfectly normal. Most of these guys will be students. Gonking is a great way to get some seriously intensive study done without using up too much of your "real" time.'

'It's like Flea. How she sees the world in slow motion.'

'Except to these guys it's in real time.'

'Is it safe?'

Tia gave a shrug. 'The studies are inconclusive. Some people have flipped out while using the drugs, gone on mad rampages. Because of that the authorities have declared these places illegal. That's why they're unmanned.' She nodded to the far wall. 'The drugs are dispensed from that vending machine. If the authorities raid the place, the owners can simply set up somewhere else.' She looked around, searching for something. 'That's what we're here for,' she said, nodding towards another device next to the drug dispenser.

Moving over to the machine, Tia waved her hand across the surface, bringing up a holopad into which she proceeded to enter a series of numbers and symbols. 'Eleanor's contact details,' she explained to a bemused Rush. After a few moments a voice came through.

'*Yes?*'

'Eleanor. I'm sorry to be contacting you using voice-only, but I thought it best under the circumstances.'

'*Who is this?*'

'I'm the person who is now a marmoset,' Tia answered cryptically, knowing Eleanor was one of only a handful of people who knew it was a marmoset monkey the girl had had her own CivisChip installed into.

There was a pause. 'Where are you calling from?'

'Don't worry. I'm in a gonkshop. Downtown. This comms console is a temp, so it won't be traced.'

Another silence followed. 'How do I know you are who you say you are? The ID label on this call says your name is Stark.'

Tia fully understood the woman's wariness. Eleanor was a well-known friend of Tia's father, and as soon as he'd been arrested as an enemy of the state, it was inevitable that the former city police chief would also be on Melk's radar.

'You don't. That's why I'm sending somebody to prove it to you.'

'Explain to me again why you can't come with me?' Rush asked. They were standing on another moving walkway, this one taking them through a long clear tunnel high in the air between two buildings. Tia told him it was best if they kept moving, sticking to public spaces so their chips weren't flagged. They must have been twenty or thirty metres off the ground, and Rush couldn't see what, if anything, was keeping the tunnel-bridge suspended.

'Thanks to your chip, you have access to the VieTech site. It's one of the reasons Juneau selected that identity for you over the one that was closer to your real age.' Rush didn't need to be reminded that the only way he was in the city at all was because somebody – a young man, no less – had died. 'Eleanor also has access to the same site, thanks to being a security advisor for the firm. It's the best way for you to meet so she'll feel sure it's not a trap.'

'That's what she does? Eleanor. Security advice?'

Tia nodded. 'It is now. Of course she used to run the CSP – the City Security Police.'

'Oh, great.' Rush rolled his eyes and stared at her incredulously. 'That's just what I imagined when I signed up to come with you. I thought to myself, if only I – a wanted "terrorist", who helped to bomb this very city not so long ago – could somehow get to meet the head of that city's police force.'

'She doesn't do that job any longer. She quit.'

'Oh, that makes me feel so much better, Tia.'

'Will you stop worrying? Eleanor is on our side.'

'No. Eleanor is on *your* side. She's probably on your father's side. But you have no idea how she'll react when she discovers who I really am and what she's getting herself into.'

'She's a good person, Rush. I trust her.' She paused. 'Like I trust you.'

He looked at her then. Really looked at her. She was beautiful, that was obvious, but at that precise moment he realised it wasn't her looks that made his heart clench whenever he was with her. It was her humanity and spirit that really made her stand out from all of the other 'beautiful' people swarming around inside the city walls. She didn't *have* to risk her own life to help him and the others, yet that was exactly what she was doing – her and her father, who was locked up somewhere in this vast metropolis. So if somebody like Tia Cowper thought Eleanor was a good person, who the hell was he to question that?

'Fine.' He sighed. 'If you trust her, I guess I do too.'

Elegant – that was the first word that sprang to mind as the door to the meeting room slid open to reveal Eleanor. She was standing before a window on the other side of a glass table, staring out at the cityscape before her. She was tall. Very tall. And in Rush's opinion her incredible height was matched only by her beauty. The tight-fitting black-and-gold outfit she wore perfectly complemented her ebony skin, as did the simple gold bands that she wore around her upper and forearms.

'Come in . . . Adams,' she said, turning to look at him.

He stepped inside and the door silently slid shut behind him. When she spoke again, she addressed her words towards a dark glass panel beside the door. 'No interruptions, please, but I'd like to be informed if anyone else should approach this room.' The command was confirmed by two short bleeps. For a moment or so Eleanor stood staring towards the door and panel as if she was expecting something to happen.

'I wasn't followed,' Rush said, finally realising what was going on.

'As if you'd know,' she said by way of a reply. If she was at all scared, she didn't show it, and she appeared to be unarmed. Despite this, Rush got the distinct impression this woman was more than capable of looking after herself if things should ever get a little 'agitated'.

Rush gave her a nod. 'I wanted to thank you for agreeing to –'

'Shh,' Eleanor said, shaking her head and putting a long, slender finger up to her lips at the same time. She walked over to the youngster and shocked him when she lifted his arms up on either side of him and started to frisk him down.

'Hey!' he said, dropping his hands and taking a large step backwards.

She smiled and shrugged. 'We can do it my way, or you can strip butt-naked for me.' She looked him up and down. 'What'll it be?'

One look at her face told him she wasn't joking. The young mutant puffed out his cheeks and reassumed the position while her hands moved expertly across his clothes and body, pulling him this way and that as she felt for either a weapon or any sort of listening device. It took no more than a few seconds.

Eventually, satisfied he wasn't concealing anything, she seemed to relax a little, stepping back round the table so that it was between the two of them again. She nodded for him to take a seat.

'I'm sorry about that, but I can't be too careful these days. You want some water?' she asked, gesturing towards a jug and two glasses on the table between them.

'No, thanks.'

'Straight to business, huh? Well, that suits me. So . . . our mutual friend – Citizen Stark? – she said you'd be able to show me something that would make me trust that she really is who she claimed to be when we spoke.'

Rush nodded.

'Well?'

'I'm it.'

She gave him a blank look. 'You're what?'

'I'm the proof. My name is Rush and I was recently involved in the bombing of your city. I'm a hybrid: part Pure, part Mute. I can do this.'

She watched as he took a deep breath and looked at the glassware on the table again. There was a jittering noise as if the tall jug was being jiggled back and forth, and then the entire thing rose, hovering about a hand's length above the surface.

Eleanor gasped. 'What the . . . ?'

As the jug began to tip, one of the glasses rose up from the table to meet the spout, catching the water as it started to pour forth from the lip. When it was half full, the jug returned to its original position with a loud *clonk!* and the glass floated, slightly unsteadily, over to hover just in front of Eleanor, who looked at it as if it might be the most dangerous thing in the world.

'Not thirsty?' Rush said, his voice sounding a little strained. Once she managed to drag her eyes away from the floating vessel and look at the boy, it was clear he was struggling to do whatever it was he was doing: tiny beads of sweat stood out on his forehead, and he looked markedly paler than he had a few moments earlier.

'You've made your point,' she said shakily.

The glass floated away from the woman towards the boy, who reached out and took it out of the air, visibly sagging a little as he did so. 'In that case, I think I'll have that drink after all.'

Anya

Despite being in the body of a winged reptile-thing, she was still able to cry, and what remained of the tears she'd shed earlier had frozen among the scales of her face. It was so cold, the wind against her as she flew aimlessly onwards like an icy slap now that the sun had slipped below the horizon. It didn't seem possible she'd been up here that long.

Her thoughts were a scrambled, ragged mess.

After her argument with the rest of the group, she'd morphed and flown away, raging at the heavens. She'd swooped and soared, hissing angrily at invisible foes, striking out into nothingness with her taloned fists and feet.

She hated them.

She hated the way they ignored her, or shut her down when she spoke, saying she was being negative and unhelpful.

She hated the way they'd formed into little groups – groups that seemed to have no place for her.

Most of them could go to hell. Most, but not all. She cared about Rush. But she was furious with him as well. Because he too had turned on her. Why? Why would he do that? She wanted so much for him to want her in the same way she wanted him, but he didn't.

She 'screamed' into the skies again, except it wasn't a scream; this body was incapable of making that sound. Instead a loud, harsh *hiss* came out.

Why? Why couldn't he see her? He saw the Pure girl all right! He seemed to see nothing but Tia.

Anya punched out at the air again, before folding her wings and plummeting towards the ground. The wind roared in her ears, the ground rushing up at her with sickening speed. She could end it. She could stay like this and smash head first into the ruined land so that nothing but an ugly smudge was left.

Instead she pulled up at the last moment, the muscles where her wings joined the back of her torso screaming out in pain as she did so.

Tears came again.

She flew on into the night.

Tia

Eleanor stared at the teenage girl sitting across from her. 'First things first,' she said. 'Who is Stark, and how is it you're masquerading as her?'

'I won't be for long. I've got a little over ten hours left before I have to get out of the city. I'm officially dead.'

Eleanor raised an eyebrow.

'It's a loophole,' Tia said.

'Pretend I didn't ask.' The former police commander looked out of the window and nodded her head in the direction of the mutant boy. Rush had decided to leave the pair to talk alone in the eatery they'd chosen as a safe place. 'So he really is one of them?'

'One of whom?'

'The mutants who bombed this city.'

'In order to save their friend.'

'You're defending what they did?'

The severity of her tone took Tia aback, and she wondered if she was doing the right thing by being here. 'No, just clarifying the situation.'

Eleanor studied her companion. It was difficult to pinpoint exactly what it was that had changed about her, but she was a different person to the young girl she'd first met not so long ago in the safety of her home. Back then she'd come across as a little immature – spoilt. Now there was a steeliness to her, and she seemed more self-assured and . . . harder. She looked a lot like her father, and unknowingly mimicked a number of the facial expressions he made when he was in the debating chamber, determined to get his point across.

'What have you got yourself mixed up in, Tia? I helped you leave this city so that you could document the mutant plight. That's what you told me when you originally came to me. Your father also believed that was what you were doing. Now you tell me you're mixed up with a group of individuals who were illegally created by President Melk?'

Tia nodded in Rush's direction. 'He's part of the mutant plight. Look at him, Eleanor. He could pass, *does* pass, for one of us. He didn't ask to be cooked up in some secret laboratory any more than you or I asked to be born. If Silas hadn't rescued him and the others, who knows what Melk would have done to them. Silas believes he was planning to create a super-army by cloning them. That in itself is outrageous. Rush isn't the terrorist here, Melk is. The man's a monster. You know that as well as I do, and I can't just sit on my hands and do nothing if I have a chance of exposing him as such.'

Eleanor remained silent for a few moments, still looking at the mutant boy outside. 'He's cute.'

'Is he?'

'Oh, come on, Tia.'

'We're friends.'

'Just friends?'

The suggestion angered Tia, but she held her tongue. She refrained from pointing out to Eleanor how she'd been a long-time activist for mutant rights and was not just some sappy, doe-eyed fool. This conversation was too important. She certainly didn't want it reduced to anything as trivial as 'cute boys'.

Eleanor stared at her. 'I'm just trying to establish the motive for your actions, Tia. Trying to figure out if you've got yourself mixed up with these "freedom fighters" because that boy has used his romantic charms on you? Because if that *is* the case, I'd –' She stopped when the girl laughed. 'What's so funny?'

'Rush? Romantic charms? He's about the least charming

person on Scorched Earth. If either of us has feelings for the other, it's me for him.' She paused, frowning, surprised at how she'd blurted out those words, finally admitting her feelings for him aloud. 'I'd appreciate it if you kept that to yourself. He has no idea. He's . . . oblivious to that sort of thing. In one way I find that quite endearing; in another it's utterly infuriating.'

'I know how that feels.'

Tia caught the tinge of sadness and said what she'd often wondered but never dared ask.

'My father?'

'Let's just say that by the time he realised how I felt about him, it was too late. He and I danced around each other for too long. We flirted and hinted about our feelings, but neither of us had the courage to come out and say it. Then your mother came on the scene. She didn't play silly games – she came straight out and told him she was in love with him– and they married shortly after.'

'I'm sorry.'

Eleanor waved the apology away. 'I just wanted to be sure you were involved in this for the right reasons.'

'Regarding the bombings,' Tia said, glad to bring the conversation back on track, 'there really was no other choice. Melk wouldn't release Brick, another of the kids – the healer I told you about. Our "beloved president" wanted to cut him up to discover how Bio-Gen could best use his unique powers. The bombs were the last resort, only to be detonated if Melk refused to hand his prisoner over.' Tia leaned forward, her eyes locked to those of the other woman. 'But those explosives were judiciously placed to cause damage to infrastructure, not cause death.'

'You make it sound as if you knew it was all going to happen.'

'How couldn't I? I helped them plan the entire thing, and got them inside the Wall.'

Eleanor gasped. 'You did what?'

'Until now, all I've ever done is document the things I've seen happening on the other side of the Wall. I shot footage, commented on the thuggish actions of the ARM, made the odd cutting remark about Melk or the Principia, then packed up my stuff and hurried back to the safety of C4 and my father's fortune. But sometimes it's not enough to stand on the sidelines and watch. Sometimes you have to take action to change the world. Especially if that world is as cruel and barbaric to some of those living in it as this one is.' She knew she sounded preachy, but she meant every word. It occurred to her that she would never again feel the same about the world she'd grown up in. She looked about her; the place was still almost empty, the staff preparing for the midday influx when workers would fill the place. 'How is my father?'

'They're treating him well enough – for now at least. But if the trial goes against him, he'll be made to wish he'd never said the things he did. There's talk of sending him to TS1.'

'They can't! That place is a hellhole.' TS1 was a high-security prison set on an island in the middle of a toxic lake. Nothing was allowed on to the place except those sent there as criminals. She'd done a speculative piece on the prison a year or so back. The worst offenders (murderers, rapists and violent thugs) were housed there, and just the thought of her father among such men was enough to cause a rising sense of panic in her.

'Treason's a serious charge.'

'Who's representing him in court?'

'As you might imagine, he has the best lawyers money can buy. But with Melk and eighty per cent of the Principia desperate to make an example of him, he's going to find it hard to get off.'

'Not if somebody could prove Melk was a criminal who'd broken just about every law the Six Cities have ever devised.'

'Proof?'

'Melk's brother. He is living proof that my father wasn't

lying when he said Melk had caused all of this to happen. Silas is willing to give evidence about a secret installation Melk set up to perform illegal activities. He's a former citizen, so his testimony should be taken seriously.'

'Former – exactly. Melk would try to discredit him, and at the end of the day it would be one man's word against another; the big difference being that one of those men is the president.' She sighed. 'Things are different here since the bombings. The people are different. Melk has realised he's the kind of leader they want right now, and he's taking advantage of it in every possible way.'

'What if I had proof in the form of videos and interviews?'

'How would you air them? Your father's media corporation has been "temporarily off air" since his arrest. All we get on our screens at the moment are state-sanctioned broadcasts. I tell you, Tia, we're about this far away –' she held out her forefinger and thumb – 'from being a military state.'

'Could I get the news channels up and running again? Challenge Melk's right to take them down?'

The former police chief narrowed her eyes as she thought this through. 'Possibly. But you'd have to be inside the city to do that.'

'That's where I'm hoping you can help. Do you know where Buffy is?' Tia asked, referring to the marmoset monkey she'd had her chip placed inside in order to fool the authorities into thinking she'd never left the city in the first place.

'Of course I do. As soon as I heard of your father's arrest, I made arrangements to have the animal brought to me. As far as the authorities are concerned you're living in my apartment, too upset about your father even to go outside.' She stared at the girl again. 'What you're planning is very dangerous, Tia. I'll help you as much as I can, but this could get nasty, very nasty.'

'I've seen plenty of nasty, Eleanor. Besides, I don't have much choice.' She stood up. 'I think it's time Tia Cowper came out of hiding, don't you?'

Steeleye

The ARM soldiers stood at the back of their troop carrier watching the strange behaviour of their cyborg commander. Standing about twenty metres ahead of them, the Mute had been staring at the ground for what seemed an age, occasionally looking off in one direction or another. When he went down on one knee to peer more intently at something, one of the men swore he saw Mange lick his finger, dab it into the dusty soil, sniff it, then lick it.

'What on Scorched Earth does he think he's doing?' another man asked. 'I tell you, this freak is –'

'Shhhh,' Blake, the recently appointed captain, hissed. 'Guy's got the hearing of a bat.' Despite his voice being barely audible, he eyed the man-machine warily as he gestured for the men and woman in his charge to gather together back inside the vehicle. Everyone safely inside, he closed the rear door and spoke to them in an urgent whisper. 'Listen, from what I can make out, this madman intends to lead us off deep into the Wastes in his search for these rebel kids. That's out of our jurisdiction. Way out. Who knows where we'll end up if we continue to blindly follow this crazy son of a bitch?'

'Those were our orders though, sir.'

Blake shook his head. 'The Agency for the Regulation of Mutants, that's who we are. And why did we sign up to the ARM, hmm? I'll tell you why: to keep a handle on these Mutes. To stop them from contaminating our cities and our blood with their filthy mutant genes. That's the reason I signed up anyway. What I *didn't* sign up for was to find myself being ordered around by one.'

'So what do you propose we do?'

The captain turned to the woman standing by his side. 'Sergeant Loyas, you're the best shot here, am I right?'

'Yes, sir,' Loyas said without hesitation.

Addressing the group as a whole, Blake continued: 'Then I suggest tomorrow morning, when that freakosaurus is out front, running with the wind in his hair, Sergeant Loyas puts a bullet in his head. We leave him where he falls, to be picked apart by the scavengers. Then we head on back to our families and civilisation.'

'A bullet? Sir, we haven't used ballistic firearms for a

long time now. The Principia banned such weapons after the –'

Blake, who had removed a long box hidden beneath the bench on his side of the compartment, flipped open the lid to reveal the antique weapon inside. It was his grandfather's high-powered rifle, complete with a long, black telescopic sight mounted on the rear of the barrel. One of the soldiers gave a low appreciative whistle. Where Blake's grandfather had got it was anyone's guess, but following his death the old man, himself an ardent hater of the Mutes, had left it to his grandson to show how proud he was that the boy had joined the ARM.

'Our former captain didn't deserve to be shot in the way he was,' Blake said. 'I went to visit him before we left, and thanks to that thing out there –' he nodded in the direction Steeleye had been standing – 'Cap might never regain the use of his left arm. Now I don't know what special defences Melk and his scientists might have built in to the cyborg, so I don't trust our pulsed-energy guns against him, but this . . .'

'May I?' Loyas said.

'Be my guest.'

The sergeant bent down and picked up the rifle, swinging it into her shoulder and looking down the scope. 'It's beautiful,' she said.

'Wait a minute,' one of the newer recruits said, the apprehension in his voice clear to everyone present. 'What do we tell the authorities? They're bound to ask what happened to their new pet project and why we didn't bring him back. Hell, I can't begin to imagine how much those bionic augmentations of his must have cost. And President Melk said –'

'I couldn't care less what anyone said,' Blake cut him off. 'We'll tell them that we were ambushed by a marauding gang who killed the commander. We did our best to repulse their attack, but there were simply too many of them. We saw them haul his body off. There was nothing for us to bring back.' He shrugged and bent down to the viewing window to stare out at the cyborg. 'As far as I'm concerned, the guy signed his own death warrant when he shot Cap like that.'

The rest of the group murmured their agreement.

'So it's settled. Tomorrow morning.'

With the promise of bad weather, the platoon woke up early the next day. Dark clouds hung in the air. Every now and then the men and Sergeant Loyas caught the distant rumble of thunder somewhere off to the east. In his usual position, up ahead and away from the others, Steeleye looked out across the severe landscape laid out before him, his human eye seeing the scene in one way, the other 'eye' superimposing a weirdly coloured image atop it. It was this secondary visual representation, an ultraviolet filter of some kind, that allowed him to see the trail clearly left by the transporter taken by the rebel children. The vehicle must have had a small leak in its cooling system, nothing serious, but enough that every fifty metres or so, a drip of coolant fell on the ground. When he'd analysed these tiny seepages, he found out he could see them clearly by switching his cyborg vision to one particular mode, and now their route was laid out before him like Hansel and Gretel's breadcrumb trail. All he had to do was join the dots for his chance of revenge.

The albino.

Of all the renegade children he sought, the one called Jax – the one who'd first come to Steeleye and messed with his head, implanting nightmare visions so that the mutant gangster was rendered a quivering coward in front of his own men – would be made to suffer the most. Him *and* the kid with the freaky telekinesis, the one responsible for the brain damage that had nearly killed Steeleye, injuries that *would* have killed him if Melk hadn't rebuilt him into the thing he now was. Those two would know what real pain was before he finally dispatched them. As for the others? He thought he might capture them alive. Take them back as a present to Melk and Razko.

Steeleye was so caught up in his diabolic fantasy that he didn't notice the troop carrier had stopped some distance away from him, the driver swinging the vehicle round so the opening at the back, the door now thrown wide open, was facing him. Neither did he notice the momentary glint of the sun reflect on the front lens of the telescopic sight as Sergeant Loyas swung the rifle up and centred the fine crosshairs on the cyborg's head.

Instead it was pure luck that Mange twisted his head to the right to take in the mountain range that stretched off in that direction at the precise moment Loyas squeezed the trigger with her forefinger.

The bullet should have taken the Mute's head off. Instead it hit the metal half of Steeleye's skull, careening off into the air after blasting the cyborg from his feet so he landed face down in the dirt. Carried by the momentum of the impact, he rolled over two or three times before coming to a stop against a small rock sticking up out of the ground. Inches from his face, a small scorpion, brown in colour, scurried out from a crack in the rock and waved its barbed tail at him.

Mange sucked in a deep breath. His vision swam, and he thought there was every chance he would give in to the curtains of grey pushing at the edges of his vision. *What the hell had just happened?* Warnings, accompanied by a loud blaring noise, flashed across his HUD, informing him that certain systems were down and others were malfunctioning. Fighting to maintain consciousness, and trying to get his thoughts straight, Steeleye focused on the data from his scanners, desperate to ascertain where the attack had come from. He knew the crew in the troop carrier to his rear would have seen him being hit, and that they'd be rapidly dispersing to deal with the threat. Calling up the control panel on his heads-up display, he scrolled down until he found what he wanted, the selection turning green as he activated it. A small panel slid away from his bionic right arm, the shiny black globe inside emerging on the end of a metal rod. *DEPLOYING SPY DRONE* flashed across his vision a split second before the sphere shot out, hovering in the air just off the ground for a moment before ascending straight up into the sky. Via the tiny remote device, Steeleye could see everything below him as if he was flying up there himself, and not face down in the dirt, fighting for his life. Despite everything, he refused to give in and close his eyes, knowing that to do so might mean never waking up again. He switched the camera to a combination of optical and thermal, so the warm bodies of the ARM agents would stand out in stark contrast with the cold ground. One of them had remained in the vehicle, the agent's heat signature visible above the heat from the troop carrier's engine. The others had disembarked and spread out in two groups. Steeleye paused, trying to make sense of what he was seeing. Instead of fanning out from the vehicle to discover where the attack might have come from, the agents, all armed, were approaching him. They had split into two groups, a pair closing in from one side, three from the other as if they were . . .

The reality of the situation dawned on Steeleye. The attack had *come* from the ARM vehicle! These traitors were trying to kill him!

Anger had always served Steeleye well. In the slums, as head of a vicious criminal gangland, he'd been renowned for his ruthlessness, especially when dealing with rival factions who sought to take over from him. Calling upon all his reserves and fuelled by rage, he forced himself to focus. Keeping face down, and as flat to the ground as possible, he scooted himself round to put as much as possible of the small boulder between him and the shooter, who was no doubt at this very moment trying to make a target of him again. Despite the incredible pain in his head, the cyborg's face twisted into a grim smile. *If this was the way they wanted it to go, so be it. He'd show them precisely what happens when you screwed with Steeleye Mange!*

On his HUD each of the little figures below acquired a small red triangle, the symbol tracking their progress as they made their way towards him. Two triangles appeared over the troop carrier.

Showtime, Mange thought as the words *MINI GUIDED AP MISSILE LAUNCHER ACTIVATED* flashed across his vision in green.

Another small panel slid away, this time from his shoulder, revealing a small cylinder. The device was packed with twenty or thirty small rocket-shaped objects, each one no thicker than the tip of the cyborg's little finger and of about the same length. At his silent command, seven of these missiles flew up in the air, separating after fifty metres or so and each taking its own path as it honed in on its allocated little red triangle.

The first five missiles exploded almost simultaneously. Steeleye grinned as, on his display, the small red triangles over the moving figures flashed brightly in time with the blasts. Then they, and the little figures they accompanied, disappeared from view. A split second later, the last two missiles found their mark. Steeleye was already on his feet as the transporter was destroyed, the thing instantly turned into a fiery mass from which torn and twisted metal flew off in every direction. With a roar he pumped the air with his fist, revelling in the destruction of his enemies.

The drone, having been summoned back, returned, hovering in the air in front of Steeleye until he reached out and took it in his human hand and placed it back inside his robotic arm.

During his time in the slums, in order to rise to the position of power he'd come to enjoy, Steeleye had been forced to kill on numerous occasions. The act had never kept him awake at night, and this time would be no different.

'Pure?' he muttered to himself, looking about him at the desolation. 'Pure garbage.'

The grin that was forming on his lips slipped away almost as quickly as it had appeared. His water and supplies, not to mention various pills he was supposed to take to stop his body rejecting his bionic augmentations, had been in that vehicle. The doctors back at C4 had impressed on him the importance of the drugs, but they'd omitted to tell him what the consequences might be should he fail to take them. Swearing under his breath at his own stupidity, the mutant cyborg spat a bloody blob into the dirt, turned his back on the scene of destruction and set off on the trail of the stolen transporter and the rebel kids he'd been sent out here to find.

Anya

She was trapped. Trapped inside the body of the hideous creature she'd conjured up in a moment of anger and frustration, the thing she'd become after arguing with Silas and Rush. And now that body had become a permanent vessel for her mind. *Stupid!* She had stayed in this form for too long – flying for extensive spells and neglecting to transform back when she returned to solid ground. She had no idea how long she'd spent aloft, flying through clouds and across open skies, but she knew the sun had risen and set at least once since she had assumed this form. And she knew how dangerous that could be for her. She should do – being trapped inside another body had happened to her before, but never for this long, and never with the resulting pain she was now experiencing when she tried to morph back.

She had no idea how long she'd been struggling to turn. Hours? Days?

Taking a deep breath, she tried again.

Not that anything without wings could get up there, but had anyone been unfortunate enough to pass the shallow cave on the mountainside at that moment, seeing the snake-headed creature writhing grotesquely on the floor, they could have been forgiven for believing the chimeric beast was in its death throes.

The thing twisted and bucked violently back and forth, as if pushed and pulled by huge unseen hands. The serpent mouth, stretched impossibly wide, emitted shrieks and hissing noises that were every bit as terrifying as the sight of the creature making them. The face seemed to change, distorting horribly, caving in and puckering in places, bulging and distending in others, as if something was alive beneath the surface – alive and trapped and trying to force its way out. A nose appeared and then disappeared again; the eyes shifted and changed, large and reptilian one moment, smaller and more human the next. The mouth too stretched and shrank; a ghastly slit became an oval of human pain before reverting to something between the two, and as it changed, the noises coming from it altered too – rasps and hisses became screams and gasps. It went on for maybe a minute, although to Anya it felt much longer, and then the Anya-thing stopped, the creature going limp, its abdomen heaving up and down as it struggled for air.

A keening *heee!-heee!-heee!* sound came from its mouth. Agony didn't even begin to describe the all-consuming pain Anya had just experienced, and yet she was still trapped. Something had changed, she was sure of that. She reached up and felt her face. Except it was not her face. She tried to speak; something she had not been able to do since her initial transformation into this body. '*Trapped*,' she said, the word sounding as ugly and distorted as she felt. Her half-serpent, half-human voice had an eerie, breathy quality to it, but at least she could form and utter words now.

Getting to her hands and knees, she tried to stand, but fell to one side, crashing painfully back down where she stayed, tears running down the tight scales that made up the skin of her face.

Exhausted, she slept for a while, and when she woke she knew: this was *their* fault. Silas and Rush and that do-gooder Tia Cowper. *They* had alienated her and pushed her out of the group. Tink had come for her. Tink had been the one to rescue her and bring her to the others. They had been happy to *use* her, oh yes. Happy for her abilities to aid them in their plans. They had *needed* her help with the raid on City Four. *She* had been the one to set most of the explosive devices. She had been the one to catch Silas as he leaped from the top floor of the skyscraper, taking him up in her hands and flying him to safety. But once that was done, once they had made their point and proved to the Pures what they could do, she was no longer needed and had been pushed out.

It was all too clear to her now – the way some of them, especially that Cowper girl and Rush, spoke together in hushed voices, stopping or changing the subject when she came near. Tia was the main troublemaker! She'd never liked Anya. And poor, pathetic Rush had fallen under the pretty little city dweller's spell. Anya had watched how he'd been manipulated, the way Tia flirted so openly with him, trying to break up the group. And Silas too! He was just as gullible and weak.

That was why *they* had been chosen to go to C4 together, while she had been expected to stay back in that dead place. They'd known she would react. They might even have planned it. Now this. Now, because of them, she was confined in this body, unable to get out. Tia Cowper. Anya pounded angrily at the ground, imagining it wasn't the earth she was hitting but the Cowper girl's face.

Why couldn't they see? Tia wasn't one of them, would never be one of them. Silas wasn't either. There were only five people who could ever know what it meant to be one of President Melk's freak experiments: Rush, Flea, Jax, Brick and Anya. They should have stuck together, *always.* But now they couldn't even trust each other.

Anya forced herself to her feet, staggering a little but managing to stay upright this time. Dragging herself out of the cave, she shivered when she came into contact with the cold air. But it was just what she needed, and she gulped huge breaths of it to clear her head. The mountains reminded her of the place where she had grown up. She could think here. Feeling stronger, she stepped forward and jumped off the ledge, her heart leaping in her chest as she plummeted towards the ravine below. Unfurling her wings, she was instantly caught up by the air, and she flapped her huge bat-like appendages until she started to gain height.

She would go back. Go back and show them what they'd done. Then she'd work out a way to get even with them.

Steeleye

It was clear to Steeleye that a number of things were wrong. His HUD, designed to keep him informed of everything around him, kept winking out when he least expected it. Every time it did this he realised how much his brain had come to depend on the information constantly being streamed to it. There were mechanical gremlins in the system too. His left leg was making a weird whirring noise when he moved, alarming enough to make him give up on the idea of travelling at anything but a moderate pace in case the damn thing just packed in altogether. In addition, his cyborg right arm had started to jerk uncontrollably one moment, refusing to move at all the next.

He stopped and scanned the land ahead of him, looking out for the telltale spots on the ground. As he did so, he reached up with his human hand and felt the area where the bullet had impacted with his metallic skull. The dent was larger than he'd first thought, and it was without a doubt the reason for the malfunctions of his 'augmented self'. Who knew what damage had been done to the high-tech equipment, not to mention his real brain. Ever since the attack he'd had a raging headache that refused to shift, and for some reason the pain inside his skull made him think of Svenson, and how she'd react when she saw the damage; no doubt she'd have him under the saw or knife as soon as he walked in the door. *If there was anything of him left to walk through the door.* He might have been imagining it, but he had the distinct impression that the areas where his human body parts interfaced with the bionic augmentations were more tender than they'd been when he'd been taking his medication. He certainly wasn't imagining the red and puffy, sore-to-touch skin at the 'interface zones'. *Maybe my transplants are being rejected?* he thought, and the idea made him laugh out loud. The sound had a harsh braying quality and didn't sound to his ears like the laugh of a completely sane person. *Too much heat,* he thought, and guffawed again.

Thank goodness the sun was setting. Although he was both dehydrated and hungry, his mood was lighter than it had been for some time now. No longer having the whingeing and whining ARM unit with him was part of it, but it was also because he was close. He didn't know how he knew this, but he did. Soon he'd be at the place where those freak kids were hiding out, and then he would settle the outstanding business that existed between them.

The HUD dropped out again, and with it the filter he'd been using to track the stolen vehicle, returning his view of the world to that of a one-eyed human. Swearing aloud, the cyborg banged at the side of his head with his bionic hand, the impact making a dull clanging noise and doing nothing to diminish his headache. This hit-and-hope trick had worked last time: the heads-up display had returned, along with a stream of data about faulty systems and diagnostic faults, all of which Steeleye Mange had ignored or deleted. This time there was nothing.

'Dammit!'

He raised the fist again, ready to give his skull an almighty whack, when he stopped. He'd been so reliant on following the data provided by his cyborg equipment, he'd almost forgotten to take in his surroundings. He'd finally made the crest of the hill he'd been climbing, and below him, spread out at the bottom of a shallow valley, was a desolate city. That there was anything left of it at all after the Last War was a wonder, and Steeleye reasoned that the geographical layout of the land all about it – hemmed in as it was by the hills – was the reason. He didn't need infrared or heat vision to tell him this was the renegade children's encampment. He *knew*. It was perfect. If he'd been on the run in the same way they were, he wouldn't have hesitated to go to ground here. Grinning, he looked down at his own feet. Sure enough, there, next to them in the dirt, was the smudged impression of a tyre track, and he was sure that if he'd had his HUD working there would be a small speck of the telltale residue somewhere in the dirt around it.

His shadow stretched out off to his left, and he turned his head to glance at the swiftly setting sun. A small slither of intense orange peeked back at him over the horizon. It would be gone in a few minutes, and that suited Steeleye just fine. Looking for a way down into the basin below, he spotted the walkway at the far end of the ruined flyover. Humming to himself, he strode towards it, ignoring the clunking noises his leg was making. Maybe today wasn't going to be too bad after all.

The dead city was eerie, made all the more so by the silver moonlight it was bathed in now. It was too quiet, and the silence gave him the impression that the mummified dead who occasionally stared out at him from the shattered earth might at any moment rise up and attack him, the unwelcome interloper. Steeleye liked the place. It had a menace to it that he could relate to.

'HELLO!' he shouted. 'Come out, come out, wherever you are!'

He paused to take another look around.

Where? Where would be the best place to hide a six- or seven-strong group of individuals among all this wreckage and –

He spotted it. He must have looked over it already, but now he was looking at it from another direction he could see how the opening in the ground wasn't just a cave-in as he'd first assumed. It was too regular in shape, and the area around it too ordered, as if much of the rubble had been cleared recently. But the real giveaway was the pair of trousers he could now see spread out on top of the mangled concrete outcrop not far away, no doubt put there to dry.

The mutant cyborg picked his way over to the concealed entrance, staring down into the rectangular opening and the stairs that led down into a perfect blackness. He'd heard of such places. It was rumoured that huge subterranean transporters had operated between the six underground cities, or Arks, that the Pures had hidden in throughout the Last War and the years that followed it. If that was indeed true, it made sense that the pre-war inhabitants of Scorched Earth might have had something similar. He wondered what it must have been like back then, living in a world where humankind was all *one.* No Pures or

Mutes, just one homogenised species called *people*. He decided he didn't like the idea. Division causes fear and mistrust, and those were two things Steeleye knew how to use to his benefit.

There was a faint whiff of something on the air coming up out of that place. Fuel? He banged the side of his head again, hoping to jolt his visual feedback systems back to life, but nothing happened. Night vision might have been nice right now.

Screw it, he thought. Having come all this way, he was damned if he was going to creep around like some goddamn sneak thief. He'd take these little upstarts on, mutant to mutant.

'Little pigs, little pigs, let me come in!' he shouted down into the shadows. 'Or I'll huff and I'll puff and I'll tear your underground hidey-hole apart!'

Silas

'What was that?' Silas said, looking up from the sock he was darning with a needle and thread. He thought he'd heard a crash, like something falling down outside, followed by what might have been a human grunt. He looked over at Brick, but the big mutant clearly hadn't heard anything and sat, oblivious even to Silas's question, humming tunelessly to himself. If the mutant colossus had asked how long it would be until Rush would be back once, he must have asked a hundred times.

Slowly getting to his feet, Silas took a few steps towards the entrance and then stood perfectly still, listening. Nothing.

They're fine, he told himself, knowing his edginess had everything to do with his anxiety for the four children currently not with him: the three he'd sent off to C4, and Anya, who'd not been heard from since she'd transformed and gone off on her own. Flea had volunteered to go out and scout the surrounding land, looking for her, but each time she returned, exhausted from her extensive searches, she did so alone.

Silas was about to turn and return to his work when he froze. There it was again, louder. This time it was unmistakably the sound of a man's voice carrying down the stairs from above.

Brick too had heard it now. The big guy quickly scrambled to his feet and stared across the room in the direction of the gate-like shutter separating the stairs from the area where they'd set up home. Silas gestured to Brick to stay silent when he was struck by the expression on the other's face. It was almost as if he recognised . . .

Silas gave a small gasp as it dawned on him why Brick was staring agog like that. He also knew the voice. He should do – he'd locked horns with Steeleye Mange before, back in Muteville. If Mange was up there, his arrival could only spell trouble.

'Brick!' he hissed, jabbing a finger in the direction of a small pile of blankets in one corner. 'Wake Flea.' As the big guy did as he was directed, Silas moved towards the stairs to check the security gate was locked.

Having woken up almost the instant the giant mutant's

hand had touched her shoulder, Flea suddenly appeared at her guardian's side. Her transition from deep asleep to fully awake was as quick as everything else about her. He beckoned Brick over too.

'What?' Flea said, the word dragged out a little so it sounded odd: *wh-a-a-t?* Her powers made it hard for her to work at the speed of the others. Her perception of the world and the people in it was that they were super-slow-moving, and even though she'd gone a long way to being able to control this aspect of her special ability, learning to slow herself down so she could function more normally, she still struggled to form words and make herself understood.

'We have to go down into the tunnels,' he said. Brick groaned with dread. 'I'm not going to lie to you, Brick, it's very dark down there, but Flea and I will be with you. We can't stay here.' He turned to Flea. 'Do you remember the man who captured you on your way to the C4 slums? The man who made you steal for him? The same man that captured Brick here?'

'Bad man,' Brick said to Flea. He pointed to his face. 'Silver ball for eye.'

She nodded.

'That's who is up there. I don't know how he found us, but he has. So you see, we don't have any choice. We have to go. Now.'

* * *

They paused at the top of what had once been an escalator. Dark didn't even begin to describe the sucking blackness below them. The strange ridged metal steps disappeared after only a few metres. Beyond that, nothing. When they'd first arrived and set up camp, Silas had made some torches: metal rods around the top of which he'd wrapped fuel-soaked rags. But even though he and Flea now each held one, they knew they mustn't light them until they were well out of sight and in the underground tunnels themselves. Brick wasn't allowed to turn on his own little dynamo-powered torch either, but he held the plastic contraption jammed up against his face, tears rolling down his cheeks as he forced himself to step out, down into the darkness.

They were almost two-thirds of the way down when the voice from above boomed for them to halt.

Steeleye

Luck was on the cyborg's side. Or maybe it was something more than luck. Maybe it was destiny that was aiding and abetting him. Why else had he turned his head a split second before the ARM sniper had squeezed the trigger, avoiding certain and instant death? Why else had he been led here by a trail of chemical droplets that only he could see? And why else, when his leg momentarily failed on the second step down to the underground hideout, sending him tumbling down the rest of the stairway and causing him to smash his head on the concrete floor at the bottom, had his HUD suddenly blinked back to life? *Destiny*. He was being tried. Fate was playing games with him, testing his ability to keep going and overcome the obstacles it threw up in his way. And if that was the case, it could only mean one thing: he was being groomed for greatness. He'd always known as much – that he was destined to be so much more than the gangland boss of Dump Two. No, he was far better than that, and when he took these hybrid kids back to Melk and won his citizenship, he'd show the Pures what it was to be powerful. How long might it take for an individual like him to rise to the level of power that someone like Melk enjoyed? Not too long, he thought.

Steeleye picked himself up off the floor. Although working again, the heads-up display wasn't completely functional. It winked off and on again three times before finally settling as a fuzzy, blinking version of what it had once been.

A security gate separated the bottom of the stairs from the rest of the underground space. The thing was made of metal and, when pulled across into the thick concrete walls as it was now, looked as if it would be difficult to shift. A quick shoulder-charge confirmed this to be the case. Gripping the gate and placing one foot against the wall next to it, Steeleye leaned back and heaved, enjoying the screech as the metal began to buckle and give way under the immense force. When he'd created enough of a gap to squeeze through, he paused to assess how best to proceed. The head-mounted light appeared to be operational, but if anyone was waiting to ambush him on the other side of this gate, it wouldn't do to give them such an obvious and easy target. Not until he knew what he was dealing with. There were other ways to spot rats in the sewers. He switched to thermal instead and carried on.

Before leaving they'd taken the time to turn off the generators that had powered the lights, but the stink of them still filled the underground space. The things they'd recently touched glowed in his new view of the world. If indeed this was a place Old Earthers had come to journey underground, there must be a series of tunnels that their vehicles had travelled through, and he was betting this was the escape route the rebel children would take now. He didn't have to go far to find the top of the stairway leading deep down, further into the ground. Almost at the bottom, the thermal imaging picked up the three fugitives slowly descending. Three human-shaped harlequins, different colours glowing where their bodies gave off most heat, carefully making their way through the blackness.

He could have taken them in the dark. That would have been the easiest thing in the world, just fire down on them from his elevated position and snuff their miserable lives out. But he wanted the albino, and if the white-skinned freak was one of this trio, simply eliminating him so quickly in this manner wouldn't do. Oh no. Besides, what was the point in having all this high-tech gear if he wasn't able to have a little fun?

He liked the way they cowered and grabbed at each other when he shouted down at them to stop. One of them stepped back a little too quickly and would have fallen down the rest of the steep staircase had the others not grabbed them. Now they all clung to each other in the blackness, staring this way and that for any clue as to where he might be.

'Look at you,' Steeleye taunted them. 'Three blind mice. Maybe we should shed a little light on this scene before I come after you with the carving knife, eh?'

He activated the light on his HUD, turning it up to maximum brightness so he could get his first real look at the trio. He knew them all. The big guy – Brick? – was the one he'd captured and taken back to C4 for Melk not so long ago; the smallest of the three, was a petite redheaded girl he'd forced to become a pickpocket for him. But it was the third member of the group that he was most pleased to see. The older guy had accompanied the white-skinned freak on the first occasion they'd met and had directed the albino to crawl around inside Steeleye's head, making him hallucinate and see terrible things. He was their leader. He'd openly threatened Mange in front of his own men, and when he'd left, taking the redhead and her guardian with him, he'd turned back and grinned. Well, he wasn't grinning now.

Silas. That was his name. The man turned to the other two and shouted for them to run, shoving them down the stairs away from him as he did so. Then, wielding what looked like a metal pole with a bunch of rags tied to one end, he came charging up the stairs, heading straight for Steeleye.

Maybe it was Steeleye's astonishment at the gall of the man, maybe it was an electronic malfunction, but what happened next was a terrible error on the cyborg's part. He should have simply used his shoulder-mounted PEG to shoot the man. His HUD had already locked on to the target, the crosshairs tracking Silas's surprisingly swift progress up the stairs. All that was needed was for Steeleye to blast him back down before turning his attention on the others. Instead, he got his command sequences mixed up and called up the miniature rocket launcher he'd used against the ARM agents. The crosshairs disappeared, replaced by a small red triangle. Steeleye ignored the additional red warning signals that flashed in front of his eyes, dismissing them as just another bunch of dumb system errors.

It was only as the tiny anti-personnel rockets hissed upwards out of the launcher that he realised what he'd done and what the warnings had been trying to tell him. Silas was almost on top of him, but Steeleye paid him little heed; he was frantically trying to access the abort command for the rockets. Only as the steel pole swung down towards him did he take evasive action, lifting his metal arm to ward off the blow just as the rockets smashed into the ceiling overhead. The explosion in the confined space was deafening, and Steeleye was vaguely aware of the redhead girl emitting a loud scream before disappearing in a blur of motion.

The ceiling came crashing down, great chunks of concrete hammering into flesh and bone and metal, burying everything beneath it.

Flea

She'd been so close! As soon as she saw the rocket fired by the cyborg, she knew she had fractions of a second to react. But even fractions of a second could be a very long time to somebody as fast as Flea. As she set off she watched the pencil-sized rockets' propulsion systems firing, and she instantly recognised what was going to happen. The rockets, two of them, moved quickly even in her super-slow-motion version of the world, but she thought she could reach Silas in time. She had to. Between Silas and the bottom of the staircase, where Brick and Flea were, there must have been forty or fifty stairs in all, and she was only three or four steps away when the rockets struck the ceiling and exploded. Flea glanced up to see the flames spreading out from the point of impact like a deadly flower slowly opening its petals. She stretched forward and grabbed a handful of Silas's shirt from behind, peering past him and registering the look of horror on Steeleye's face as the full implications of what he'd done dawned on him. Her plan had been to simply yank Silas back towards her, even though doing so meant there was a good chance the two of them would fall down the full length of the escalator, but his momentum as he swung the pole at the cyborg carried him forward instead, sending them both off balance.

She'd misjudged how long she had.

She dodged the first few chunks of stone as they rained down around her, but one caught her a painful blow on the leg. She twisted about but was struck again, this time by an even larger hunk of stone that connected flush between her shoulder blades, forcing her to her knees. From that point, she knew there was no getting up. Writhing in agony, she watched in horror as a slab of concrete almost as big as she was plummeted down on to her.

The noise of the explosion in the narrow confines was terrible, and the shock wave that followed threw Brick backwards, smashing his head against a stone column near the bottom of the escalator. There was a loud *crack!* inside his skull – something breaking there – before he passed out. Now, as he came round, having been unconscious for only a few moments, he was aware that his skull was already mending: fibroblasts and chondroblasts producing collagen and fibrocartilage at a rate that should have been impossible. He had stopped bleeding – the open wound having already knitted together – and by the time he got back to his feet Brick's skull had already started to form the callus that would bridge the two pieces of bone together in his cranium. His ears were ringing, but his perforated eardrums, like the rest of him, were also healing. The disorientation was not so swift to remedy. He shook his head, fighting to work out where he was and what had happened. Somehow he'd managed to keep hold of his torch, and he switched the thing on now, shining it up the grooved stairs at the site of the cave-in.

Letting out a low groan he hurried towards the steps, taking them three at a time.

After the initial agonies there was no pain. That, like her life, was slowly leeching out of her. She'd screamed as the huge block of concrete came crashing down on her, but even that sound had been cut short as its weight forced all the air from her lungs in one go. Things had snapped or been crushed in her small frame, and the relief she now felt from those first few moments of torture was immeasurable. Not that she wanted to die. She was too young and had too many things she wished to do. But she didn't want the pain either.

Flea felt herself drifting – drifting towards nothingness . . .

She became aware that Brick was holding her hand. Not aware in a physical way – she was well beyond that – but aware that he was there with her. It was good not to be alone. She felt a halt in that drifting sensation, a jarring shudder. And with it was the awareness that Brick was trying to bring her back from the brink. She also somehow knew that it was hopeless, despite his powers. She was too far gone. She felt his . . . essence, his soul in those moments, and understood what a truly good person he was. She would miss him. And Tia. She would miss her friend Tia most of all.

Aware that the slab that pinioned her had been lifted free, she looked up to see – really see – Brick kneeling over her. She felt him trying so very hard to infuse her with his own life force. And then she felt nothing.

The thick dust made Brick want to cough, but that would have made him drop the plastic torch clamped between his teeth as he threw the rocks and debris out behind him. The din of the masonry crashing down the metal escalator steps hardly registered with him. Neither was he aware of the wounded-animal-like moan emanating from him. Tears streamed from his eyes, making salty tracks through the grime that covered his face before they fell down into the rubble. Somebody, maybe everybody, was alive in there – he could *feel* it. He stopped for a moment when he saw the small, slender arm. A delicate bracelet, little metal flowers with blue centres – a gift Tia had given Flea – around the wrist. Resting the torch down, he grabbed the hand in his own, closing his eyes and praying he wasn't already too late. He could heal almost anything, broken bones, disease, terrible wounds, but he couldn't reawaken a body if life had already departed.

There was the tiniest glimmer of life force remaining, a solitary star in a nothingness of space. But it was receding. Concentrating hard, Brick pulled the darkness out of his friend, swallowing it up into himself. This was how he healed others: he took their hurt. He wasn't sure how he healed himself afterwards, but he always did. But it wasn't working on Flea. She was too far gone. With one hand still holding on to hers, he shifted more debris, the weight of the stuff fully registering now that his own strength was ebbing away. There was a large slab of concrete on top of her, too big for him to shift one-handed. He hated letting go of her, even for the few seconds it took for him to heave the mass from her broken body, but he had no choice. He threw the thing behind him and looked back down, grabbing for her hand at the same time.

'Flea,' he said.

Their eyes met, a last flicker of recognition registering in her pale blue irises before slipping away. He was too late, and Flea's tiny star winked out forever.

The roar that escaped the huge man filled the space more completely than the exploding rockets had. Sobbing, he lifted her gently from the debris and carried her up to the top of the steps, where he laid her down.

He wanted to stay with her. It didn't seem right to leave that small ruined body all alone up there, but he had no choice. Because he could feel that there was still life down there. He spoke to her as if she was merely asleep, and before he moved away he wet the pad of his thumb on his tongue and removed a smudge of blood from her cheek. Then he clambered back down over the wreckage to where the explosion had hit.

The two remaining bodies trapped in the rubble were almost on top of each other, as if they'd carried on their struggle even as the ceiling came crashing down. He uncovered Silas first. Face down on the rubble, Brick's friend and childhood saviour lay unmoving. Brick didn't need to reach out and touch the man to know there was nothing he could do for him.

Which meant that the life force he could still sense was . . .

Brick stood, panting with exertion, struggling to control the rage that quickly bloomed inside him. With his fists he pounded the thick black rubber handrail at his side again and again, crushing and buckling the metal underneath until he was finally spent. Then, in the same way he'd done with Flea, he gently carried his friend away.

He was in no hurry to go back down. Instead, after wrapping their bodies in blankets, he took each of his dead friends up out of the underground hideout, into the fresh air. He didn't want them down there with that . . . thing. He lit a fire and placed them by its edge. Silas would have prohibited it, argued that it would draw attention, but Brick doubted that mattered right now. All he wanted was for their cold bodies to be near some light and warmth. He stood, staring down into the dancing flames, letting the smoke and the heat wash over him.

'Must go back down,' he said, half to himself and half to his dead friends.

Brick's mind, often muddled and slower than everybody else's, was a jumble of confusion now. A part of him wanted to leave the man-machine-thing there, but a bigger part of him knew that wasn't the right thing to do. He wished his best friend in the whole wide world was here. Rush always knew what to do for the best. But Rush was gone. Gone with Tia and Jax. *Jax!* Brick let out a loud sob at the thought of how the albino would react when he discovered that Silas, who had been like a father to him, was dead. Brick had never had a father. But he'd had Maw, and she had been like a mum and a dad all wrapped into one. He thought about her now. Maw had brought him up, just like Silas had brought Jax up. She'd loved him and told him what was right and wrong – she was very big on that. And when he needed help on those things, right and wrong, he always tried to think about what his guardian would do. So he imagined her here now. He remembered how she looked at him when he did something foolish or stupid, and how her expression was very different when he did something bad. He imagined her standing next to Silas's and Flea's lifeless bodies, and he imagined asking her what he should do – what the *right* thing to do was.

He knew what she would say. It didn't *feel* right, but deep down, he knew it was.

With a sigh he tipped his big head back so he could look out at the stars twinkling and dancing up there in the void of space. Then, after taking a couple of deep breaths of the cool, fresh air, he walked back down the steps, returning underground to dig his friends' murderer out from beneath the rock and stone.

Jax, Rush and Tia

Standing in a darkened doorway at the very end of the alleyway, Jax peered out at the group guarding the passage. The woman in charge might be his only problem. Briefly reaching out and touching their minds with his own, Jax had deduced she was the least susceptible to the type of psychic trickery he planned. Still, he felt reasonably sure he could pull it off.

Jax had made his way here after Rush and Tia had failed to meet up as they'd agreed. It hadn't been easy finding the place – this Juneau character had done a good job of staying off most people's radar – and Jax had been forced into some fancy detective work, dipping into people's heads in an effort to discover something that would lead him to his friends. The information had eventually come from an unlikely source: a city guard just north of here had

had some illegal surgery done in the past and knew exactly where the bioengineer could be found.

Now Jax was here, he was faced with the not inconsequential task of getting access to the man. The albino thought there was a good chance that Juneau had double-crossed them, taken the young mutants captive so he might hand them over to the authorities and claim whatever reward was being offered. His only hope was that the scientist still had the youngsters in his keeping and he was not too late to free them.

Movement ahead drew his attention back to the task in hand. As one of the lookouts broke away from the others, Jax remained perfectly still, waiting patiently for the man to come closer. Jax's black clothing helped him remain unseen, but even if he'd been dressed in a bright orange jumpsuit the man would have had trouble spotting him, thanks to the 'fuzz' Jax had placed in his mind. As soon as he'd gone, Jax stepped out and headed back towards his group.

'Hey, Boz. What you doing back so soon?'

'Forgot something,' Jax said. In the group's eyes he looked exactly like the individual who had just left: clothes, hair, walking gait, everything. 'Yesterday Juneau asked me to take something to the market. Need to pick it up from the surgery.' It wasn't proving difficult to make four of the five people see what he wanted them to. The only one he was having to work hard to convince was the tall woman, and he was fairly certain that she too was buying the phantasm he'd created in their minds. He was almost at the door when he spotted the small wooden lean-to beside it. A shallow metal bowl of water had been left there, and beside that the savaged remains of what had once been a large bone. When Dotty poked her head out from the lean-to she recognised Jax immediately and jumped up at him. It would have been obvious to those watching that the gesture was a friendly one had she not been suddenly pulled to a halt by the short metal chain attaching her to the wall. Jax, taken aback by the sight of the rogwan, momentarily allowed the illusion he'd created in the others' minds to slip.

'Boz?!' the woman shouted.

Jax turned and looked at her, noticing the flicker of confusion in her eyes.

'What?'

When the woman looked from him to the rogwan, it was clear she thought something was up.

'Dammit,' Jax mumbled under his breath.

And that might have been the end of Jax's ruse if Dotty, somehow understanding what was happening, hadn't taken up an aggressive posture – head low, muscles tense, baleful eyes fixed on the man in front of her. Deep *hurghing* noises, in complete contrast to the friendly greeting she'd initially gave him, came from the rogwan, who topped the display off by peeling her lips back, treating him to a glimpse of her lethal-looking teeth.

The tall woman's attention was redirected to Dotty, giving Jax a chance to reinforce his illusion in her mind so that when she looked at him again, Boz was back. 'Mind you don't get too near that thing,' she said. 'You know what happened to Grubs when he tried to take its bone away!'

The rest of the group, with the exception of one man, who gingerly reached across to hold his left forearm, laughed.

'Dotty, you are a clever girl,' Jax said to the rogwan under his breath.

With that, he slipped through the door and entered the building.

'Who the hell are you?' Juneau said as the tall albino walked into his secret laboratory from the waiting room. 'And how did you get that door to open? And why didn't my security buzzer sound?'

'To take your questions in order: I'm Jax; I didn't – you opened it; and when your buzzer went off, you chose to deactivate it.'

'Now hold on just a –' The bioengineer paused, deep frown lines creasing his forehead. The buzzer *had* sounded and he *had* disabled it. Not just that, but he'd gone on to activate the device around his neck to open the hidden panel. *Why had he done that?* He'd been working on cracking the security-code problem that Tia Cowper had left him when he'd suddenly come over a little dizzy, a brief touch of vertigo that had made him a little queasy. Then, for no good reason, he'd reached down and pressed the button to let this guy in and . . .

The frown disappeared, replaced with a look of realisation. 'Oh, wait a minute. I get it. You're another one of them, aren't you? One of those hybrids or whatever. The ones the Cowper girl is mixed up with?'

'I'd like to ask you some questions.'

Still peeved at whatever trickery he'd been subjected to, Juneau shook his head. 'Won't do you no good. Doctor–patient confidentiality is the buzz-phrase here, my pasty-faced friend.' He pointed a long finger from one of his extra hands at the albino. 'Say, I could sort out that melanin-deficiency thing you've got going on there. Wouldn't be too expensive. Let's say about –'

'Where are Tia and Rush?'

The strangest thing happened to Juneau then. At one level he believed he was giving his albino interrogator the standard spiel about not divulging client information – he could almost feel his lips forming the words and then saying them aloud to this intruder – but on another level he was aware that he was in fact telling the white-skinned freak everything he knew, the words seeming to be spoken by him and *not* by him at the same time.

'So you chipped them? Both of them?'

No. 'Yes.'

'Why?'

Why what? 'So she could help her father.'

Juneau shook his head. *What the hell was going on here?*

'If I find out you've done anything to endanger my friends, I'll –'

'We're fine, Jax.'

The albino spun round to see Tia standing there smiling back at him. Perched on her shoulder was a small monkey. Behind her were Rush and Dotty.

'Nice to see you, Cowper,' Juneau said. 'In fact, I'd go so far as to call your timing impeccable. Now perhaps you'd be so kind as to tell Whitey here to get the hell out of my head.'

Once Tia and Rush had convinced him that Jax would not be listening in to his every thought – something the backstreet bioengineer seemed to find a truly terrible prospect – Juneau returned to his usual cocky and brash self. Holding court around a vis-unit that he'd put the image of the nanobots on to, he made a big show of producing the security-encrypted holo-player, placing it on the desktop alongside an omnipad so they could all see it.

'Now,' he began, when he was certain he had everybody's undivided attention, 'as you know, the file we wanted to access was highly protected. Only a person of almost genius-level intelligence could crack such a cipher.'

Rush groaned, but the bioengineer ignored him.

'However, it just so happens that I *am* a genius. A much maligned genius, but a genius nevertheless. If I'd been born on the other side of the Wall I'd have been lauded as a –'

'Could you just cut to the chase?' Tia said. She turned to Jax. 'Or maybe you should go back into his head and find out what it is we need to know.'

'That won't be necessary,' the four-armed man hastily said. 'In fact, I was on the verge of trying to access the file for the first time myself before Dax, or whatever his name is, bust in here and started doing his little mind tricks. So your coming back when you did is a double bonus. We can see what's on it together.' Leaning over and opening a drawer, the scientist took out a weird-looking device – not unlike a gas mask – and placed it over his mouth and nose.

'What the hell is that thing?' Tia asked.

'Vocal imitation apparatus. Neat, isn't it?' her own voice answered her back. She stared at Juneau, who winked, clearly enjoying the startled look on the young woman's face. He waved a hand over the holo-player and tapped a series of figures into the holopad that appeared in the air above it. When he spoke again it was neither in Tia's nor his own voice. Instead it was the unmistakable accent and intonation of the President of the Principia. 'Cracking the code is only half the task, so it's a good job I had this thing programmed with Melk's voice, not to mention those of a number of other high-ranking city officials, a while ago. Following Melk's most recent broadcast, I was able to fully update the voice records I had on him.' He gave them all a sly look. 'You'd be amazed at the stuff you can get done if you place orders in the voice of that old nutjob.' Gesturing for them all to turn their attention to the holo-player, he continued. 'Security access code five-nine-alpha-four-four.' There was a bleep. 'Play N22 research file, number forty-six.'

An image of a laboratory appeared in the air above the player, and Juneau enlarged it. There was no sound, only a faint *hiss*, like low-level static. When a man wearing rubber gloves and a long white coat appeared, the camera operator honed in on him. White Coat proceeded to approach a number of rabbits housed together in a large cage. Three of the animals were a dark grey colour, the remaining trio pure white. One by one, the scientist removed the white rabbits from the pen. Holding each one still on the work surface, he reached out his other hand into small polished steel dish and withdrew a syringe which, except for being about a tenth of the size, was identical to the twelve hundred or so that lined the hidden walls of the hijacked transporter back at the dead city. The scientist injected the blue liquid into each of the white furry animals, holding them firmly while they kicked and bucked for a second or two. The rabbits were returned to the cage with the others, where they seemed unfazed by their experience. Having recorded this, the camera panned across, focusing on the structure beside the rabbit pen. There was something about the way the cameraman concentrated on the large metal cylinder that made the watchers uneasy, even though it had no markings to identify what it might be or do.

'What –' Tia began.

'Shhh,' Juneau said, despite there being no soundtrack for her to disturb.

After a few seconds the camera operator pulled back, widening the field of view so both the cage and the cylinder could be seen.

Beside the cylinder was a small box of the same colour with a large red button on it. Taking this device in his hand, the man moved to one side to give an unobstructed view of the pen and the creatures inside it. Then, being very deliberate to show his actions, he pointed at the cylinder and pressed the red button.

Nothing happened for a moment or two; the camera operator zoomed in a little, filling the view with the cage and its furry inhabitants.

The grey creatures suddenly became more animated; sniffing at the air with their twitching noses, they began to run around the pen. Then, en masse, they started to back away from the paler rabbits. Within a few seconds they were jammed into the corners, pushing themselves up against the edges of the pen to get as far away from the others as they could. At the same time, the white rabbits began to shake. The movement was slight at first, but very quickly the tremors became increasingly violent. Two of them opened their mouths, and despite there being no sound, it was clear that the creatures were crying out in distress. One of the animals began to run around wildly, crashing headlong into the edges of the enclosure as if it was trying to break out. The blood came from their eyes first. Within moments it was leaking from every orifice, looking all the more ghastly against the pure white of their fur. Their pain and suffering was watched by the greys, and it was only a matter of seconds before the three injected rabbits, convulsing uncontrollably towards the end, became a mass of bloody gore and collapsed, dead.

The camera zoomed out to reveal the man in the white coat again. He looked at the camera and simply nodded his head. The holo-image ended.

Nobody said anything. One by one their attention shifted away from where the holo-image had been to the vis-unit with the image of the squid-like nanobots, complete with their blade-tipped tentacles.

Juneau broke the silence. 'So much for the theory that this stuff was being made for medical purposes. I couldn't have been more wrong, could I?'

'They've been injecting the inhabitants of Muteville with that stuff,' Jax said. 'The mutant population is being relocated to new reservations in the east. Part of the registration means allowing yourself to be "vaccinated" against disease. The authorities are pumping mutant veins full of these microscopic killing machines and –'

'Oh no. No, no, no.' It was Rush, and he was suddenly looking almost as pale as Jax. 'Go back,' he said. 'Rewind the clip.'

'I don't want to watch that again,' Tia said, her voice little more than a whisper. The marmoset monkey sitting on her shoulder must have picked up on her owner's discomfort and gave a little screech of its own.

'No, go back to the part where they show you that black cylinder. The thing the guy operated with the remote control.'

The bioengineer waved his hand across the machine's display until he got to the part Rush was talking about. He paused the holo-image.

'What?' Tia asked.

'That. Whatever it is,' Rush said, 'I've seen one before.'

'Where?'

The young mutant seemed unable to speak. He reached out, his forefinger held level so that when he put it through the floating image, the black cylinder looked as if it was balancing on it.

'Rush, where did you see it?'

'On the back of a transporter – a massive one. It was when we did the first raid.' He looked over at Jax. 'Do you remember when I went up into the hills with my telescope to see if I could spot a vehicle we might be able to ambush? While I was up there I saw this big carrier in the distance. It was way off, but you could tell it was huge. The thing on the back was like that –' he nodded at the frozen holo-image – 'but much, much bigger.'

'Where was it heading?'

Incapable of taking his eyes from the thing on the screen, he frowned and gave a little shake of his head.

'East. Over the Salt Basins and away from the rest of the cities. I didn't think anything of it at the time; it was just a big black cylinder.'

'That must be where they're building this mutant reservation,' Juneau said, thinking aloud. 'Where the old City Six was.'

'Pardon?'

'The *former* C6. The current C6 was once the seventh city.'

'I thought there were only six Arks.'

'No. The story goes that the former sixth city was responsible for a lot of hush-hush research, and because of this it was deliberately removed from the other metropolises. It seems they were looking into a new form of energy production when something went wrong. There was a total meltdown and the place became a ghost town overnight. The authorities denied everything of course, but pretty soon they just shut the gates and seven became six. But . . .' he said, opening a drawer and rummaging around until he came out with a number of large rolled-up maps. Selecting the one he was looking for, he spread it out on a table for the others to gather round. The map showed the landscape containing the Six Cities and the connections between them. Holding it down with two hands, he gestured with a third. '. . . I'm guessing *this* is still in operation.' Juneau was pointing at two perfectly straight dotted lines, close together, stretching out from the area marked as 'C4'.

'What is it?' Tia asked.

'A tunnel. It goes right under the Salt Basins in the direction your telekinetic friend here saw that carrier heading. Unless I'm very much mistaken, folks, that there –' he tapped at the map – 'is how our twisted President Melk is going to transport his mutant deportees. Right before he wipes them out.'

Rush closed his eyes, but all that was waiting for him was the image of the blood-soaked rabbits, their mouths open in a silent scream. That, and the memory of that giant cylinder disappearing off into the distance. Melk had to be stopped. Whatever it took, the lunatic couldn't be allowed to carry out his diabolical plans.

'We have to get to that tunnel and see if there's any way we can stop the transportation going ahead,' Jax said. He turned to Juneau. 'Thank you for your help, and I'm sorry I doubted you. I should have known to trust Tia's judgement. I'd appreciate it if you didn't tell anyone about what you have seen and heard here today.'

'You don't have to worry about me talking, but if you think I'm done with all this, you're seriously mistaken. I'm going to continue working on things from here.'

'Why?'

'This involves me every bit as much as it does you. Now, I mightn't have any magic tricks like you and your friend here –' he nodded at Rush – 'but I'm damned if I'll stand by and watch my people get wiped out. I'm smart. Not street-smart like Tia here, but I understand technology and how things work. Maybe I can figure out how to stop Melk's murderous little machines.'

'You could get caught, Juneau,' Tia pointed out. 'If that happens, you might not get to spend that fifty thousand credits I had my friend transfer into your account.'

'If everyone else is dead, there isn't going to be anywhere to spend it, is there?'

The three outlaws looked at each other for a moment. Although none of them spoke, it was clear that they were in agreement about Juneau's proposal. The bioengineer picked up on the silent exchange too. 'That's agreed then. I'll do what I can to figure out how these things are activated.' He glanced from Tia to the monkey that had now taken up position at the other side of the room. 'I'm guessing the presence of our simian friend here means you want your old identity back?'

'That would be useful. We also need to ask you a favour. We'd like you to look after some things for us while we're gone.'

'Things?'

'Buffy for one.' Tia nodded at the marmoset.

'And Dotty,' Rush added.

'What is this, a petting zoo?' The bioengineer shook his head in dismay, but it was clear he was going to agree. 'Anything else?'

'I don't think so.'

'OK. Then let's get your chip out of the monkey and back where it belongs. Won't take me too long to do.' He gestured for her to follow him, but they were both stopped in their tracks by Jax, who gasped, his hand going up to his head as if he was in pain.

'What?' Rush asked.

'It's Silas. I can't . . .' He placed a finger to his temple, a look of dread writ large on his features. 'I can't feel him any more!'

'I don't understand.'

'Ever since I was a small child, I've always been able to sense his presence. Nothing big, no details, just some kind of link that's existed between us. But he's just . . . not there.'

'What does that mean?' With each question he asked, Rush felt himself fill with fear at what the answers might be.

'I don't know. Maybe . . . nothing?' Jax replied, but his expression suggested otherwise. 'I have to go back and find out what's happened.'

'Brick and Flea are there too,' Rush said in a small voice. 'And Anya must have returned by now.' He felt sick. Something must have happened for Jax, who was usually so rational, to be having this reaction. What if Melk had found them? Or a drone had spotted them and another ARM unit had descended on his friends?

'Should we come with you?' Tia asked.

They were all thinking the same thing: the more they spilt up, the weaker they became. Despite his rising panic, it was Rush who finally broke the silence. Despite his love of the team members they'd left back at their base, he couldn't leave the mutant population of City Four to its fate. Not even for the sake of friendship. 'OK, you go and find them, Jax. Make sure they're safe. I need to stay here and work out how to stop Melk.' He looked cautiously at Tia. In the relatively short time she'd known Flea, the two had become like sisters. 'It's up to you whether you stay or go – there's no right answer.'

She looked straight back at him. 'I'll stay with you and Juneau. Jax will find the others and bring them back here.'

Jax was already at the door. He stopped briefly, turning to give each of them a curt nod. 'Stay safe,' he said. 'I'll find you when I've got the others.'

Tia and Rush

They sat beside each other outside a small shop in the slums. The man who served them their sweet tea drinks had declared they were made from filtered water, but the slightly sulphurous aftertaste made them doubt the veracity of this. It was late in the day, and the market in the square was packing up, the traders laughing and joking with each other as they put away their wares and secured their stalls. Despite the noise, the two teenagers seemed largely oblivious to the hustle and bustle going on all around them.

'You'll be on your own,' Tia said, tracing the edge of the cup with her finger. The effects of the painkiller Juneau had given her were beginning to kick in. A second operation in almost as many days had left her leg sore, but at least her original CivisChip was back in place.

'Hardly.'

'You know what I mean.'

'There's no other way. I have to try and stop that underground train or, failing that, get inside this camp of Melk's and see if there's anything I can do there. The only way I can do either of those things is to register as a resettler.'

'And what do you really think you can do then, hmm?'

'I have no idea. But I can't just stand by and do nothing.'

'You'll be injected with those things.'

Rush looked about him. From what he understood, he doubted there was anyone in the market square who'd not already signed up for Melk's semi-enforced relocation. Every Mute here had already been 'inoculated'. The difference was that they were all blissfully unaware of what had actually been done to them.

'Then we'll have to find a way to stop them being activated, won't we?'

Lost in her thoughts, Tia lifted the cup and took another sip before hastily pushing it away from her again. She took a deep breath. 'I . . . I care about you,' she said, the words coming out too quickly, and not at all how she'd wanted them to.

'I care about you too, Tia.'

'When I say I care about you . . . I mean . . . a lot.' She couldn't help but blush, and it was this, not her words, that finally revealed to Rush what she was trying to say.

'Oh. Er . . .'

'I'm sorry. I know it's the wrong time for us to be talking about this, but I just wanted you to –'

'No, no. Don't apologise, please. I, er, well, I like you too – a lot.' He reached out to grab her hand, almost knocking the cup over, his clumsiness making them both laugh and relieving some of the awkward tension that had built up.

'It's not just me who is going into the lion's den,' he pointed out. 'You'll be putting yourself in danger the moment you set foot inside that wall again. Melk will be forced to try to keep you quiet.'

'I have one or two surprises up my sleeve yet for our beloved president.'

He looked at her quizzically, but she just smiled, not willing to reveal what she was alluding to.

Across the market square an ancient clock, maybe a relic from before the Last War, rang out the hour, the bell sounding tired and muffled.

'Well,' he said, getting to his feet, 'I'd better get going. Don't want to miss my chance to register and get my injection of microscopic killbots, do I?'

Tia stood too, her chair making a loud rasping noise on the ground.

'Bye,' he said.

'Bye.'

Rush gawkily proffered his hand as if to shake hers, and was completely taken aback when, ignoring it, she stepped forward and kissed him.

It was the first time he'd ever been kissed by a girl.

He breathed her in, closing his eyes and relishing the feeling of her soft lips on his own. His heart did a weird thing inside his chest: stuttering momentarily, as if it too was shocked by the kiss, and then speeding up to a heavy and thumping rhythm that made his head swim. And then it was over. He opened his eyes, noting how she did the same thing at precisely the same time, and they simply stared at each other. It was like looking into her soul, and he knew this brief moment had changed everything forever.

'That was nice,' she said.

'Mmmm.'

She smiled, and the moment was broken. She reached out and touched his hand briefly with the tips of her fingers. Then she frowned, realising something. 'I don't know your last name.'

He shook his head. 'Neither do I. The terrible thing is, I guess it must be the same as the man responsible for giving me life. If that's true, I think I'd rather not have one.'

'Be careful, Rush.'

'You too, Tia.'

They parted then, going their separate ways. It struck Rush as he walked away that he might never see her again, if it all went wrong. But he couldn't turn back. He was going to be relocated with the rest of the inhabitants of Muteville. Relocated in a place where a deadly black cylinder was waiting to deal out death to the mutant population.

Anya

She flew high despite the cold, a part of her relishing the pain that the near freezing temperatures caused in her extremities. She welcomed the solitude that flying at such heights afforded her. The cold and the aloneness matched her mood. Her anger with the others at their mistreatment of her had grown, and with it so had the realisation that she was no longer one of them. They didn't want her around. They had made that quite clear that last time they'd all been together. Jax and Rush were the chosen ones. Oh, and Tia – Tia, a rich little brat who wasn't even a mutant, never mind a hybrid like the rest of them! They were Silas's favourites.

Screw them, she thought. She didn't need them, any of them.

Anya swooped down low before catching a thermal

thrown up from the range of hills stretching far below. Carried effortlessly on the air, she scanned the landscape. She was close.

Although she had made up her mind that she wanted no part of their stupid little gang, she was damned if she was going to let them get away with how they had treated her. Her plan might be a petty one, but it was better than nothing.

Away to her left, looking like an ugly scar on the landscape, she spotted the dead city. A smile formed on her face, the mouth of the serpent head stretching wide to reveal the black fangs within.

She frowned as she swooped down out of the night sky. They appeared to have set guards. There was somebody not far from the entrance to the right of her, and she wondered what had happened to make the group start posting lookouts. Stranger still was the fact that the sentry, far from being discreetly hidden, had made a fire, announcing their presence to anyone approaching the area. Maybe they had been posted to keep an eye out for her, but she doubted that. They'd probably said good riddance to her leaving.

She landed almost silently, her leathery wings beating downwards at the last moment to stall her in the air before she dropped the last metre or so and alighted, legs bent to soften the sound further. Even so, she glanced over at the sitting figure to check they hadn't been alerted to her presence. Closer now, she recognised the silhouette – it wasn't difficult, only one person here looked like *that*. Slumped forward at the edge of the fire was the big dummy, Brick. Something, *some things*, were on the ground near to him and for a moment she thought they might be sleeping figures. But that was silly. Why would they be sleeping out here? Unless something had happened to their little underground hideout . . .

She crept over to the entrance and slipped noiselessly down the stairs.

It was darker than she'd expected. Only one of the lights was on, and from the sound of the generator – they always made more noise when they were first started – it had not been on for very long. She needn't have bothered being so stealthy – there didn't appear to be anyone down here.

Had she not been so hell bent on revenge, Anya might have stopped to consider where Silas was – he rarely left the site – but the thought didn't even cross her mind. Instead she set about carrying out what she'd come here to do. She strode over to where the group kept their food: a storage area on the far side of the former ticket office.

Opening the door, she pulled out the foodstuffs– many of which had been liberated from ambushed vehicles – ripping at the packets and cartons with her clawed hands and throwing everything on the ground. On to this she poured the drinking water from the big containers stored in the same place, producing a sodden mess which she finally kicked here and there, mixing it with the muck and dirt of the ground until it was utterly spoiled. She kept one vessel of water back, and this she carried across to the generator fuel tanks that powered the lights. She would have liked to torch the place, set fire to the fuel and watch it burn, but she was far from certain that her beast claws had the manual dexterity to create a flame without causing harm to herself. Instead, bypassing the one with the working light, she opened the tanks and poured the water in. It wouldn't necessarily ruin the machines, but it would cause damage in the short term until Silas had a chance to clean them out and fix them. Petty, she knew. But it felt good nonetheless.

Finished, Anya looked about her at her handiwork. The damage she'd done hardly seemed an adequate response to the group's ostracising of her, but it was better than nothing. Silas would quickly figure out who was responsible, and her only regret was that she wouldn't be around to see the look on his face. Still, she was satisfied that she had made her point. She planned to go back to the mountains far away from here. Not the hills she'd just come from, but those where she'd grown up. How she'd hated that place when she was small, but now its isolation and solitude seemed just what she wanted. Kerin might still be there. Anya and her guardian had not seen eye to eye before she had left, but she thought the woman would have her back – and maybe, eventually, help her find a way to transform back into her human self as they'd done in the past.

She approached the only remaining working light and turned it off before setting about spoiling that generator too. She would have to find her way out again in the darkness, but she was confident she could do so and . . .

The glow in the murk made her stop. Straightening up, she looked behind her in the direction of the stairs leading down to the tunnels. The light was coming from down there. Not the consistent illumination that the arc lights up here emitted, but a shifting, wavering glow that could only be a flame. If somebody was down there, the sensible thing to do was leave immediately, but her curiosity was piqued, and she approached the escalators.

Something had happened. Not only were the stairs strewn with rubble, but the area at the bottom also appeared to be covered in the stuff. She stared up at the large hole in the ceiling, trying to imagine what might have caused such an isolated rockfall. It explained the dust everywhere. Maybe there had been an earthquake. She shrugged. It wasn't her problem. Nothing that happened here any longer was her problem. As she turned her back on the scene to make her escape, she heard the groan. Somebody was down there in the murk, and from the sound of things they had been hurt.

Without knowing quite why, she carefully began to make her way down through the mess, struggling with the water container she still held in her hand, until eventually she made it to the bottom. Illuminated by the flickering flame of a burning torch jammed into a crack in the floor, she stared at the source of the noise.

The thing had been tied up. Loop after loop of strong thick wire had been used to truss up the prone figure, so there was no chance of it moving, let alone escaping. In addition, a black sack had been placed over its head. But Anya hardly registered these things because her eyes were immediately drawn to the legs, made as they were out of a dull brushed metal. She extended a foot and kicked at one, her claws making a harsh noise on the surface, noting how solid and heavy the things were. The right arm, pinioned to the side of the body with wire, appeared to be made of the same stuff, but this had been battered and damaged in places; deep scratches and dents were evident towards the top of the limb, and the same maltreatment had been meted out on a small device mounted on top of the shoulder; the thing – crushed, bent and ruined now – appeared to have been a gun of some kind. The cyborg – she was sure that was the correct term for it – was covered from head to toe in dust and dirt and had clearly been involved in the cave-in.

She jumped when another groan came from beneath the heavy black sack. Reaching forward, she took hold of the material and pulled it away, revealing the full man-machine.

Anya let out a small gasp. She recognised him. At least she recognised half of him. He had not been half man, half machine the last time she had seen him, but it was definitely the same person who had burst through a door into an alleyway back in Muteville and captured Brick. He had almost got Rush and Jax too, and would have, had Anya not helped them escape by wrecking the aerial spy drones put up by the ARM to assist them in their mission. Silas and his pathetic gang of renegades had needed her then, hadn't they? They had been happy to keep her around while they had a use for her, only to shun her now. And here was this . . . man-thing again, no doubt sent out by Melk and his people to complete the job he'd failed at last time. If that was indeed the case, it appeared as if he'd once again been unsuccessful.

An idea formed in Anya's mind. She'd been disappointed by her efforts upstairs. Despite destroying their den and food supplies, she had wanted to make more of a statement – show them what she really thought of them all, her mutant so-called brothers and sisters. Now this cyborg, trussed up with wire and left here near the tunnels, might be her way of doing just that.

She looked down at the water container in her claw. Lifting it, she poured its remaining contents on the cyborg's head, watching as he coughed and spluttered back to consciousness.

'Hrngh? What the hell?' Steeleye spat into the dust at his side before turning his attention to the chimera looming over him. The creature was part snake, part ape, part human, with huge bat-like wings folded along its back. It was staring back at him. Despite the fog in his head, he guessed it was the shape-shifting polymorph he'd previously encountered. There was nothing friendly about the look the thing gave him, but he defiantly held its gaze.

'What you waitin' for?' he said. His lips, smashed and bruised, struggled to form the words properly. 'Get it over with.'

The creature made no move towards him. Hell, there

was nothing he could do even if it had, trussed up like he was. And even if he'd not been bound tight with wire, every flesh-based part of him was in pain, a pain that increased tenfold at even the slightest effort. The 'other' aspect of him – the machine part – seemed to have fared little better. Inside his head, his HUD, blinking on and off sporadically, was a rolling stream of warnings and alerts – a sea of red accompanied by alarms – that he swiftly shut off to stop himself from going mad.

The thing still hadn't moved.

'You know,' Steeleye slurred, 'if you're gonna kill me, the least you should do is let me see what you really look like. Hiding in the body of a creature like that is kinda cowardly, don't you think? Like the axemen of old concealing their identity with a mask.' He spat again.

There was a low cough and then the thing spoke in a weird hissing voice that was every bit as unnerving as its appearance. It was clearly struggling to form the words. 'If I were you, I'd be quiet,' it said.

Had he imagined it, or was there something about the way the creature reacted when he'd spoken about transforming back? He paused, thinking things through. In his previous life, as a gangland boss, he'd learned a thing or two about unspoken communication. Everybody around him lied and deceived, and Steeleye had become very adept at interpreting body language and facial expression to gauge the truth behind people's words. He narrowed his eyes as he studied the monster.

'Perhaps you're not a coward. I might have been a little hasty there.' He was talking aloud, shooting his mouth off in the hope that he might buy himself some time to figure a way out of this mess. 'Maybe you're ashamed. Ashamed at what you've been tasked to do, so you don't want me to see the real you?' No, that wasn't it. 'Or maybe you *can't* change back, and you –'

'I said, *shut up*!'

Aha! He'd hit upon something. The only question now was, how could he use the information to his advantage?

He narrowed his eye at the thing. 'I know that look,' he said, nodding at her and instantly regretting the action as a new wave of pain ignited behind his eyes. 'I should do – I've been wearing it ever since I had half my body hacked off and replaced with these machine parts.' He paused. *Anya*. Her name popped into his head from nowhere. Melk had spoken about the rebel children, and Steeleye was certain that Anya had been the name of the shape-shifting girl. 'You're stuck in that body, aren't you, Anya?'

The thing looked over its shoulder up the escalator – the gesture alerting Steeleye to even more about what was really going on here.

'And they don't know you're here, do they?' He paused, then continued, hoping to get a response. 'I bet it was something to do with that Silas guy. After all, he's the boss here, isn't he? He's the one calling the shots. What happened, eh? They kick you out because you did something to upset them?' He shook his head, tutting.

'You and I are alike, you know that? You're stuck in that body, I'm in this one, and we're both where we are because of those freaks up there. *They* put us in this mess. They attacked me and left me for dead in that alleyway all those months ago. You know that's true – you were one of them. Of course, you didn't attack me personally. You were in charge of taking down the "eyes in the sky". But those others – that Jax guy and the one called Rush? – they smashed my old human body up pretty bad. They're responsible for me being this way, just as they made you what you are right now. Am I right? Well, am I?'

He let his words hang in the air, hoping that something would have had the desired effect on her.

'Yes,' she said, and tears began to form in those reptilian eyes. Whether they were tears of sadness or anger or impotence was difficult to tell, but he guessed they were a combination of all three. She'd been abandoned by her friends, and that could only be a good thing for him.

'We should pair up,' he said quickly. 'We could escape

together and work out a way to get back at them. Look what they did to me. Look what they did to you! They care nothing for anybody but themselves, and we clearly don't fit in their little clique.'

She made a little growling *hiss* noise, and he knew he'd hit upon something. Something that he might be able to use to save his hide. Now he just had to press home his advantage.

'You don't have to be alone, Anya. I can help you. And if you want to get back at them, I can help with that too.'

He considered going on, but realised he ran the risk of sounding too pleading and needy if he did so. She might see that as weakness and decide she didn't want anything to do with him. Instead he shut up and stared up at her. The reptilian eyes were impossible to read, and he was starting to wonder if he'd wildly misinterpreted her presence here when, with one last *hiss*, the creature bent forward and with a scaly talon began to undo the wire holding the cyborg prisoner.

Melk

President Melk was only vaguely listening to the military officer as she finished her report. It was hot in the room, and despite already having undone the top button of his shirt he was sweating again, the heat and the boring woman's droning voice made him want to simply get up and leave. He knew he should be concentrating, but found it impossible. He seemed in a permanent fugue state of late, unable to focus his thoughts in the way he'd always been able to. He put it down to the lack of sleep. Pills didn't seem to help any longer, and when he did manage to drift off he invariably jolted back to wakefulness within a few moments, convinced that somebody – or something – was in the room with him. He'd taken to leaving a light on, but it didn't help. The thing was still there, a malevolent presence that –

'Sir?'

'Huh?'

Fretz, the man who had called this meeting, was staring at him. Melk didn't like him. He was a worm, always sidling up to him and making stupid remarks about things he knew nothing about. Either that, or he would try to tell Melk jokes. Jokes! When Melk's ancestors had formulated the idea of repopulating Scorched Earth with a new, pure race of humans, they surely had not been thinking of the likes of Fretz. The man would have to go. Him and a number of other 'parasites'. He cast his eyes around the other people sitting at the table, some of whom were shifting about uncomfortably in their seats.

'We wanted to know how you wished to proceed.'

'With?'

General Razko stepped in. 'They want to know what you would like us to do next about the cyborg. As Captain Mayer here has just reported, we know he's responsible for the deaths of the ARM team sent to assist him with this mission, and now we have lost all contact. We need –'

'Why do I surround myself with the likes of these people?' Melk spat, glaring around him before turning back to his general. 'Hmmm?'

The sudden change in the president's mood was so unexpected that the woman sitting diagonally across from him tittered.

Maybe she thought it was some kind of joke. Perhaps one of Fretz's 'funny' stories.

One look from the leader of the Six Cities told her otherwise, and the sound died on her lips as quickly as it had started.

Melk reached up to wipe away the sweat that had formed on his top lip. 'I assumed, wrongly it seems, that you people might have the mettle to make important decisions, to prove to me that you were made of the right stuff. The stuff that will be needed in the months and years ahead if we are to truly fulfil our destiny and become the one true race on Scorched Earth. But all I seem to be surrounded by is INCOMPETENCE!'

'Sir –'

'Why was I not informed of this earlier?'

Razko didn't get a chance to tell him that he *had* been told of the cyborg's actions because the president went on without waiting for a response.

'This is the sort of thing that will bring our dreams of a New Earth crashing down around our ears, you know that? You, all of you – with the exception of Razko here – are weak. Yes. Weak. Inept. BUNGLING! INCOMPETENT!' Wild-eyed, spraying flecks of spittle, Melk stared about him at each of the people in the room in turn, the feral look in his eyes striking fear into every heart.

'With all due respect, Mr President –'

Melk glared at the speaker. Fretz again. The imbecile didn't know when to shut up.

Melk imagined himself with his hands around Fretz's neck. Squeezing and squeezing until . . .

Concentrate, Melk! Concentrate, dammit!

'The mutants are out there,' the president said, although in such a low voice that those across the large table struggled to hear his words. 'Out there . . . breeding. Every second we fail to do something about them, they are producing more of their filthy offspring.'

A short silence followed, broken only by the ticking of a clock. Somebody cleared their throat.

Razko took the reins again. 'Sir. The cyborg?'

'Cyborg?'

'Commander Mange. You . . . *We* sent him out to find the terrorists.'

'Yes. And?'

'Either he's gone rogue or he's been eliminated.'

'Gone rogue?' The president slowly shook his head. The wild look was melting away, much to the relief of everyone else in the room. They watched as their leader appeared to pull himself together again. He spoke only to Razko, treating the others as if they were not there. 'What makes you think such a thing?'

'Well, as Mayer has pointed out, there has been an incident between the ARM agents and the cyborg. Our data shows that an illegal rifle in the ARM vehicle was fired, so it's far from clear who started the whole thing.'

'Bring the cyborg back in and make him talk. Torture him if you have to.'

'That's the problem, sir. We don't know where he is. The tracking systems have gone down.'

Melk closed his eyes and took a deep breath.

Father . . .

'Not now,' he mumbled. 'Please . . . not . . . now.' Melk hardly dared open his eyes in case the bloody spectre of his dead son was there on the other side of the room, staring back at him with his own face.

'Mr President?' Razko reached out and almost put a hand on Melk's arm, but wisely stopped short. The general had thrown his lot in with Melk, and his future was intimately tied up with the other man's. At first it had been the obvious choice: Melk controlled the Principia in a way no one before him had. But the man's behaviour of late had the soldier doubting not only the politician's abilities, but his very sanity. Whispers about his mental state had been heard in the corridors of power, and added to this were the rumours of damaging evidence that might come to light if Towsin Cowper wound up in court. Maybe it was time to think about jumping ship. If Melk couldn't be relied on to keep him in power, Razko had to consider who could.

Melk's eyes snapped open and he looked about him as if he'd come out of a daze.

'You,' he said, pointing at the officer, Mayer. The woman visibly flinched in her seat, dreading what was coming. 'I assume you have reliable intelligence on the last known location of our cyborg?'

'Yes, sir.'

'Good. Then you personally –' he jabbed his finger at her – 'will appropriate a vehicle and travel out to that point.'

'Me, sir?'

'Yes, you! In case you haven't noticed, we are in the process of transporting a huge number of mutants away from their slums outside this city, which means that everyone, including you, must do their part.' He waited, daring the woman to answer him back. 'Once you reach your location, you will conduct a search, broadening it steadily until you find Commander Mange's body – either living or dead. Regardless of which of these states he might be in, you are to bring the cyborg back here to City Four. Do you understand these instructions – ' he glanced at her insignia – 'Captain?' Another idea occurred to him. 'Oh, and you can take Fretz here with you.'

The politician looked at him aghast. 'With all due respect, sir,' he spluttered, 'I'm not trained for duties of that kind. I think –'

'ENOUGH!' Melk slammed the table again. 'Are you disobeying a direct order from your president, Fretz?'

The man slid his eyes in Razko's direction – and received the tiniest shake of the other man's head. 'No, sir. Of course not.'

'Good,' Melk said. He rapped his knuckles on the tabletop: two quick knocks that seemed to punctuate something only he understood. He looked about him and smiled, his mood seemingly transformed.

'Why is there no air conditioning in this damned room?'

Nobody dared tell him he'd ordered it turned off at the start of the meeting.

'Well, I think that was a useful discussion, don't you?'

Another of his advisors tentatively raised a hand. 'Mr President, sir, I, er . . . I thought we'd planned to discuss the repairs to the south-east section of the wall, with the aim of –'

'Another time, I think,' Melk said with a waft of his hand. Standing up, he paused, frowning as if considering this response. 'Yes, definitely. Another time. The walls? Who knows – maybe we won't be needing them for much longer, eh, General?' Signalling for Razko to accompany him, the president turned on his heel and walked out of the room.

The people he left behind in the meeting room looked desperately at each other for a few seconds before one dared to break the silence.

'What the hell was that all about?'

'He's under a lot of strain,' suggested the woman who'd almost laughed out loud.

'Strain?' Fretz said, visibly shaken at the thought of leaving the safety of the city to go into the mutant wilderness. 'He's out of control, that's what he is. Did you see the way he was talking to himself? Who does that, hmm? I'll tell you who: a madman, that's who. The man is deranged!'

The woman shot him a look. Fretz held a position in the Principia she'd always hankered after, and in her opinion the man was not fit for office. 'I hope for your sake that this room isn't bugged. I'd imagine your little trip out to the Wastes could be very interesting, if what you just said was brought to our beloved president's attention. I mean, who knows how he'd react?'

All colour drained from the man's face. He started to say something and stopped. First he looked about the table, trying to gauge if anyone there would know if the room *was* bugged or not. When all he received were blank looks, he started to scan the walls and ceiling for possible places a listening device might be concealed.

'Well, I'd better be getting ready,' Captain Mayer said, standing up and straightening her uniform. 'I should have a vehicle powered up and ready to go in about an hour. I'll meet you down by the loading docks in Sector C, Principal Fretz?'

As things transpired, Melk's plan for Captain Mayer and her reluctant travelling companion turned out to be a good one. She travelled to the site of the confrontation between Steeleye and the ARM agents, and despite her misgivings about successfully finding anything in that harsh wilderness, she quickly ascertained the direction they had come from. Reasoning that this was as good a direction as any to begin her search, she carried on along the same bearing. As a soldier, Mayer was used to complaints from the men and women under her. Orders were usually met with grumblings or outright objections, but the civilian next to her took whingeing to a whole new level: first it was the heat inside the vehicle; then, when she opened a window, the dust was a problem; her driving came in for criticism next, and when all that was done he started in on the terrain. The man seemed unable to just shut up and get on with things, and the thought of having him alongside for much longer was enough to drive her to distraction. But luck was on the captain's side. She'd gone no more than ten kilometres from the start point when she saw a pair of figures come over a low rise, heading her way.

Mayer pulled to a halt and watched them.

The cyborg could hardly move; the man-machine was hanging on to the nightmarish creature that appeared to be accompanying him; that hellish creation appeared exhausted, only just bearing the strain and effort of the weight placed on it. Concentrating as they were on staying upright, the pair initially failed to see the vehicle ahead of them.

Like Mayer, Fretz was speechless for a moment. When he did speak, it was in a horrified tone. 'Get us out of here,' he said. 'Just put this thing into reverse and get us the hell out of this place before they notice us.'

'Those are not our orders, Principal,' Mayer said, although in truth the exact same idea had occurred to her.

The cyborg was bad enough: bloodied and ruined, it looked as if both flesh and mechanical elements had been put through a threshing machine. But the thing with it, a truly terrifying monster that Mayer thought would haunt her nightmares, was enough to make even the hard-bitten soldier shrivel inside.

Nevertheless, she reluctantly undid her seat belt and

climbed down out of the cab, calling out and waving to get their attention. Upon spotting her, they straightened up a little and began to make their way over.

Captain Mayer drew herself up to her full height when the half-man, half-machine was in front of her. Even weakened and damaged, he was a formidable sight. 'Commander Mange,' she said, trying her best to sound a lot braver than she really felt, 'my orders are to take you back to C4 where you will face a court martial.'

'Get me into that carrier,' he said, the lips and tongue of his smashed and ruined face not working properly. 'This is Anya. Get her in too.'

Mayer hesitated, then reached for the wrist restraints hanging from her belt.

'She's my rescuer, not my prisoner,' Steeleye slurred, shooting the soldier a withering look with his one good eye.

'I'm to take you back, Commander. I wasn't instructed to take anyone or *anything* else back.'

'Well, I'm telling you now, Captain. She goes with me. And if it was Melk who gave you the order to come here and find me, you'll be glad you obeyed my directive.'

Mayer paused for a moment and then gave a curt nod. 'The pair of you will be more comfortable in the back. There's water in a canteen there and a first-aid kit in the storage compartment in the footwell.' As the pair made their way to the rear of the vehicle, Mayer walked round to the passenger door. She opened it and looked in at the politician, dabbing at his forehead with a blue silken handkerchief. 'Get out,' she said to Fretz.

'What?'

Up until she'd laid eyes on her new passengers, this had been the part of her mission she'd been dreading the most. 'Out. Now.'

'Who do you think you're talking to, Captain? I am a member of the Principia, not one of your –'

'I know all too well who and what you are, sir, but my orders were twofold: bring *him* back, and leave *you* here.'

The politician's eyes grew wide as he stared back at her. 'W-what? Are you insane? When did you receive such an order? Who would dare to issue such a preposterous –'

'A few moments before we left. The president contacted me personally. He was quite clear. He also said that I was to tell you that he hopes you'll use your walk back, *if* you should make it back, to think up some more of your excellent jokes. He looks forward to hearing them.'

'Do you have any idea what you're –'

'Get out, Principal Fretz.' Her right hand moved down to her hip, the thumb releasing the flap that secured the pistol in its holster. The movement was not lost on the politician, and he stared at the hand that now rested on the butt of the weapon.

Tears slid down Fretz's face. Gathering what little courage he had, Fretz nodded once and silently did as instructed.

'Here,' Mayer said, handing the man a small canteen of water. It was contrary to what she'd been ordered, but she didn't think it would matter.

Getting back into the vehicle, she sat for a moment, then turned the engine on and began to back away.

'What was that all about?' Steeleye asked from behind her.

'Nothing that concerns you, Commander.'

As she drove off, Mayer glanced in the rear mirror at the receding figure of the politician. Without any warm clothing, shelter or means to defend himself against the wild animals that roamed these parts, she doubted he would make it through the night.

She made a mental note to herself never to tell President Melk any jokes.

Jax

The vehicle had hardly come to a halt when Jax was out of the door and hurtling headlong down the hill that led to their encampment. The albino ignored the dangers of going so quickly down the rubble-strewn pathway in near total darkness, and when he fell, badly twisting his ankle, he was straight back up again, in spite of the searing pain in his leg, as if it wasn't there. At the bottom he headed for the fire, only limping to a halt when Brick got to his feet and turned towards him. Nothing was said. The big man just stood, tugging the bottom of his shirt back and forth between his hands as if trying to wring some invisible matter from it. Jax's gaze moved from his friend to the two broken bodies on the ground, where he lingered for a moment or two before turning back to the big man.

Brick looked terrible. It was clear he'd recently used his

powers of healing, and that it had left him utterly spent. His eyes were sunken – deep shadows under yellowed bloodshot orbs – and the network of veins and arteries beneath his sallow skin was dark, appearing almost black in the firelight. From the dried blood on his face and in his hair, it seemed he'd been injured too.

Jax had never been able to look inside Brick's mind. Even when they'd been young boys together, back at the Farm where Melk had created them – the two of them being earlier, 'less successful' experiments – he had been unable to access his friend's thoughts. Nevertheless so, he felt the waves of pain, sadness and anger emanating from the big man. Approaching him, he reached out a hand and was shocked when the huge mutant flinched as if he thought the albino might strike him. 'It's OK, Brick,' Jax said, placing the hand on the other's shoulder and giving it a squeeze. 'It's OK.'

With that, he moved towards the fire and knelt beside the two bodies. Pulling at the blanket covering the smallest figure first, he already knew what he would find underneath. Looking down at the little girl's broken body, he sighed and shook his head. 'Sleep now, little Flea,' he whispered, covering her again.

'Brick tried,' the big man rumbled. 'Brick got to her real quick, but the hurt was too much. Too much.' Jax turned to look over his shoulder at his friend. 'Brick couldn't get it out. Useless . . . Brick . . . Couldn't . . . Get . . . Hurt . . . Out . . .' With each word, the big mutant, tears running down his cheeks, hit himself, slapping at the side of his head, until with some difficulty Jax, on his feet now, managed to grab hold of his hands, urging him to stop and reassuring him he knew just how hard Brick must have tried to save her. After a few moments, when he'd finally managed to calm the big guy down again, Jax turned to the figure beneath the second blanket. He took a step in its direction, then stopped, not wanting to uncover it and confirm what he knew lay beneath.

'Silas,' Jax said, when he was finally able to speak again.

Brick groaned.

'What was it, Brick? A cave-in? Before he disappeared from my mind, I thought I sensed something like that. I sensed . . . rocks falling, and –'

'Not cave-in.' The two friends' eyes met. 'The bad man did it. The man who came looking for us.'

'What bad man?' Jax's entire demeanour changed, the grief quickly giving way to an even stronger emotion.

'Metal man.'

'Brick, please talk sense.'

'One-eyed man. Brick dug him out too.'

There was a pause as Jax took this information in.

'Where is he?'

'Down there.' Again Brick wouldn't make eye contact. Now he looked down at the ground with a shamed expression, as if he expected to be reprimanded. 'Had to, Jax. Couldn't just leave him there. Not right. Maw would have been mad if Brick had done that.'

'It's OK.'

'Brick didn't heal him though. Oh no. No.' He went back to twisting the bottom of his shirt. 'Tied him up with wire. Broke his guns. Smashed them with my hands. Did a good job. Had to. To stop him getting away.' He looked at Jax for reassurance, the younger mutant nodding to let him know he'd done well.

'Show me,' Jax said, heading for the underground entrance.

'He was here!' Brick wailed, looking down at the place he'd left the broken and injured Steeleye. They looked down at the mass of tangled wire. 'He was broken. Couldn't get out. Brick made sure!'

'Maybe you didn't –'

'Brick made sure!'

Jax looked over at his friend. It was clear, in his mind at least, that Brick thought it impossible the murderer could have escaped. The big guy had a wild-eyed look about him, staring this way and that for some clue as to how it could have happened.

Tuning Brick out, Jax stared down at the wires and discarded sack that Brick had used as a hood over Steeleye's head. Something felt wrong about the scene. Taking the flaming torch with him, he went back up the escalator stairs and approached the generators again, frowning when each in turn failed to start. As he got to the last one, he was struck by a smell. In his hurry to get to the man responsible for killing his adopted father, he had not noticed it, but it was clear now. There, on the floor, was a ruined mess of food. A short distance away, the door to the storage unit was still open.

An idea occurred to him.

Jax, on his haunches with his hand in the scattered food, closed his eyes and tried to tune into the place, reaching out for a clue as to how Steeleye could have got away. It wasn't an easy thing to do. Jax could read people readily, tune into their thoughts as effortlessly as if he was listening to them speak, but what he was trying to do now was pick up on the ghosts of thoughts: things that had happened in a place previously. In his experience it only worked if these 'ghost feelings' were associated with strong emotions. The first thing he sensed was fear and he allowed himself to open up to it, letting that dread sensation creep through him as he vicariously experienced some of the horrors his friends had suffered as they fled down the stairs in the inky darkness. Next came a harsh panicky sensation, then more fear, then pain. Steeleye was included in these newer sensations, the mutant's psychic footprint different from the others' but just as strong, and it became clear to Jax that the killer too had been scared witless in those moments before the roof had come crashing down on them. Brick's fright and terrible sadness washed over the albino next, but then came a new phantom, this one more recent and different again. Despite the intense concentration and effort he was having to expend, Jax was aware that Brick had come up to join him, the big man hovering beside him. As if through thick glass, he heard Brick say his name and ask him if he was OK, but Jax ignored him, all of his focus on this new emotion and the person associated with so much anger and resentment.

He had felt the same thing from the same person before. It had never been as strong as this, but he recognised that psychic footprint.

When he opened his eyes, Brick was in front of him, wringing his hands together and shuffling from foot to foot, unsure what to do for the best.

'Anya,' Jax said, feeling the strength suddenly drain out of him. He was light-headed, and as his legs gave out he would have fallen to the ground had the big man not easily scooped him up. The energy trickled back into him, and he knew Brick was responsible for helping to rejuvenate him, despite being drained himself.

'What?'

'It was Anya. She was here. She's the one who made this mess, and she's the one who set Mange free.' He frowned as two more things occurred to him. Brick set him on his feet again. 'She let him go because he promised to help her get back at us, and – ' he groped for more understanding of the ghost emotions he felt – 'she helped him without knowing that he'd killed Silas.'

Brick took a moment to process this. 'Poor Anya,' he eventually said.

A sudden flame of anger welled up inside Jax, but he swallowed down the harsh words he was about direct in Brick's direction. Giving in to anger was what had caused this tragedy. And the big man was right. Anya was every bit as much a victim as Flea and Silas had been. She'd fallen in with a damaged and ruthless individual, a man who would stop at nothing to realise his ambitions. Jax's only hope was that she too might come to realise this before the man was able to completely poison her.

They didn't want to bury Silas and Flea in that dead place. It didn't feel right to simply add them to the vast number of nameless bodies there. Instead Brick carried them both to the top of a hill where Jax prepared two graves, side by side, at the peak. They lowered a body into each grave as gently as they could, then stood, shovels in their hands, neither wishing to begin piling the cold earth back over their friends' bodies. It was Brick who finally broke the impasse, the big man telling Flea that he was sorry, before throwing a handful of dirt down on to the blanket in which the small body was wrapped. Jax did likewise, and then the two, without another word, continued the dreadful task until both graves were complete.

After burying the bodies, the albino and his friend formed two stone cairns. On top of one they placed a large, pure-white rock that Jax found. On the other, Flea's flower bracelet.

'At least they're together,' Brick said, and he stepped forward. Kneeling in the space between the graves, he gently placed the wind-up torch he'd taken from his pocket on the ground. He stood, noting the confused expression on Jax's face. 'Don't want them to be in the dark out here.'

'What about you? Won't you need it?'

The big guy took a deep breath and shook his head. 'Worse things to be scared of than the dark. Time Brick realised that.' And with that he left his friend to say his own goodbyes and moved off in the direction of the transporter that they were to take back to City Four.

Rush

He was second in line now. It seemed that most of the inhabitants of Muteville had already completed their registration, and the remainder were either reluctant stragglers hounded into the undertaking by their loved ones, or those who had, for whatever reason, been unable to do so until now. Like Rush, the people around him seemed tired of the long wait they'd had to endure. Unlike him, they stood in the line oblivious to the ultimate consequences of the thing they about to undertake. *Like lambs to the slaughter*, he thought. A part of him wanted to shout out to tell everyone what was going on, but he knew that wasn't an option. Almost all of Muteville had been injected now, and he couldn't hope to get around the thousands of people inhabiting the slums. No, he had to find a way to stop the killings happening at source, and that meant playing dumb and going along for the ride.

The security had become more obvious the closer he got to the front of the queue, and the nearer he got to the guards and ARM agents, the more Rush was sure one of them would somehow realise who he was and arrest him. He doubted that his dyed hair or the cap he wore were really going to fool anybody, but he'd refused Juneau's offers to surgically alter his face a little – 'Nothing major, just a little reconstruction to your cheeks and jawline' – trusting that the sheer number of people they had to deal with would mean the security forces were too stretched to pay any real attention to any one individual.

The man behind him gave him a nudge. Turning, he was surprised to see a hunk of bread thrust in his face.

'Go on, take it,' the man said with a nod. 'You've been in this line as long as I have, and I haven't seen a crumb pass your lips.'

Rush was touched. Food, any food, was scarce in the slums. 'That's kind of you, but I'm –'

'Don't be stupid.' The man pushed the piece of bread into Rush's hand and went back to talking to the woman he was with. 'Besides, there's supposed to be food aplenty where we're going. They say there's land that's fertile enough to grow on, and that those who want it will be allocated plots. They say –'

'Next!'

Lost in his thoughts, Rush hadn't realised he was now at the front. Stuffing the food into his mouth, he hurried forward past the guard and entered the registration building.

'Pull your sleeve up,' a stern-looking blonde woman said. Everything was white inside the makeshift medical centre, the place all the more stark thanks to the bright strip lights hanging from the ceiling. There was a harsh, acrid smell of cleaning product that made Rush's nose itch.

'Your sleeve?' she repeated, raising her right eyebrow and reappraising him as if she thought he might be a little slow. In her right hand, the woman – Rush assumed she must be a nurse – held a syringe full of an all-too-familiar blue substance, and his pulse began to race even at the sight of it. If he'd believed he could control his fears about what was about to happen to him, he'd been wrong. Every part of him screamed out that he mustn't go ahead with this lunacy, but he had no choice. Registration would get him on to whatever transport Melk had planned for his victims, and if Rush was going to help, he needed that access. Just *how* he was going to help was still not clear, but he knew this was the first step he had to take.

'Scared of needles?' the woman asked. 'You're not the first. Best thing to do is close your eyes. You'll feel a small pinprick and it'll all be over.'

'Just explain to me why I have to have this injection again?'

Her face changed. Impatience replaced the faux concern she'd projected seconds up until now. 'Your registrar should have explained all this to you, Mute. The injection is to protect you and your fellow resettlers against any communicable diseases.'

'One injection protects everyone from all contagious diseases?'

'You'd be amazed at the things the scientists can do these days.' She smiled at him, but there was nothing friendly about the look. 'Now pull up your sleeve, please.'

Rush took her advice and closed his eyes. As he did so, he remembered the feeling of Tia's lips pressed against his, her warm breath on his cheek, the smell of her soft skin. That last time, he'd opened his eyes to find her own staring back at him, now he opened them to the sight of the stern woman jabbing a needle into his arm. He wanted to see Tia again, not be sitting here in this den of lies having microscopic death machines introduced into his bloodstream.

The nurse frowned down at the syringe. Despite her applying pressure with her thumb to the plunger, the thing wouldn't go down.

'That's odd,' she said.

A bead of sweat broke out on Rush's forehead.

Stop it, he told himself. *You knew what you were doing when you came here. This isn't about you, and it isn't about Tia; it's bigger than that.* Nevertheless he found it hard to relax his mind and relinquish his hold on the syringe. But as he did so, the woman's thumb pressed the plunger and the deadly blue liquid slid down the steel shaft and into Rush's body. The syringe was consigned to a yellow container. He noticed how the thing was half full with them.

'Your registration card,' she said, holding out her palm.

Rush couldn't stop the trembling of his own hand as he handed the transparent plexicard over, watching as the woman entered it into a machine before handing it back to him.

'I don't suppose you can read, can you, Mute?' she said, giving him a surprised look when he told her that, yes, he did in fact possess that skill. 'Well, that makes this part a whole lot easier then.' She nodded at the card in his hand. 'The details of your transportation are on that card. The first group will be leaving tomorrow morning. There are no allocated spaces, and places are on a first-come, first-served basis. Don't worry if you miss one – the Principia have seen to it that there are plenty of vehicles, and you'll be able to get on a later one. However, we do recommend you try to get to the reservations as quickly as possible, before all the best accommodation is taken up. Enjoy your new life, Mute.'

She turned away and began to enter data into a screen. Despite this clear signal for him to leave, Rush stayed sitting on the bench for a few moments more.

'Nurse?'

The woman looked back at him, clearly peeved that he had not already left.

'How many of these injections have you given?'

'I don't know, hundreds, maybe a thousand.'

'And you believe that they are for the benefit of the mutants you're giving them to?'

She seemed genuinely flummoxed by the question.

'Of course. Why?' She sighed. 'Look, you people need to take this opportunity for what it is: a chance for both Pures and Mutes to make a fresh start. The mutants get a new place to live; the citizens of the Six Cities get rid of the terrible slums on the other side of the Wall. And you and the other Mutes going to the very first reservation will be the pioneers! Why, I would have thought a handsome young man like you would jump at the chance to live in a place like that.' She did that thing with her eyebrow again.

He scanned her features, looking for any sign she might be lying. There was nothing. It seemed the Pures of C4 were as much in the dark about Melk's plans as the Mutes. Rush stood up and gave the nurse a sad smile, realising that she too had been duped in all of this. If the president's plans succeeded and the Principia were unable to cover up the truth about the killings, this poor woman would have to live the rest of her life in the knowledge that she, and others like her, were responsible for injecting countless innocent people with those needles.

Of course, Rush had other more pressing reasons than the nurse's guilt to hope Melk's plans were thwarted, the main one being that if they weren't, he'd shortly end up dead.

Steeleye

Captain Mayer pulled to a halt in the underground space below the ARM headquarters and peered out at the dozen agents surrounding her vehicle, all of whom were pointing weapons in her direction. It occurred to the captain that this would not be a good time to exit the transporter. Moving slowly and keeping her hands in plain sight in case one of the armed guards was a rookie with an itchy trigger finger, Mayer followed the instructions given by the leader of the little welcome party.

'The cyborg and the mutant?' the man asked as she approached him.

'In the back.' She glanced at the gun, noting how the thumb dial next to the stock was right up to maximum. 'There's no need to be quite so nervous, Lieutenant. They won't give you any trouble.'

As soon as she had been close enough to C4 to get a signal, she'd radioed ahead. Told to wait, she was caught a little by surprise when General Razko's distinctive voice came over the airwaves, asking her for an update on the outcome of her mission and an ETA. Now all she wanted was to hand the pair over, get out of her uniform, into a bath and do her best to forget the entire episode.

'Commander Mange,' the lieutenant called out, throwing the doors at the back of the vehicle open. Mayer noted how the man still used Steeleye's official rank, although the word seemed to stick in his throat. 'You and the mutant accompanying you are to step out of the vehicle. We are instructed to take you to . . .'

The man failed to get any more words out. The sight of the cyborg and the hellish monstrosity alongside him shocked him into silence, and it was clear from the gasps of the other men and women in his unit that they felt the same way. The cyborg looked out at them. Despite the pain he was clearly in, his one eye swollen almost completely shut in a face covered in bloodied cuts and grazes, the man-machine grinned and threw the assembled soldiers a lazy salute. This seemed to bring the ARM officer back to his senses.

He straightened up. 'All right, everyone, let's do what we were sent here for.' He nodded to the group closest to him. 'Take the prisoners –'

'Prisoners?' Steeleye interrupted, speaking for the first time. 'Let me tell you something, soldier. We are not your prisoners, so I'd appreciate it if you didn't refer to us as such. Anya and I are here of our own free will. I'd like to speak to the president right away.'

'In that case, you're in luck. Because President Melk and General Razko are eager to see both of you too. So if you'd like to follow my colleagues here, we can arrange for that meeting to take place.'

Steeleye muttered something under his breath but complied, limping off after the ARM lieutenant and his men, closely followed by Anya.

Razko and Melk sat on the opposite side of a long table from the cyborg and the shape-shifter. Since telling them to take a seat, the politician had not said a word and seemed unable to tear his eyes off the girl/creature, making her squirm in her seat.

Despite the injuries and damage Steeleye had sustained, the man seemed positively buoyant since they'd arrived in the city. Anya by contrast seemed scared half to death, the sights and sounds she encountered at every turn making her jump and stare around her in alarm.

Eventually Melk broke the silence. 'I would urge you, Commander Mange, to consider carefully your responses to the questions I am about to ask you. My initial reaction, upon hearing certain reports about your mission, was to have you eliminated on sight –' he held up a hand as Steeleye looked set to interrupt – 'but the general here convinced me that, as an officer of rank, you should be dealt with by the military courts.' His eyes took in the mutant girl-thing. 'But your turning up with this creature here leads me to believe that even *that* might not be necessary.' The look he gave Anya did nothing to lessen her discomfort. 'My, how you've grown.' He smiled when the thing hissed back at him. 'I sympathise with the frustration you're feeling right now. Even when you were a baby, it was clear to me and the other scientists that your "gift" – cellular metamorphosis, they labelled it – was difficult to control.' He paused, frowning a little. 'If I remember correctly, and unfortunately all my data from the place where you were created was destroyed – the more complex the form you chose to transform into, coupled with the length of time you spend in that body, means that you sometimes have a hard time reverting back to your original form. Do I have that right?'

Anya nodded, twisting her mouth to form the word 'yes'.

'Hmmm. Well, I think I can help.' His voice was different now, like a benevolent older relative talking to a young charge. 'Here at Bio-Gen we change people all the time. In the bad old days, we would use surgical methods, but now we have other means – we can tinker with the cells at a molecular level. Eye colour, skin tone, rate of hair growth –' he waved his hand in the air – 'we can alter these and more. But people here are fickle, and after they've had these changes tend to want to go back; they want their old bodies and faces returned to them. So we've developed a rather clever machine that detects changes cells have recently undergone and reverses them. It was originally designed as a treatment for cancers, but as with most things in the Six Cities, somebody has found a more asinine use for it.' He made another vague gesture in the air. 'Not really my field of expertise, but I'm told it is not only effective but is completely painless. I believe it would be worth your trying it out to see if your latest cellular "reimagining" can't be reversed.' He gave her a smile. 'I'm hoping it works – I'd rather like to see how you look after all this time.' The smile was that of a kind old uncle. 'So when some of my people turn up at that door in a moment, I'd like for you to go with them. Will you do that? Will you give it a try?'

The bat-snake-human thing managed another strained 'yes'.

No sooner had the word left her serpent mouth, than there was a knock.

'Ah! Perfect timing.' Somewhere beneath the table, Melk pushed a button, revealing the scientists waiting at the door. A woman walked in. She was tall and elegant, her hair piled up on top of her head in a tight bun. She peered over the top of her glasses at Anya. If she was shocked by what she saw, she made a good job of covering it up. 'Come along . . . er, young lady,' she said.

Anya glanced over at Steeleye for encouragement. The cyborg gave her a nod and she got up and followed the woman out of the room.

The door slid closed again, and as it did, so too did the smile slip away from Melk's expression. The look the politician gave Steeleye was anything but friendly. 'Now, *Commander*, perhaps you'd like to tell me what the hell is going on? Maybe you'd like to start with why you murdered every member of the ARM unit I sent out to accompany you on your mission? And after that, you can explain how, one –' he held a finger up – 'you appear to have wrecked the bionic augmentations we, at enormous expense, fitted to you, and two –' another finger – 'why I appear to have only one of my hybrids back here. I'd have expected at least the heads of the others if you were forced to kill them.'

Steeleye paused for a moment. 'Can I talk now? That OK?'

Melk bit his lip, but managed a curt nod.

'First of all, I'd like to say thank you for the warm welcome. You know, I was almost moved to tears at the sight of the armed response team sent to escort me safely from the vehicle that I came back in. Although, I think next time we might consider having them line up facing each other so they can throw flowers at my feet?' He sniffed, before continuing: 'Now, to answer your questions. The first one is simple enough. Your ARM agents' untimely deaths. What happened to those fools was as a result of *them* attacking *me*. Now I tried to warn you there might be some "friction" between us – I suggested as much to you before we left – but you and the general here insisted that they accompany me. Despite my reservations, I didn't for one second expect them to turn on me the way they did. Oh no. They bushwhacked me good and proper. This –' he indicated the huge dent in the metal part of his skull – 'is a result of that cowardly attack. They shot me with an antique of some kind! A bullet!' He shook his head in disbelief. 'Can you believe that? In this day and age? A bullet! What choice did I have but to launch counter-measures in order to protect myself?'

Razko spoke. 'How do you know they were all in on it? Maybe there was a lone shooter and the rest were innocent of that person's intentions?'

Steeleye tapped at the dented metal with the tip of his finger. 'There are – correction – there *were* some pretty sophisticated gadgets and gizmos working in here before it all got smashed up. I launched a probe. It showed the shooter in the vehicle and the rest of your beloved agents creeping up on both sides of me in a pincer movement. I think it's pretty safe to say they were all in on the gig!'

Melk looked pointedly at his military advisor. The general gave a small shrug. 'His account does seem to concur with what Mayer found at the site of the skirmish.'

'There you go then,' Steeleye said, sitting back in his seat a little.

Melk looked at the cyborg closely. Although the man was trying his best to hide it, there was something in his attitude that made the politician a tad uneasy. It was as if Steeleye was only just managing to hold himself together. Anger, that's what he was sensing. The 'borg was angry and doing his best to keep a lid on things.

'OK, so let's assume we buy in to your little tale about being attacked. What happened next?'

'I carried on with my mission.' He looked pointedly at each of the men in turn. 'You sent me out there to do a job, and despite what you might believe to the contrary, Steeleye Mange is a man you can rely on. Out there in the slums? I made myself a reputation as somebody who gets things done, you know what I mean? You strike a deal with me, I deliver. And deliver I did.' He motioned with his head towards the door.

'One. You delivered one,' corrected Melk. 'There are five hybrid children. Not to mention my brother, and you were sent out there to –'

'Four.'

'What?'

'There are three of your mutant creations out there now. And you don't have to worry about your brother either.' He paused. 'There was an "incident". Something went screwy with these "enormously expensive" augmentations you had me fitted with. They malfunctioned. There was an explosion that caused the place that housed your other little creations to come tumbling down around my ears! Your brother Silas? He's no more. Neither is the speedy little kid with the red hair and freckles.' He stopped again, shaking his head at the memory.

The president narrowed his eyes at the mutant. Maybe it wasn't anger he'd sensed after all. Could it be that the cyborg was feeling regret at what had happened?

'She was an accident,' Mange went on. 'Nothing I could do to stop that one.'

'Where. Are. The. Others?'

Steeleye shot the politician a baleful look. 'Did you hear what I just said? The little one, she's dead! Doesn't that mean *anything* to you?'

'The "little one" you forced into slavery, you mean? The cute freckle-faced kid you made steal for you or risk your hurting the woman who had raised her? Is that the one we're talking about, Mange?' He snorted humourlessly. 'Excuse my cynicism, Commander, but I'm having a tough time believing you of all people have suddenly acquired a conscience.'

'Whatever.' The cyborg shrugged. It wasn't lost on him how Melk hadn't even blinked at the news that his own brother was dead. The man was cold. Ice cold. And Steeleye knew just how dangerous such men could be.

'The others – where are they?' Melk insisted.

'The only other one there was the big guy. The one they rescued from under your own nose not so long ago, remember?'

'You're on thin ice, Mange. I wouldn't go stamping your feet if I were you.'

'After the rockfall, the big guy dragged me out and tied me up with wire. I'd still be there now if Anya hadn't come along. She doesn't know about Silas and Flea. If she did, despite the anger she's feeling towards the others, I don't think she would've helped me escape. We need to keep it like that. Keep her in the dark and find some way to use her.'

'I agree.'

Melk and Razko exchanged a look. The general looked down at something he was holding in his lap.

'What's going on here? You –' Steeleye didn't get to finish. Despite the severe damage to most of his systems, it appeared as if the lockdown failsafe they'd installed in him was made of tougher stuff. Razko was able to render him inactive at the touch of a button. Mange froze. The cyborg was unable to do anything more than look about him, trying to work out what was going on. Behind the two men another door slid open. Standing there, smiling back at him, with that mouth he'd imagined on countless occasions smashing his big metal fist through, was Dr Svenson. The woman nodded at the orderlies with her, who hurried in pushing a reinforced steel gurney, on to which they manhandled the paralysed Steeleye.

Although his jaw wouldn't move, turning the words he was trying to make into garbled gibberish, it was clear to all present that the cyborg was using just about every swear word known to man to tell the surgeon what he would do to her if she laid a hand on him.

Flat on his back, he stared up as Svenson leaned over, her brunette curls framing her heart-shaped face. Her perfume was strong, and he recognised the scent immediately. He should do; it was the smell he always came round to after surgery, when this sadist had hacked him up and put him back together again. She smiled, reddened lips parting to reveal perfect teeth. 'Let's go and get you fixed up again, shall we?'

Melk

The president got the message from the scientists about an hour after the meeting with Steeleye and Anya. Thanking the woman before waving his hand across the holo-image to disconnect, he rose quickly to his feet.

He smiled to himself, recognising the emotion he was feeling as what it was – excitement. It had been a long time since he felt that particular sensation, and he took a moment to pull himself together before setting out for the Bio-Gen suite.

Anya was pale-skinned and dark-haired. Still growing into her young body, she looked a little gangly and awkward, but it was clear she would develop into a beautiful young woman. She should do – the embryo she'd been created from had been from some of the best stock in his company's Liqi-Freez storage facility. All five of the hybrid children came from the same stock, even if something had gone wrong with the earliest experiments, and the boys Brick and Jax had suffered . . . setbacks. Anya, on the other hand, could pass as a Pure. Having said that, there was something a little 'off' about her. She looked . . . harsh, as if the things she had seen and experienced had shaped her looks as much as her original genetic make-up.

Melk held out a hand to her, happy to touch her now she was no longer trapped in that hideous chimeric form.

The girl tentatively stepped forward and slipped her fingers between his.

'Let's give you the full no-holds-barred tour of this place, shall we?'

Tia

She was surprised to have got back into the city quite as easily as she did. The guard gave her a cursory glance and waved her through, already moving on to process the person behind her.

As she emerged from the fissure in the wall she understood why. Four members of the CSP, the city police force, were waiting for her.

'Citizen Cowper,' said one of the officers, 'perhaps you'd be so kind as to come with us? We have some questions we'd like to ask you.'

'Am I under arrest?'

'That could be arranged,' the man at the front said, although it was only because of his voice that she knew it was a man at all. All of them had opted to keep their front visors down, masking their faces from her. 'For now let's just say that we'd like you to help us with some enquiries. Follow me, please.'

Trying to look as nonchalant as possible, she gave a shrug. The leader turned his back on her, as the other three officers flanked her on all sides, penning her in.

You knew this could happen, she told herself. Nevertheless she couldn't control the sudden quickening of her pulse as they set off in the direction of the walkway leading to the CSP headquarters. She'd gone no more than thirty or forty paces when the palm of her right hand pulsed with a purple light. At the same time a small voice inside her right ear told her that an unknown caller was trying to get in touch. She'd only been outside the city for a few months, but during that time her palm-com hadn't functioned at all. Initially she'd thought it broken, and after a while she'd forgotten about it all together. Lifting her palm to the side of her head, she pressed the tip of her forefinger to her ear to take the call.

'It's me,' said a voice she knew she recognised but couldn't identify.

'Who?'

'Juneau.'

'Wha–'

'Stop talking, Tia. If we had more time I'd be happy to bore you senseless by telling you how I remotely reactivated your palm-com, and the cunning and clever methods I had to employ to hack into the C4 comms system, but we don't, so be quiet and listen to what I have to say. You remember that thing I spoke to you about before you left? The thing I thought might be the answer to our problem.'

'Yes.'

'I think I might have discovered where one is. Now listen carefully.'

She'd been sitting in the same seat for what felt like hours now, and although she'd been allowed to leave the room twice for 'comfort breaks', she'd been immediately returned to her stark little cell. Tia glanced at the door again. Her escort, a small stocky woman who looked as if she might have represented C4 as a power lifter in the InterCity Games at some point, stood on the other side of it.

Boredom had replaced fear. There was nothing to see in the interview room No windows, and as far as she could tell, no cameras were set into the walls or ceiling. It was just a blank place. The coffee-flavoured drink they had left her had gone cold so that a thin, congealed skin now floated on the surface. It was strange how her brain had filtered out some of the things that had initially set her on edge when she'd been brought here. Like the smell in the room that made her nose wrinkle when she'd walked in: a nasty, slightly sweet stink reminiscent of overripe fruit; the repetitive banging noise that came from somewhere down the corridor was less noticeable too. She wondered if her father's cell was like this, although she doubted he had the luxury of a chair, even one bolted to the floor like hers. The only thing of any interest came via the light hanging directly above the table. The bulb, housed in a wire cage, presumably to stop anybody smashing the glass had attracted a visitor. Every few seconds there was a little dull *plink!* as a moth attacked the source of the light, slamming itself into the immovable object over and over again, releasing tiny dust motes each time. She had no idea what the little insect hoped to achieve by its actions, but she admired its determination.

The noise of the door opening made Tia sit up. She wasn't entirely surprised when it was President Melk himself who entered.

She watched as he closed the door behind him before turning and slowly walking over to take the seat across from her. Trying to shuffle the chair forward, he frowned when he realised that his, like hers, was secured to the concrete floor. He sat, saying nothing for a moment or two. Just staring across the table at her.

The *plink-plinks!* continued overhead, but he appeared not to notice them.

'So,' he eventually said.

She knew this game. She'd used it herself when interviewing reluctant sources. He wanted her to blink first. Before she'd left the city all those months ago and seen the things she had, she wouldn't have just *blinked* first, she'd have crumbled before this man-of-power's unwavering stare.

Instead she gave him a blank look in return. 'So, what?'

A hint of something flashed across his eyes. Anger, maybe. But it was gone as soon as it had appeared. Pleased with this tiny victory, she allowed herself to look more closely at him and was immediately surprised at how he'd changed in the short time she'd been outside the walls. He appeared to have aged considerably; dark crescents underlined his eyes, and his face had a pinched, gaunt aspect to it. He made a small sighing sound and gave her a condescending smile. 'Miss Cowper. Tia, isn't it?'

'I prefer Miss Cowper. Only my friends call me Tia.'

'As you wish.'

'Is it normal for the most powerful man in the Six Cities to come into police interrogation rooms like this?'

'Is that what this place is? An interrogation room? Put like that, it seems rather unpleasant, doesn't it? I thought it was merely a room in which we might have a little chat. And to answer your question, no, it's not a place I'm used to frequenting.'

'I suppose you have plenty of goons to terrorise young girls for you. I'm flattered.' Her tone made it quite clear she was anything but.

'I had hoped to find you a little more amenable, considering the predicament you find yourself in.'

'And what predicament is that, I wonder?'

'You've been dodging us for some time.'

'I don't know what you mean.'

'After your father's arrest, we wanted to have a little talk with you. We knew you were staying with your father's friend Eleanor, but every time we showed up at her apartment, you seemed to have just . . . disappeared. The only person there to greet our officers was the former police chief herself, with her pet monkey. Eleanor was, of course, extremely apologetic about it all, but it did become a thorn in my side for a while. That was before I moved on to other, more pressing matters.' He angled his head to one side as if he expected her to say something, giving a little sigh when she didn't. 'And now it seems you have been consorting with the dead.' Melk threw the line out almost casually.

'Granted you don't look too good, Mr President, but I

think "dead" might be pushing it a bit far. Of course, I doubt I'm alone in thinking that the Six Cities will be a better place once that unfortunate event eventually befalls you.'

'You have your father's gift for sardonic wit, Miss Cowper.' Tia hated the offhand way in which the politician referred to her father when it was *he* who was responsible for him being locked up in a prison cell. 'Let's get back to the dead, shall we? It seems you left the city with a walking corpse only yesterday. Our records show that your CivisChip and that of a corpse exited, but only one of you returned. When the officer manning the gate was questioned he could only recall seeing a girl roughly matching your description and a . . . monkey. Now that information, coupled with our recent difficulties in tracking you down, might lead a more suspicious man to conclude that our former police chief's little simian friend isn't all he appears.'

'She.'

'Pardon?'

'Buffy. It's a she, not a he. And as for the other stuff, I really have no idea what you are on about, President Melk.'

'There it is again. You really are your father's daughter, aren't you?'

The president began to speak again, but the repeated mentions of her father had angered Tia to such a degree that she was only vaguely listening now, his words drifting over her until she forced herself to focus again.

'. . . people might be a little suspicious. Particularly in light of the fact that you have hardly left Eleanor's apartment in the last few months. Now I'm beginning to wonder if –'

'I wonder what the people of C4 would think if they knew their president was a criminal?' she said. 'I mean, the Principia is full of men and women who bend the rules for their own benefit, we all know that, but you, sir, are in an altogether different league from the usual thieves and liars who govern us, aren't you? My father is in a cell right now for "treason". Treason? And yet –' she raised a finger in the air – 'he never created a secret laboratory to create super-Mute–Pure hybrids, did he?' She looked across. The politician was doing an incredible job of hiding his emotions. If Melk was in the slightest bit worried, he didn't show it. When Tia was twelve her father had taught her to play poker, schooling her not just in the value of the cards and how to play your chips, but also in maintaining a neutral facial expression to hide what you might, or might not, have in your hand. Melk would make a great poker player. Tia went on. 'Nor did my father, upon discovering that his little creations were still alive, set out to destroy them, sending ARM units out to the regions where the cities have no jurisdiction.'

Still nothing.

'And then there's the matter of human cloning. Granted, it pales in comparison to taking Pure embryos and crossing them with mutant DNA, but cloning *yourself* and putting that person in the Principia in the form of your "son"? That would surely raise a few eyebrows, wouldn't it? I'd imagine that must go against the principles of what tiny sliver of democracy we still pretend exists here. I say "pretend", because in a democracy the people don't sit idly by while megalomaniacs lock innocent people up for daring to criticise them.'

She'd spotted a reaction this time. The only surprise was that it had not come at her name-calling. No, a slight tick had set up residence beneath Melk's right eye at the mention of the clone he'd created. Not just that, but on Melk's previously smooth brow a faint sheen of sweat had appeared.

'Those are very interesting theories,' he said. His eyes briefly left hers and shot across to the corner of the room behind her.

'Oh, you and I know they're more than theories, don't we?'

'You've been busy, Citizen Cowper. One wonders how you've managed to be quite so industrious when, if what you claim is true, you appear not to have left the city walls in all this time.'

That shift of the eyes again, as if he was looking at somebody behind her. If it was a ploy to unnerve her, it was working. Scolding herself for being silly, Tia craned her head around and afforded herself a look. There was nothing there.

'What do you keep looking at?' she asked.

'Pardon?'

He's playing with you, Tia, she told herself. *Trying to fluster you.*

Melk shook his head and mumbled something under his breath.

What the hell?

The man took a deep breath, and when he looked at her again he seemed back in control of himself; none of the creepy mania he had been displaying seconds before.

'You've been a bad girl.'

It was a weird thing to say to a young woman who had just accused you of terrible and heinous crimes. Strangely, it chilled her more than anything else so far.

'Let me guess, you're going to declare *me* an enemy of the state too? Like my father?'

'Or I could just have you killed.'

Her blood ran cold. She had known this could happen. While drawing up her plans to return to the city as herself she'd weighed everything up, thinking through the various scenarios and not dodging even the most terrible outcomes like torture or murder. Even so, having the man opposite her threaten her in the flesh sent an icy shiver through her. 'I wouldn't do that if I were you.'

'Oh? Why not?'

'Because my disappearance would trigger a series of events that would eventually expose you for the monster you really are. Call it my insurance policy.'

Melk sucked his teeth as he sat back in his chair, appraising his opponent.

'You're bluffing,' he said. 'If you had that kind of power, you would have used it against me already.'

'Not so. Because you have something I want. That's why I'm here. That's why I walked back through the Wall straight into the clutches of your goons.'

'So I give you your father?'

'Yes. And you drop all charges against him.'

He actually laughed. 'And what do I get in return? This all seems a bit one-sided to me. Although I have to admit, I'm rather intrigued about this "series of events" you refer to.'

'In return for my father's safe release, I'll give you all the footage I've shot in the last few months outside the city walls. Footage and interviews that would destroy the Melk name forever.'

She allowed herself a small smile as she watched the supercilious smile slip away as it dawned on him that she might just be telling the truth. 'Do you play chess, Miss Cowper?'

'No. Why?'

'Because if you did, you'd know you have just played yourself into a stalemate: a point in the game when neither side can win. *If* everything you say is true, and I'm not entirely convinced it is, you must see that it is a bad deal for me. I give you your father, and you give me your "evidence". But who is to say you have not made copies of your work? I give you the thing you want, and you simply destroy me anyway.'

'You would have my word.'

He stared at her unwaveringly, as if he could look straight into her soul and see whether or not she was lying. Then he stood up, straightened his jacket and turned towards the door. 'I will give you my decision tomorrow. I need time to think these things through.' He knocked on the door and waited as a small hatch slid away to reveal the eyes of the female guard peering back at him.

'Open up, please,' he said, stepping back as the officer did as she was bid. The politician stepped through and addressed the guard: 'You can release Miss Cowper,' he said. 'She has answered all of my questions satisfactorily and is free to go.' Before leaving, he turned to Tia one last time. 'You know, you really should take up chess. I think you might be rather good at it.'

The guard rolled her eyes theatrically when Tia demanded to speak to the commanding officer, claiming she wanted to lodge a complaint about her treatment in the police station. The journalist had moments earlier been given her possessions back at the front desk, and the female officer must have thought she'd got rid of the young woman when she made the announcement.

'That'll take time, sweet cheeks,' the woman said, giving her a look that said she'd also be wasting her time. 'And that means you'll be stuck in this place even longer. Is that what you really want?'

'I believe it's my right as a civilian. Or are we living in a police state now?'

'Fine,' the guard said, although it was clear from her tone that she thought it was anything but. 'I'll go and get an omni with the necessary forms loaded on it.' The woman ushered Tia into a room next to the booking-in desk and was about to close the door when Tia stopped her.

'You can leave the door, thank you.'

'What?'

'The door. You can leave it open. After all, you heard the president – I'm not a prisoner. I'm here as a free citizen of C4, of my own free will, so I'd like to be treated as such. You can leave the door open while you go and get whatever it is you need.'

The woman opened her mouth as if to say something, then closed it again. 'Whatever,' she said, before walking off.

Tia counted to thirty in her head and then left the room. Telling the desk officer that she needed to use the toilet, she headed towards the emergency stairwell at the end of the corridor.

Deep beneath the earth, in the bowels of the CSP headquarters, Tia stopped outside the door to the police armoury, swiped her palm to activate the comms unit and lifted her hand to the side of her face. She wasn't surprised when the call was answered almost instantly.

'I'm here,' she said.

'Good. Now wait a second.' She could hear Juneau humming to himself as he looked something up on the other end of the line. 'OK, the code for today is as follows . . .' He went on to relay a series of numbers and letters to her, saying them slowly as she entered them into the screen beside the door. 'Now place your palm on the reader,' he instructed her.

She hesitated. 'You're sure this will work?'

‘As far as that reader is concerned, your right hand is that of the quartermaster in charge there today.’ There was a pause. ‘That is if the rota I hacked was correct. I mean, I guess the guy could be ill or something.’

‘Juneau, I don’t need self-doubt and uncertainty right now.’

‘Right. Look, I have to believe the information I have is good. So put your hand to the screen and offer up a prayer for city police efficiency.’

Tia hesitated. It was hot as hell down here, and she wiped her forehead before placing the same hand on the scanner. An involuntary titter of relief escaped her when there was a loud buzz followed by a series of clunks as huge bolts slid back out of the wall into the body of the steel door in front of her.

‘You’ve got precisely one hundred and twenty seconds until the block I’ve put on the door-open alarm is deactivated,’ Juneau said. He’d already informed her that the palm-com wouldn’t work inside the steel shell she was about to enter, so he quickly and efficiently gave her the last-minute details she needed, finishing with, ‘Good luck, Tia Cowper,’ before cutting the connection between them.

It wasn’t too hard to find the case Juneau had described, although how the four-armed bioengineer had discovered exactly where in the police station it was kept was anybody’s guess. Setting it on the floor and opening it, she peered down at the thing she'd come here for, thinking how it looked nothing at all like she'd expected. Swapping her ill-gotten gains for the clothes and shoes in her backpack, she heaved the now considerably heavier bag over her shoulders, praying that the straps wouldn't give out under the weight, and returned the case full of dirty laundry to the shelf. Walking out and hitting the door closure button, she had nine seconds to spare before the entire police force would come storming down to the basement floor to discover who was in the armoury.

'Piece of cake,' she said to herself, willing her hands to stop shaking and her heart to quit trying to smash its way free of her chest. She'd beaten the odds to obtain the thing she'd come here for. Now all she had to do was get it out of the building and out of the city.

The female police officer gave her a look like thunder when, having returned to the waiting room with the necessary equipment to register a complaint, she was informed by Tia that she'd changed her mind and no longer wished to lodge her objection. Somehow the woman managed to hold her tongue, although it was clear she wasn't at all displeased to see the young woman with the heavy-looking backpack finally leaving her police station.

From there, trying her best not to look as panic-stricken as she felt, Tia hurried to the omnipad repair shop Juneau had told her to go to. With every step she took she expected a hand to land on her shoulder, or the sound of a city police officer bellowing at her to stop where she was.

The shop was dingy, the interior as dark and unwelcoming as the man sitting behind the counter who barely glanced up from whatever it was he was working on as she came in.

'Help you?' he grunted.

'I have a problem.'

'Uh-huh?'

'Some kind of virus. And I think it has mutated. My friend sent me here. He said you have a particular knack with this kind of thing.'

There was a pause and then the repairman finally put down the tools he'd been using. Nothing else was said; he just held out both hands, she handed him the backpack and he turned to a recycling chute behind him, slid the door open and put the bag inside. When he closed the door again, her hard-earned contraband would be carried away on a series of conveyor belts to Dump Two, one of a pair of huge refuse centres outside the Wall, where a couple of Juneau's most trusted henchmen were waiting for it to arrive at the top of a vast mountain of discarded electronic equipment.

Tia was almost out the door when the man spoke again.

'Good luck,' he said. 'I hope you manage to get your old man out of prison. He's a good guy.'

Rush

'Move right down, please!' the ARM officer, using a voice-amplifier, bellowed over the heads of the mutants pouring down the steps behind him and out on to the platform. As at registration there was a system in place, but the sheer number of people keen to be on the first trains to leave was causing problems.

Rush had chosen to sleep out in the open the previous night, setting himself down close to the disembarkation point where the transporter vehicles were to pick the mutants up the following morning. He was far from being alone in this decision – indistinct shapes, some out in the open like him, some under hastily erected tarpaulin lean-tos, could be made out in the murk. It had been a cold night, and with no blanket or warm clothing he'd hardly got a wink of sleep, but he must have dozed off just before dawn because he woke, stiff and full of aches, to the sound of approaching vehicles. Each was capable of carrying about fifty passengers at a time, and Rush soon found himself on the fourth transporter out.

In the back of the windowless vehicles the living cargo was thrown around like rag dolls. Unlike the people around him, who whooped and cried out, excited to be on such a wonderful machine for what was probably the first time in their lives, Rush found his mood getting darker by the minute, especially when the bumps smoothed out and it became clear that they were on a tarmacked road. It was also apparent that it sloped steeply downwards – Juneau had been right; they were going to use the old underground transportation system.

If any of his fellow passengers noticed his surly manner, none of them said anything, and Rush in turn spoke to nobody during the long trip. When the vehicles finally stopped and the rear doors were thrown open, he peered out at the huge circular subterranean space, before climbing out. Orders were shouted as the transporters spewed their mutant cargoes before swinging back around and returning to the surface so they might pick up the next batch of resettlers.

Exiting the vehicles, Rush and the others were urged down a wide staircase, the men and women doing the directing telling them it led to a platform where a train waited to 'take them to their new home'.

Rush's heart sank when he saw the heavily armed guards concentrated towards the front of the train. He'd harboured a hope that he might be able to get near to the driver or the engine cab and sabotage it somehow, but that was clearly going to be impossible. His only hope if he was to try such a thing would be to see if he could make his way through the carriages once they were en route.

As he reached the bottom of the stairs, a feeling of nausea, strong enough to make him gasp, swept over Rush. His stomach lurched, and he felt a familiar sensation inside his head that made him stop abruptly and stare about him in all directions. Eager to keep moving, people *tut-tutted* or simply pushed into him from behind, but he remained frozen, even when the guard shouted for him to get going. In any case, he was only vaguely aware of any of these external voices because another spoke to him, one that filled his entire head so that he couldn't have ignored it even if he'd tried. When he did glance over in the official's direction, he saw that the ARM officer had set off towards him, the man's angry expression making it clear what he thought of the teenager partially blocking the bottom of the stairway he was in charge of. Rush also noted that the man was reaching for the stun baton hanging from his belt. Concentrating on his would-be assailant's helmet, Rush bent the item of uniform to his will. The guard was no more than ten paces away when his headwear somehow slipped down over his eyes, causing him to stumble into the moving tide of people, where he was buffeted about and almost went down under the crowd of moving feet and legs. Swearing loudly, the agent managed to keep upright, but when he pushed his helmet back he saw that the young mutant boy had gone; no doubt swept along with the others towards the train.

Back at the top of the stairs Rush watched as the next wave of transporters returned and offloaded their passengers into the circular disembarkation area. The unpleasant feeling of nausea continued and now he had the odd sensation of another mind looking out through his eyes, the experience so disorientating that he hardly noticed a little blonde girl and what appeared to be her brother approaching him.

'Hello, Rush,' the girl said, slipping her hand into his. 'Shall we go?' The small boy accompanying her had a grubby backpack over his shoulders, and he shifted it about as if to make it more comfortable before his hand also entwined with Rush's. The disorientation was slowly ebbing away, so Rush, without a word, turned on his heel and led the pair back down the staircase he'd just come up.

It was only when they were all on the train, the three having made a small space among piles of luggage and hastily packed boxes so they might talk without being overheard, that Rush's head completely cleared and he was able to see Jax and Brick clearly for who they really were. He'd known it was them – Jax had communicated to him inside his head – but even with that knowledge Rush had been unable to separate the reality from the illusion.

'I hate it when you do that,' he said, grimacing and pressing his palms against his eyes. Something occurred to him. 'How long have you been in my head?' He was thinking about the kiss with Tia and hoping that Jax had not been piggybacking on his consciousness then.

'Not too long. I first made the link when you were in the medical room having your injection. You shouldn't have done that. You should have waited for me.'

'I had no idea when, or if, you would return, Jax. I couldn't just sit on my hands and do nothing.' He looked over at Brick. The big guy hadn't said a word to him since boarding the train, and sat, eyes fixed on the floor between his feet.

'Brick?' Rush reached over and placed a hand on his friend's. 'Are you OK?'

The big guy shook his head. 'Gone. Brick couldn't help them. Metalman did it.'

Rush remembered how Jax had reacted back at Juneau's when he'd felt his 'disconnection' with Silas. He didn't want to ask the next question, as if putting it into words might make more real.

'Silas?' Rush asked in a small voice. It was only one word, but he found it almost impossible to get out.

'He's dead,' Jax said.

Rush's head spun. The man responsible for rescuing them all way back when they were little more than babies, the man who had saved them all again thirteen years later, was gone. He felt tears slip from his eyes, and would have given in to his grief completely had he not suddenly registered what Brick had said moments before. 'Them? Brick, you said *them*. Who else couldn't you help?'

Jax looked at his friend, a terrible expression on his face. 'Flea's gone too,' he said in a whisper.

Rush sat trying to take the news in, his body gently buffeted from side to side as the train sped through the tunnel. 'What happened?' he finally managed.

'It was the mutant, Steeleye,' Jax said. 'He's working for Melk as some kind of bounty hunter, and it seems that we are his quarry. Brick says he's different now: half man, half machine – a cyborg of some kind. He found our hideaway in the Dead City.' He paused. 'It seems brave little Flea died trying to get Silas out from under a collapsing ceiling. From everything I can gather, their deaths . . .' Quite suddenly, his emotions got the better of him and he tailed off.

'It's OK, Jax. You don't need to –'

'No. You need to know.'

The albino took a deep breath and cleared his throat before going on. 'Silas and Flea's deaths do not appear to have been premeditated. In fact, they might not have occurred at all if Silas hadn't attacked Mange. There was a cave-in and all three of them were buried. And despite what he says to the contrary and feeling that he failed, Brick did everything he could to save them both. When that wasn't possible, he did the next best thing and captured the cyborg, who somehow survived beneath the rubble.'

Another thought occurred to Rush. 'Anya – was she there?'

A pained look flashed across Jax's face. 'Anya, for reasons I can't imagine, set Steeleye free and helped him escape.'

'What? W-why would she do such a thing?'

'She doesn't know about Silas and Flea's deaths; Brick had already removed their bodies. Mange must have manipulated her into releasing him. I think we have to assume that Anya is lost to us now, and maybe that Steeleye or Melk will seek to use her in some way.' There was another long silence. 'We stopped by Juneau's place on the way to the transportation lorries.'

Rush scanned the albino's face for some clue as to what this cryptic announcement might mean. As always, his friend's expression was impossible to read, but Jax nudged the bag that Brick had been carrying all this time in his direction. Rush pulled the drawstring loose and stared at the contents. The thing looked for all the world like a series of grey tubes surrounding a larger central one. On top of the main drum was a small domed light above two red push buttons marked 1 and 2.

'What is it?'

'I don't really know. He gave it a name, but then went into a whole load of science babble – something about a non-nuclear transient electronic disturbance – that I didn't understand a word of and didn't have time to ask. But if our friend Juneau is correct, it might be the only thing that can stop Melk's plans to wipe out all of C4's mutants in one fatal blow.'

'Jax, are you sure you're –'

'We'll mourn Silas and Flea later. But right now the three of us have to get on with the task in hand.'

Tia

Her father looked awful. He'd lost a lot of weight, which gave his face a sunken, skeletal look that was exacerbated by the deep shadows beneath his eyes. The overall effect was that he appeared to have aged ten years since she'd last laid eyes on him only a few months earlier, and the sudden change shocked her. He was sitting in a room not unlike the one in which Tia herself had waited for Melk to arrive the previous day. This one had a screen of some kind set into one wall, that allowed her to see in, but prohibited him from seeing out. Not for the first time since learning of his arrest, she wondered if this was somehow her fault; if her father had spoken out in the way he had, inviting Melk's backlash, as a reaction to her disappearance. If that was indeed the case, it was even more important that she do everything in her power to secure his release.

'He does look bad, doesn't he?' Melk said. The man was standing at her side and had clearly noticed her reaction.

'You should be ashamed of yourself, Mr President. This is not the way a civilised society acts towards its own people.'

Melk grunted. 'If it were up to me, I'd have shipped him off to TS1 some time ago.'

'Without a trial?' Tia asked, doing her utmost to hold herself together.

Melk merely waved a hand in the air, the gesture leaving Tia in no doubt as to what the elderly politician thought of the Six Cities' judicial system. How had things got so bent out of shape so quickly? Yes, the Pure–Mute situation had always been unjust. Yes, the political situation in the Six Cities was known to be flawed and, yes, a number of people inside the Wall pretended that these things didn't really matter. But this? If a man like her father could be locked away simply because he dared to criticise Melk and his cronies, then nobody was safe. It was a dictatorship, and the man next to her wielded all the power.

Get a grip, Tia, she told herself. *Now is not the time to lose your nerve.*

'Let's get down to the matter in hand, shall we?' Melk nodded in her father's direction. 'You might have observed that your father is wearing a rather snazzy bit of neckwear.'

Tia had indeed noticed the collar around her father's throat, but had incorrectly assumed that it was some sort of prisoner identification device, due to the red winking lights set into a small screen at the front.

'When we spoke yesterday, Miss Cowper, you told me of your "insurance policy", and how, if anything should happen to you, your supposed findings would be revealed, destroying not just me, but my family name. A bold play, I have to admit, and one that forced me to take notice. Well done, young lady – you managed to get my attention.'

Tia waited.

'Well, the device around your father's neck is *my* insurance policy. It's a variation on something we have been using in a cybernetic experiment I'm conducting. The collar contains an electrical unit that can be remotely activated at any time, killing the wearer instantly. The same thing would happen if anybody should attempt to cut the collar off.' He paused and pretended to remove a piece of dust from his jacket sleeve. 'One of my people came up with the idea as an alternative to prison. More civilised in some ways, don't you think?' Tia was staring at the thing in horror, and her reaction wasn't lost on the politician. 'Yes, I thought you'd appreciate it, Miss Cowper. You see, it's a perfect counter to your own strategy.'

'You won't get away with this,' she said. 'The people of

C4 will not tolerate this kind of thing. My father has friends in high places, he'll –'

'*Au contraire*, my meddling little friend. Your father is an enemy of the state, and the people of City Four have recently, at first hand, experienced what can happen when such people are not controlled. It was, after all, enemies of the state who detonated bombs here. Towsin Cowper's so-called friends have, largely, forsaken him – as you would know if you'd been around instead of playing at being a journalist with a bunch of extremist mutants.' He paused, enjoying himself. 'I will make an announcement informing the people that I have magnanimously agreed to free your father. He can cover that thing up quite easily and go about his business as he did before. But you and I will know the consequences of betrayal in this matter. Towsin is perfectly safe, as long as you keep your end of our bargain and never release the information you claim to have on me.'

Tia was struggling to control her terror. 'I gave you my word. That isn't good enough for you?'

'I make a habit of never listening to such paltry pledges. No, this –' he gestured in her father's direction again – 'is a much better solution for all concerned. *You* have your insurance policy; *I* have mine. It's not exactly a win–win, but neither is it a lose–lose situation. It keeps both of us . . . honest.'

Tia placed her hand on the glass as if she might be able to reach through it and touch her father. Of all the scenarios she'd played out in her head, this had never been one of them. She'd thought she was being *so* clever, but she should have known Melk would not take her threats lightly. *That's what happens when you make a deal with the devil,* she thought. Nevertheless, he *was* offering her a chance to free her father, albeit under terrible circumstances. She glanced at the politician. Melk wouldn't consider this the end of the matter. The man would, as they spoke, have as many people as he could muster trying to find out where she'd hidden the files. Should he succeed, the stalemate would quickly turn into checkmate, and then both she and her father would 'disappear' forever. She was about to say something when another thought occurred to her. 'Does he know what that thing is?' she asked.

'No. I thought I would leave it up to you to decide what to tell him. As far as he is concerned, it's a tracking device he must wear as part of his release agreement. He *does*, however, know that any attempt to remove it would be bad for his health.'

I don't have any choice, she thought. 'OK,' she said, doing her best not to let her emotions show in her voice. 'I agree. You free my father and I will sit on those files.'

'Not so fast, young Miss Cowper.'

'But you said –'

'There are some other conditions that you and your dear papa must agree to for this to happen.'

'Do you think I'm bluffing about the information I have on you, Mr President? Because if so –'

The older man cut her off again. 'If you want to dilly-dally, do so. Your father can be returned to the cells and continue to suffer the mistreatment his fellow detainees have been doling out to him during his time here. If that should happen, it would be you, not I, who would be to blame. As I have already said, you've played the game well. However, it would be foolish to throw away all your hard-earned advantages now.'

'What are these conditions?'

'Your father is to retract everything he has said about me during the last six months and publicly state that my re-election was the right decision for the people of C4 to make.'

She almost laughed aloud. 'Anyone in their right mind would know that was untrue.'

He shrugged.

'Is that it?'

'Nearly. The other condition is that you, Miss Cowper, will remain within the confines of C4. No more little jaunts out to the mutant community. No more "roving reporter". You will be a model citizen of this city.' He gave her a cold smile. 'Now, I find it hard to believe you would deny me these two small requests to ensure the safe release of your beloved father.'

'I'll agree if you will reciprocate with a request I have.'

'Oh?'

'The collar. It only stays on as long as you are still president. Once your tenure is over, the thing comes off. And I want it in writing. Signed.'

Tia was surprised when he held out a hand, which she stared at for a moment until it dawned on her what he meant.

'You want to shake on it?' she said, rolling her eyes in disbelief. 'My word is considered to be a . . . what was it? Oh, yes, a paltry pledge, but my handshake is enough to seal my father's release?'

'Call me old-fashioned.'

She wanted to call him a whole lot of things, but old-fashioned was not on the list. Instead she bit her tongue and slipped her hand into his.

Rush

None of the three friends had any real idea how long they'd been on the train, but when it finally slowed to a halt and they got to their feet their muscles were stiff enough to elicit groans from each of them. As the doors slid open they stared around them at the other passengers, taking in the happy, excited faces, their expressions making Rush want to shout out a warning for everyone to stay on the train and get back to where they'd all come from, but he bit his lip and hung back with Jax and Brick, waiting for the main body of people to disembark before merging with the crowd.

A starkly different scene to the one they'd left behind at the other end greeted them. There were no barked commands here, no black looks from the guards. Instead a woman's warm voice drifted into the carriages from hidden speakers situated somewhere up on the curved walls all along the platform:

'*Welcome to Reservation One, your new and permanent home. Please disembark from the train and follow the green arrows. Your induction talk will commence in one hour.*'

There was a short pause and then the message was repeated.

Despite their calculated delay, Rush, Jax and Brick were forced along the platform by the sheer number of people behind them, and there was little they could do but move along with the tide while taking the scene in. The number of guards was significantly less here, and those ARM agents who were in attendance stood at regular intervals along the platform, their sidearms holstered, answering the odd question directed at them. Although Rush could now see Jax and Brick as they really were, he knew how hard the albino was working to get inside the guards' heads so that they only saw an older mutant boy escorting his two younger siblings. Because of this, Rush didn't expect Jax to talk to him at all, but the trio had taken no more than four or five steps away from the train when his friend let out a hissing noise. Glancing round, Rush saw that Jax was glaring in the direction of the nearest ARM agents.

'They know,' Jax muttered when Rush asked him what was wrong.

'Who? Who knows what?'

'The ARM agents here. Look at the smug look on most of their faces. They're not like the ones at disembarkation. They *know* what this place is and what's supposed to happen here.' His top lip curled in disgust.

Rush stared at the man whose thoughts his friend had just tapped into. The ARM agent was smiling and nodding at an older couple as they made their way past him. When the Mutes' little trolley got caught in a grille set into the floor, the guard stepped forward to help them to free it, laughing and smiling at them, and giving them a friendly wave once they were again under way.

Rush felt his own anger threaten to boil over. 'They're all officers,' he pointed out. 'Look at their insignia.'

'I'm guessing Melk feels he can only trust his most senior devotees to carry out this monstrous task. Perhaps he thought rank-and-file ARM agents wouldn't be willing to go through with it.' Jax shook his head. 'We have to get out of this crowd.'

'Why? If we stay with it, we'll get a better idea of how Melk intends to do this thing.'

Jax shook his head. 'This "induction talk" is simply a means of getting everyone together. Once that's achieved, my guess is that there will be some kind of lockdown to keep it that way and we might not get a chance to find your black cylinder or the means by which it's activated. We could all be dead by tonight.'

The crowd was moving relentlessly down the platform, a sea of mutants flowing in the direction of the bright arrows flashing from signs suspended over their heads. Rush and the others allowed themselves to be carried along by it to some extent, all the while edging out away from the train towards the fringes of the human tide. From here, a little way ahead of their current position, they spotted the small, unmarked door set into the wall between two supporting columns. With a nod to each other, they manoeuvred towards it, eliciting harsh words and hisses when they stopped in front of it.

'Locked,' Rush said, giving the handle a turn. He reached out with his mind, feeling his way through the mechanism and manipulating the tumblers and pins. There was an almost inaudible *click!* and the three slipped through, quickly closing the door behind them.

In front of them was a long, straight corridor, numerous doors leading off it on either side.

'It's a service way,' Jax said, staring down the harshly lit passage. 'It must lead out of here somehow.' He took a deep breath and shared a grave look with his friends. 'We have just under an hour. Whatever it takes, we have to find that cylinder and destroy it before then.'

'Whatever it takes?'

The albino glanced down at the bag carrying the device. 'I think we all got on that train knowing there was every chance we wouldn't survive this trip, didn't we?' He paused, letting his words sink in. 'It's funny, but I keep wondering if Silas would have been able to figure out a better way of stopping this.'

'And do you think he would? Is there a better way?'

'I don't know. All I do know is that if we fail in our mission, all of Muteville dies.'

They were halfway up the long corridor when Rush stopped, nodding towards a door on their left with a sign:

SECURITY. AUTHORISED PERSONNEL ONLY.

He was about to suggest they try to get inside, when Rush's words caught in his throat as the door opened and the trio came face to face with a burly guard who looked every bit as startled to find them there as they were him.

'What are you doing here, Mutes?' the man asked.

'We got lost,' Rush replied.

'Then I suggest you turn yourselves round and go back the way you just came. Go through the door at the bottom and rejoin the rest of your –'

He didn't get to say any more. At a nod from Jax, Brick hit the man on the jaw and he crumpled to the floor. When Rush looked over at his giant friend, the big man gave him a shrug. 'Jax told me to do it,' he whispered, and tapped his temple with a meaty finger. 'In my head.'

'He was alone in the room,' Jax said, the certainty with which he announced this leaving Rush in no doubt that the albino had gleaned the information from the man before he'd been rendered unconscious. 'Brick, would you be kind enough to drag our friend here inside with you? Oh, and close the door behind you – we don't want any further surprises.' He gestured for Rush to follow him, and the pair stepped through into the small dark space the man had emerged from. Having shoved the guard into the footwell beneath a desk, Brick joined them. There were nine screens set into the far wall, each relaying an image from a different camera. The top-left one showed the platform they had recently escaped. Mutants were still following each other and the green arrows, but the numbers were fewer now.

'That must be where everyone is meant to gather,' Rush said, pointing to the largest screen, in the centre. It showed a huge octagonal space that looked brand new and unused. Some of the early arrivals were already in there, craning their heads around in wonder. At the centre of the space was a tall tower-like structure with huge screens positioned on each side so everyone would be able to see, regardless of where they stood in the room. Currently being displayed were a series of images, each one blending into the next: a panoply of idyllic vignettes showing what life might be like on the reserve.

Except there would be no life on the reserve, Rush thought. *Only death.*

He waved his hand to activate the control panel set into the desk, and a screen floated into view before them, nine squares controlling the feeds to each of the screens on the far wall. He selected the central one and was rewarded with a series of options that appeared to allow him control of the cameras.

'Go down a bit,' Jax said. 'To the floor.'

'What for?' Rush asked, but did as his friend asked, moving the camera and zooming in.

'The entire thing is a grate. Like a drain. And look, all about the edges? Those are hoses. To sluice away whatever is left over at the end.'

It was only as the albino uttered these words that the full significance of this set-up dawned on the younger boy. And the realisation made him feel sick to the stomach. This was the killing floor. This was where Melk intended to wipe out the inhabitants of Muteville once and for all.

He'd activate the nanobots and let them turn everyone inside that place into a bloody soup. And once that was done, his goons would simply hose down the gory remains, ready for the next batch. A shiver ran through him. He quickly went back to the controls, zooming back out and panning until he found what he was looking for. It was at the top of the central structure, and anyone might have been forgiven for thinking it was merely a part of that edifice. But not Rush; he'd seen it before. Jax and Brick clearly spotted it at the same time, because neither said anything for what seemed an age.

'Is there a way to get to it?' Jax asked.

'There,' Rush said, moving the camera again and pointing it at a large gantry high up over the floor of Melk's abattoir. At one end of the suspended walkway was a brightly lit, glass-walled room. 'That has to be the control point. We have to get up there and destroy that thing before Melk has a chance to switch it on.' He was already reviewing the images on the other screens. 'Look.' He pointed to the image being relayed from camera 7. 'That skywalk – it has guards halfway across.'

'It's also only half there.'

Rush saw what his friend meant. The section of walkway between the guards and the control room was missing – there was no way across.

It took them a few minutes more of studying views from various cameras before they were certain they knew how to gain access to that space. Then, after securing and gagging the still-unconscious guard, they hurriedly made their way out of the room.

Tia

It was clear to Tia that it wasn't just her father's physical appearance that had drastically altered during his incarceration. He seemed mentally cowed too, reluctant to talk to her about anything that had happened to him during their spell apart. Back at their apartment, the first thing she'd done was get their housekeeper to fix them both some decent food, which the pair had devoured almost as soon as it had been placed before them. She'd given the woman the rest of the day off.

Now they were in the lounge together, sitting across from each other on the vast cream-coloured couches her mother had chosen for the room a few months before she'd died. It felt odd to be back here. Staring at the lavish surroundings, Tia marvelled at how much she'd simply taken for granted before her spell of exile beyond the Wall.

Here she was, having bathed in delicious hot water for what felt like hours, sitting in new clothes that had been sent out for, scrunching thick carpet pile between her toes. This had been her life for so long. So why couldn't she just slip back into it, if only for a little while?

'Daddy.'

Her father looked up at her, still wearing the same haunted expression he had back in the cell.

'There's something you need to know. About President Melk. Some friends and I have discovered something truly terrible. He's –'

Her father surprised her by holding up a hand and shooting her a warning look. When he turned the screen of the omnipad he had in his lap to face her, she leaned forward so she might read the message he'd written there:

If this is anything you don't want 'others' to hear, please stop talking right now.

Then he pointed to the collar around his neck and made a gesture of cupping his ear, as if he was listening to something.

She stared at him, then nodded, letting him know she understood.

'– We found out he's not a nice person.' It was a silly,

crass comment. The first thing to come into her head, which was swimming with a thousand different thoughts.

'I know,' was her father's response. 'But he'll get what is coming to him soon enough.' He paused. 'Your mother would have been so proud to see the way you turned out, Tia.' A ghost of a smile crossed his lips. 'When we knew we were going to have you, we were scared and excited about what kind of person we were bringing into this world. We needn't have been. You're everything we had hoped for and more.' He got to his feet. Once again she was struck by how thin he was. 'I'm very tired. I think I'll go and have a lie-down for a while. Do you mind?'

'No, of course not.' She watched as he made his way to his bedroom. He paused in the doorway and turned back to her.

'I love you very much,' he said.

'I love you too, Daddy.'

Her father gone, Tia simply sat on the couch, taking the occasional sip of iced water from a glass on the coffee table. It made sense that Melk would use the collar not just to silence her father, but also to hear anything he might be saying in secret to others opposed to the president. Her thoughts and concerns inevitably turned to Rush and the danger he had put himself in, and her heart clenched at the thought that something terrible might have happened to him. She forced the thought down, refusing to consider the possibility. No, somehow Silas and the others would meet up with him, and they would discover a way to put a stop to Melk's murderous plan. When she closed her eyes she could see how it would play out: her little friend Flea would use her incredible speed to get them access wherever they needed; Jax would confuse everyone into believing they weren't really seeing what they thought they were; Rush would use his telekinesis to deal with any bad guys who didn't fall under Jax's spell, and if any of them *were* accidentally hurt? Well, Brick would be there to heal them – patch them up as good as new so they could finish what they'd set out to do. She wondered if Anya had returned, and hoped for the sake of the group that she had; the polymorph was every bit as awesome as the other members of the group, and Tia had little doubt they would need her if they were to succeed.

And when they *had* thwarted Melk's scheme, what then? What would be the ultimate price? The mutant population had a right to know what had almost befallen them. And once aware, what would their reaction be? She knew how the people of the Six Cities would respond had it been the other way round. Melk and his military commanders wouldn't hesitate to use such a thing as an excuse for war. And if it came to a war, whose side would she be on? Could she find a way to help her mutant friends without endangering her father?

The last time she and her friends had all been together, Tia had heard Tink talk to Silas of war. She'd been in a corner, trying to get some sleep, when the pair had entered. Half dozing, she'd not been able to announce her presence in time to avoid overhearing them. Tink had explained how, in one of his extraordinary visions, he'd seen Pure and Mute clash in a way that might settle the future of Scorched Earth once and for all. Tensions between the two sides had been stretched to breaking point, so it required no great leap of the imagination to believe that this latest diabolical deed could be the spark to ignite a revolt in which the mutant population rose up against their oppressors.

That was something her father would have fought against. *Will,* she corrected herself. *He* will *fight against such injustices*. He just needed a little time. But time suddenly felt precious to her, and she had the horrible feeling it was running out for all of them.

Rush, Brick and Jax

The three mutants moved along an elevated walkway circling the auditorium, keeping to the shadows as best they could to avoid being spotted. Despite their caution, they knew they had to hurry. A klaxon had blared out a few moments earlier, the deafening noise followed by an announcement that there were ten minutes until 'induction'. Induction surely meant something terrible. Way below them, visible through the gaps in the steel lattice floor, more and more of their fellow Mutes poured into the assembly space, their excited hubbub filling the place. There was hope in those voices; Rush could hear it and it filled him with rage and fear. The voices belonged to people keen to begin their new lives in this place, voices that would soon be silenced forever if Rush, Brick and Jax failed.

As they rounded the section of the walkway they were

currently on, the two guards they'd spotted on the security screens came into view, but the three mutants didn't falter in their progress. Jax was using his psychic powers of misdirection, putting all his effort into making it appear, through *their* eyes, as if three fellow ARM agents were approaching them. As they neared the men, Rush was horrified to see how cheerful both appeared to be. As if they were standing around waiting for the end of their shift, and not about to witness the start of a genocide.

The pair straightened up as the newcomers approached, the one on the right calling out, 'Hey, what are you guys doing here? This is a no-go area until all this –' he gestured at the crowds below – 'is over. Didn't you hear the klaxon? Everything has been activated. The countdown has begun.'

Keep moving. Jax's voice was inside his friends' heads, but his lips formed real words as he spoke to the guard. 'Yeah, we know. But they sent us here to tell you there's been a problem with the –' He didn't get any further because Brick snaked two enormous hands out, grabbing the two men and cracking their heads together with a sickening crunch, the men's eyes rolling back a split second before they collapsed to the floor.

The groan that escaped Brick told Rush precisely what his friend felt about having used violence in this way. The younger mutant stretched up and put a reassuring hand on the big guy's shoulder. 'It needed doing. Don't feel bad. If you want, you can fix them up after we've got this all sorted out.' He turned to Jax. 'Did you hear what that guard said? "Everything has been activated." Some sicko has already pressed the button.' He wondered how many precious seconds had passed since the ten-minute announcement, and his thoughts turned to the millions of deadly microscopic nanobots he'd allowed himself to be injected with.

They were standing in a tubular steel archway suspended from the roof by thick metal cables. The grid-like metal catwalk between them and the control room on the far side stopped just beyond the arch. The gap between the two sections hadn't looked so big on the screens in the security room, but standing on the edge now, it appeared enormous. It must have been twenty metres wide, and the drop at least three times that. The two guards had been so lax because the brightly lit, glass-sided room didn't need protecting in the traditional sense. The only access was via a retractable skywalk. And that had been withdrawn from the other side some time ago.

Rush swore under his breath.

'There,' Jax said, pointing a long, pale finger at a small wall-mounted box on the far side. 'That must be the control switch for the skywalk. Can you activate it?'

Rush stared at the thing. On the front was a large red

rubber button. Closing his eyes, he reached out with his mind, gingerly at first, then with more urgency – he and the red button 'connecting' until the thing was as much a part of him as his own hand or foot. At a molecular level he entwined with the inanimate object, and now he willed it to activate.

It wouldn't go down. Something was stopping it. A sense of panic welled up inside Rush and he tried again, small frown lines forming on his forehead as he put more effort into it. Nothing. He gave a little whimper.

'Wait,' Jax said in a tone that said he knew what the problem was. Rush opened his eyes again. Above the screen, floating above the control box, was a holopad that had appeared as soon as Rush attempted to activate the button. The two stared at the thing, coming to the same conclusion at the same time. It was Rush who put their thoughts into words: 'Even if you could pluck the code out of somebody's head, there's no way I can enter it on that thing.'

'Seven, seven, nine, one.' Jax said, narrowing his eyes at one of the people in the room, all of whom were still completely oblivious to their presence.

Rush swore. 'Why couldn't it have been a physical keypad!'

'You'll have to get across, Rush. You can activate the

skywalk from there, and Brick and I will come across with the –'

'Are you insane?! Get across? Have you seen that gap? We haven't got any rope, and even if we did, we don't have the time. What do you propose? That Brick throws me over there?'

'You can get there.'

'How? Hmm? How can I possibly get across?'

'If I had a stone and asked you to throw it and hit that button, you could, couldn't you?'

'You know I could.'

'Because?'

'Because, unlike that damn keypad, a stone is something physical, something I can control with my power.'

'And what are you? Aren't you "something physical"? Why can't you be the stone?'

Rush stared back at his friend. He opened his mouth to say something and then closed it again, unable to think of an answer that countered Jax's logic. What Jax was suggesting was, in the face of it, madness. But in truth Rush had considered this very thing on a number of occasions in the past. If he could use his mind to influence inanimate objects, why not animate objects too?

'You know you can do it, don't you?' Jax said.

'No.'

'Yes, you do.'

'What makes you so sure?'

'I've looked inside your head many times since you were born, Rush. I don't think you understand a fraction of what you're really capable of.'

'And I'm capable of this?'

'I think so.'

'You *think* so?' Rush assessed the gap and the drop again, his insides clenching at the thought of even attempting such a jump.

A speaker positioned just over their heads went off, the sudden klaxon alarm making all of them jump in fright. As the noise died away the giant vis-monitors mounted on the central column flickered into life, revealing the face that went with the saccharine-sweet voice of the woman.

'*Welcome. Please remain where you are. We will commence your induction talk in three minutes. The outer doors are about to close for your comfort and safety.*'

The announcement was accompanied by four loud booms as the giant auditorium was sealed shut, trapping everyone inside the place. A nervous babble of excitement rose up to the trio from below.

Three minutes.

'I can't believe I'm doing this,' Rush mumbled, shaking

his head. Even as he said the words he was stepping backwards to give himself a small run-up.

Brick, watching all this, seemed unsure what was going on until that moment. When it suddenly dawned on him what Rush was about to do, he cried out and would have grabbed him, had Jax not thrown himself at the giant mutant.

Three strides. Three hurried strides as Rush's mind screamed at him not to do this. Three strides and one leap, and he was sailing out into the void.

The terror he felt in those first fractions was all consuming. A fear so great it made him cry out, but then, out of nowhere, there came a sensation of inner peace that utterly vanquished the fear. He was not calm – that emotion, like his panic, no longer had any meaning. There was the moment, and there was him, and nothing else existed. At some level he knew that he was no longer 'Rush'. Instead he was an infinitely complex mass of molecules, held together by forces he had no hope of understanding. *I'm just a physical thing. Just a stone being thrown across this gap. A stone, nothing more . . .* What he *did* understand was that Jax was right: he really was more powerful than he'd ever imagined. He had a notion of where he was in space and time, and a notion of where he wanted to be. Once he understood that, it was merely a matter of moving one of those things towards the other.

Jax and Brick, clutching on to each other, watched as Rush flew out into the air, his arms windmilling once before he brought them together, stretched out, in front of him. To his watching friends, he seemed to wink out of existence for a fraction of a second, but they would both later doubt that they had really seen that. What they *did* see was Rush shoot through the air like an arrow being shot from a bow. He crossed the space in the blink of an eye, until, at the last moment, he tucked his shoulders and curled his body, performing a perfect forward roll on the far walkway so that he was up and on his feet instantly.

You did it, Jax said directly inside Rush's head.

Rush shook his head and looked back across the void he'd somehow crossed. Had he just . . . flown?

Rush. The control box.

Forcing himself to focus, Rush hurried over to the box on the wall and entered the activation code into the floating keypad, a surge of relief filling him when he heard a loud *clank* as the skywalk began to stretch out across the gap towards his friends.

Three minutes. No, it must be less than that now. How much less?

He had to get moving. There was no time to wait for Jax and Brick. He walked towards the control room just as the three people in there, hearing the racket, became aware that the footbridge had somehow been activated.

Rush felt different, more powerful somehow, able to master this situation in a way he hadn't since setting foot on the train that brought them here. The people in the control room turned to stare at the young mutant boy striding towards them. All three, two men and one woman, were armed, and each of them reached for their weapons at the same instant. Again there was no panic, no fear in Rush. That inner peace he'd felt as he surged through time and space was still with him, and he simply lifted his hand, palm out, and blew the glass walls in so that a deadly volley of glass shards crashed through the air, the effect being that the room's occupants forgot about such trifling things as guns and hit the ground, heads bowed and shoulders hunched in an attempt to avoid being eviscerated by the airborne hail.

Glass crunching beneath the soles of his shoes, Rush calmly walked through the door and looked about the place. Projected into the air above a large desk of buttons and monitors was a countdown timer, its numbers clicking down before his eyes. There were less than two minutes left.

'Now listen up,' he told the scared and bloodied ARM officers on the floor. 'If you know what's good for you, you'll stay exactly where you are. If everything goes as planned, I'll have somebody fix you up as good as new in a short while, but for now do exactly as I say.' The guns they had dropped skittered across the glass-strewn floor into the furthest corner. Nobody budged so much as an inch.

'Wh-who are you?' one man, with a badly bleeding head, stammered.

'Me? I'm nobody. Just another Mute trying to survive in this forsaken world.' He gestured in the direction of the control panel and asked, 'Now, which button or switch deactivates that thing out there?'

'What do you know about –'

'Answer me! How do we switch it off?'

'You can't. Once the sequence was initiated from City Four we no longer had any control over it.'

'It was activated from C4?'

'President Melk himself pressed the button as soon as the first train pulled in.'

There was the sound of hurried footsteps on the stairwell. Then Jax and Brick came pouring through the door.

'He says they can't stop it,' Rush told the albino.

Jax narrowed his eyes at the man. 'He's telling the truth. Quick, the bag,' he said, pulling it from Brick's shoulders and dragging out the device so he could place it on the floor.

'How does it work?' Rush asked.

'I have no idea, but there are only two buttons, and they're marked one and two. How difficult can it be?'

'We have a little over one minute,' Rush said, pointing to the countdown timer above the console.

The pair stared down, hesitating. Both were taken by surprise when a huge ham fist reached over their shoulders and pressed the button labelled with a one, the action accompanied by a low grunt. The domed light above the button came on, glowing red. Beneath it, again only visible now the thing had been activated, were two words: *CHARGING*, and beneath that, *WAIT*. There was a shrill tone that got higher and more piercing, but the light remained red.

'Dammit!' Rush said, looking up at the timer again. Fifty-four seconds. 'Didn't Juneau tell you that this thing needed time to function?'

'NOBODY MOVE!' a familiar voice boomed out from behind them all. 'If you so much as twitch a muscle, any of you, I'll blow you to hell. Now turn around.'

'The metal man,' Brick uttered in a dread tone as the trio did as they were bid.

Rush gave a small gasp. The sight of the man he'd once encountered in a back alley of Muteville took him aback. The mutant known as Steeleye Mange was a thing of horror: half man, half machine, he was holding out an electromechanical arm, pointing what could only be a gun of some kind, mounted on the top of it, at them. His one living eye gleamed triumphantly as he took in their stunned faces.

'What's that thing on the floor behind you?'

'We don't know,' Jax answered in a voice laced with resignation.

'You don't know? You expect me to believe that?'

'Believe what you want. It doesn't really matter any more, does it?'

That piercing noise was so high now it was almost painful. Rush allowed his eyes to drift to the countdown timer: eighteen seconds. He was about to be destroyed by millions of tiny robots swimming around inside his veins as they burrowed their way through him, and all he could think about was that damned noise in his ears. So it was a blessed relief when the strident screech abruptly stopped, replaced by three short *blips*. Without needing to look, Rush knew the little domed light would now be green, and somewhere near it the word *CHARGING* had been replaced by another: *READY.*

'What the –' Steeleye said, his look going from the three of them to the thing on the floor and back again.

Rush reached out with his mind for button number two and pressed it down.

There was no explosion. Instead there was a low *WHOOMP!* that was not so much heard as *felt,* as the hugely powerful electromagnetic pulse was discharged in all directions, wrecking every electronically controlled piece of equipment within a half-mile radius. The screens showing the smiling face of the woman went grey, her voice falling mute too. The lights went out, plunging the auditorium into darkness and eliciting screams and cries from the mutants packed in down below. As mutants stumbled about, trying to find the doors in the blackness, the guards found that their communication devices, and more importantly their pulsed-energy weapons, were rendered useless. Then, as a series of generators kicked into action somewhere deep underground, a few emergency lights winked on here and there, but the meagre illumination they provided did little to assuage anyone's fears. At least the break in power meant the electronic locks on the doors had been disengaged.

Rush looked over at Steeleye, and saw that he too had been affected by the EMP. He was frozen, his human eye rolling about in his head as he tried to take in what was happening, the movement accompanied by a series of strangled moans and incomprehensible utterances. The young Mute watched as Jax stepped over to the cyborg, taking the thing's face in his hand and pushing his own into it so their noses were no more than a finger's width apart.

Rush watched as Jax reached down and snatched up the big, ugly knife hanging from the cyborg's belt. He brandished the blade menacingly beneath Steeleye's chin, so the cyborg, his head frozen in place, could only swivel his eye downwards, trying to get a look at the thing.

'I should kill you. I should end your miserable life right now while you're helpless and defenceless, just like you killed little Flea and the man who was a father to me.'

'Jax –' Rush said.

'Did it make you feel powerful, hmm? Did you enjoy ending their lives?'

'Jax. Put the knife down.'

'All it would take to rid the world of a miserable degenerate like you is one swift thrust of my hand. Just like that, and you'd be gone.' His voice had taken on a maniacal tone, and Rush was about to step in when Brick blocked his way with his huge bulk. Reaching out slowly, the big guy put a hand over Jax's wrist. He could easily have forced the weapon away from Mange's throat, but for now he just rested his hand on his friend's.

'No more hurting,' Brick said. 'No more. Not now.'

The silence between them seemed to stretch out forever.

'Brick's right,' Rush eventually said. 'Killing Steeleye won't bring Silas or Flea back. And neither of them would want you to take a life because of the sadness you feel at them being gone. Silas loved you, Jax. Don't let your anger and pain make you into a monster. If you do, you're no better than Mange.'

The albino didn't move for a second or two. He blinked, two tears sliding down his pale cheeks. A small shuddering sigh escaped him and the knife fell to the floor. He turned away from the cyborg.

'You three,' Rush said, turning towards the ARM officers on the floor. 'Up on your feet.' He waited. All three were badly hurt, but they managed to do as they were told. 'Now get this hunk of junk out of here and take him back to where he came from. You and every other citizen of the Six Cities have exactly one hour to get off this mutant reserve. If a single one of you Pures remains here after that time, we will not be as restrained as we have just been, and we will see you for what you are: an enemy of the newly founded Mutant Nation.' He paused. 'You might give President Melk a message from us too: tell him that his planned genocide has failed and that we see his attempt to wipe out the people of Muteville as an act of war. Tell him, however, that the Mutes do not seek war. Tell him that we will not be the aggressors in whatever comes next, but that we will no longer be cowed by the Six Cities and those inside the walls who would do us harm.' He looked at them, locking eyes with Steeleye last. 'I hope I never see you again, Mange. But if I do, I hope you'll remember what happened here today and realise that we are not your enemies.'

Rush and the others watched as the ARM agents

manhandled the huge cyborg out of the control room, Steeleye's robotic legs making a terrible screeching sound on the metal catwalk as they dragged him away. The three watched them go until they disappeared into the darkness. With no weapons and no means of communicating with their superiors, he had little doubt that the guards would do as he'd bid and leave.

He took a deep breath and let it out again, doing his best to calm himself after everything that had happened. Sounds from below drifted up to him, and he knew the three of them needed to get down there. They, with the help of Muteville's leaders, would need to calm the frightened people inside the auditorium. Not only that, but they owed it to them to explain what had almost happened here.

And then what?

They would need to work with those same leaders to try and form a new society, a community that now had a place to call its own. Melk's promise of a new home might have been a lie, but now these people *did* have a fresh start, and it was up to the mutants of Scorched Earth to make sure that they took this opportunity with both hands.

He turned to his friends, smiling at them in the murky half-light. 'Let's go down and tell the people of Muteville the truth. And once we've done that, let's see what we can do about getting the lights back on.'

Epilogue

The harg was as jittery as Tink had ever known it, the animal's mood perfectly matching his own as it reluctantly obeyed his murmured urgings to keep plodding forward, pulling the wagon. The canyon they were in must once have been full of water, a river that was responsible for gouging this deep scar into the rocky terrain. But that river had dried up long ago, and the wound it had left behind was as arid as the rest of this harsh landscape. The gorge was narrowing now, and as it did so the tall cliffs on either side became all the more imposing and sinister. But it wasn't the geology of the place that had the man and his beast unnerved. No, the cause of their joint disquiet was the things they occasionally glimpsed out of the corner of their eye, things tracking their progress from among the rocks. If he didn't know better, Tink might have put these vague sightings down to the heat and his own imagination, but the harg was clearly reacting to them too, and Tink trusted the big animal's instincts a whole lot more than he did his own.

'Yeah, I see 'em,' he told the animal at one point when it paused and shook its mane skittishly. Now they'd stopped, Tink lifted his head and scanned the cliffs in the hope of catching a glimpse of those watching him Away to his left something moved, and he snapped his head round. Was that a leg he'd seen disappearing behind a boulder? Small and slightly chubby, it was gone before he could properly make it out, if indeed he'd seen it at all.

Tales of the Chuni abounded in the Blacklands. They were said to be small, almost child-sized, but what they lacked in stature they made up for with a legendary ferocity in battle. One of the tales that particularly concerned Tink right now suggested they turned to cannibalism when game became hard to come by. He hoped that this year the Chuni's prey of choice was thriving in numbers so huge that the little people's bellies were swollen near to bursting. Other interesting tales about the Chuni people involved their legendary camouflage skills. It was said that they had the ability to 'blend in' with their surroundings – the skin on their hairless bodies changing colour depending on their surroundings. If that was the case, there was little wonder he was having trouble making them out against the endless expanse of orange-tan rock up there.

He sighed and turned his attention back to the route ahead. 'Get along now,' he said to the harg, giving the animal a gentle flick on the rear with the reins.

Had things been different he would not have come this way, but the more circuitous route he'd planned on taking had become impassable due to a massive landslide not far from where he'd set off. Up ahead he could just make out the end of the gulley, the shadowy half-light giving way to brighter sunshine beyond the cliffs. He reasoned that in twenty or so minutes he'd be beyond this place, but he had a nagging feeling that whatever was dogging him through the gulch would not be content to simply watch him ride out of it unchallenged.

The harg started to plod on again, only to pull up immediately with an alarmed cry, the tentacles on the side of its face waggling wildly as three arrows thudded into the ground a mere arm's length in front of it. The arrows had come from three different directions, but the target and timing of the shots left Tink in no doubt that it was a coordinated action. The low, reassuring noises he made did little to calm the startled beast, but he and the animal had been with each other long enough to know that neither was going to do anything silly to endanger the other. Tink forced himself to be calm again. The accuracy of the aim told him that, had the archers wanted to kill either the harg or the driver, they could easily have done so. With that in mind, he took the warning shots for what they were meant to be. Digging into his coat pocket, he took out his pipe and smoking pouch. Moving very slowly, he filled the pipe and lit it, sticking it between his lips and clamping down on it with his teeth. Then, still moving at a speed that made his old joints complain loudly, he stood up on the jockey box and raised his hands above his head. He was still none the wiser as to who had fired at them, but there seemed little point in calling out, so he just stood, waiting for a sign as to what he should do next and hoping that sign didn't come in the form of an arrow buried in his breastbone.

He didn't see the small person making its way down the ridge just ahead of where he'd stopped. It wasn't until the harg made a noise and shuffled back, almost causing Tink to lose his balance, that he looked down to see one of the Chuni standing directly in front of him. Two of the three arrows had already been removed from the ground and stowed in the quiver slung around the hunter's back; the third was notched and was aimed straight at Tink's left eye.

Despite the danger he was in, Tink took a second to study his assailant.

The first thing that struck him was that, despite the Chuni having not a stitch of clothing on its body, he didn't have the slightest idea if he was looking at a male or female. The anatomical area that should have made it obvious was devoid of any clues. The face was neither masculine nor feminine, and the absence of any hair whatsoever did nothing to help. Tink was left flummoxed by how he should address this person. The small person opened its mouth and made a hissing noise, revealing teeth that had been filed down into sharp points.

'I'm not here to cause any trouble,' Tink said, careful to keep his hands up in plain sight. 'I just want to get to –'

The Chuni let out a series of high-pitched whistles, yelps and clicks, the result being that, seemingly out of nowhere, from the cliffs above, emerged a dozen or so identical individuals, all of them armed with the same weapon made to the same design. One of them descended, leaping gracefully and noiselessly from rock to rock until it was on the canyon floor, where it joined the leader. The pair communicated in the clicking, whistling tongue before the newcomer turned to Tink.

'This is Chuni territory,' the new arrival said in a weird voice that was high and shrill one moment, deep the next.

'I don't want to trespass on your lands.'

'And yet here you are.'

'Out of necessity, yes. But I'm merely passing through.'

The Chuni waited.

'I came this way despite knowing the fearsome reputation of your people. Armed with this information, you must see that I would not have done so if I had some other choice. I am trying to get to the Blacklands settlement on the other side of these hills. I am here to see the mutant, Corem.'

'We know. He told us you were coming.'

More clicks and whistles followed. When the translator looked up at Tink again, a humourless smile accompanied his savage expression.

'Step down from your vehicle.'

Reluctantly Tink did as he was told. He didn't hear the small Chuni approach him from behind. Nor did he anticipate the expertly placed blow that turned the world black as he was rendered unconscious.

He was lying on his side, still fully clothed. Despite being on the ground, the mound of skins and furs beneath him made a comfortable bed. Tink let out a loud groan as he opened his eyes. His head was pounding, the pain accompanied by a rolling sensation in his stomach that had him clutching at it in an effort not to throw up.

He was in a cabin of some kind – the walls constructed

from the glass-like black rock that gave these southern lands their name. A fire was burning not far away, and from the smell coming off it he guessed animal dung was being used as fuel. The smell did nothing to quell his lurching insides. He reached up slowly, testing the area where he'd been hit and noting how his head had been bound up with cloth. A noise behind him made him start, and he instantly regretted the sudden movement. A face, upside down, loomed into view. It was a face like no other – craggy and puckered, it was ridged in places so the visage was almost lizard-like. The mouth broke into a broad smile displaying badly cared-for teeth. Despite the terrifying appearance, Tink thought he'd never been happier to see his cousin, although one look at the other's expression told him the feeling wasn't entirely mutual.

'Since when have you relied on the Chuni to guard your borders?' Tink asked, sipping from the foul-tasting infusion he'd been given as a drink to alleviate his pain. If it was not in a cup right in front of him, he wouldn't have believed it possible for anything to taste and smell so bad.

'We don't, but lately there have been some unwanted visits from outside these parts, and I asked the Chuni to keep an eye out. We do the same for them.'

'Unwanted visits?'

'Rogue gangs. Blacklander scum.'

'Even so, they make strange bedfellows. I just hope their food doesn't run out, or both you and these rogue gangs might find yourself on the menu.'

'Needs must, cousin. You of all people know about getting into bed with the enemy. Do you still trade with the Pures?'

Tink ignored the jibe.

Outside the wind picked up, blowing across the chimney on the roof of the hut, causing it to moan eerily. Neither man spoke for a few moments. Tink put his cup down on the floor, nudging it away as he decided an aching head was preferable to drinking any more of the stuff it contained.

'The visions,' he said, breaking the silence. 'You still get them?'

Corem nodded. 'You?'

'Not as often as I used to, but when they come they're . . . intense.'

Like many in their family, the cousins both had the power of foresight. As young men they'd shared numerous premonitions – visions of possible futures – but they would argue about the significance of the things they saw. Their failure to act appropriately in response to one of their shared visions – an attack on their family home – had resulted in deaths, and the incident had driven a wedge between the two young men to such a degree that Tink had left the Blacklands and headed north towards the cities, where he hoped he could make a difference to the inhabitants of the mutant slums. He returned occasionally, but things were never the same between the two of them. Corem had gone on to become a tribal elder for his people – somebody they would come to for advice and wisdom – and Tink had become a travelling man, a trader who roamed the lands far to the north, keeping a sharp eye on the world he believed would one day have an impact on the one he'd left behind.

'War is coming to Scorched Earth, Corem.'

His cousin paused. 'Yes.'

'And?'

'And I think my loyalty lies here with the Blacklanders, not with those who chose to leave these lands and go off to live in slums, picking over the city-dwellers' scraps and cast-offs like vermin.' Tink's cousin did nothing to hide the scorn from his voice.

After the Last War, the Blacklands were perhaps the most dangerous place on Scorched Earth. And in a world as utterly ruined as Scorched Earth was back then, that was truly saying something. Scarred and ruined by the sheer mass of weapons used there, it was clear the biological, nuclear and chemical fallout would never be fully cleansed.

Unlike those who sat out the effects of the war in the Arks, safely ensconced miles beneath the surface, the people who had survived in this brutal place were as scarred and damaged as the landscape itself, and when these survivors' children – and their children's children – continued to be born with horrific abnormalities, many Mutes began to talk of leaving, setting off for lands that were not so harsh in the hope that their future generations might stand a better chance.

Although a long time had passed since the exodus, the memories of so many Mutes leaving the Blacklands to find 'a better place' still played on the minds of many who had chosen to stay behind.

'This man – Melk – he won't stop,' Tink said in a voice that was barely more than a whisper. 'Not now. After he's wiped out those who are on his doorstep, do you really believe he'll continue to ignore you?'

His cousin gave him a stony look. 'These children – the ones in our shared vision – they are the root cause of this problem. It would have been better had you not helped that man Silas to rescue them all those years ago. Maybe if we just let Melk do away with them, things would go back to normal.'

'You don't really think that.'

'Don't I?'

'Help us, Corem. Talk to the people of the Blacklands and convince them that they should come to the aid of their kin.'

'Their kin?'

'Yes! Their mutant cousins. Just as you and I are cousins.'

Corem hissed and shook his head. The two men sat in silence for a while.

'What are you thinking?' Tink asked eventually.

Corem sighed. 'I'm thinking I should have let the Chuni shoot you.'

'Then you'll help? If war comes, you'll help?'

'We'll see. That's all I'll say to you. We'll see.'

About the author

Steve Feasey lives in Hertfordshire with his wife and kids. He didn't learn much at school except how to get into fights and chat up girls – he wasn't particularly successful at either – but he was always a voracious reader. He started writing fiction in his thirties, inspired by his own favourite writers: Stephen King, Elmore Leonard and Charles Dickens. His first book, *Changeling,* was shortlisted for the Waterstones Prize and became a successful series. *Mutant Rising* is his second book for Bloomsbury and is the sequel to *Mutant City*.